A Symmetry of Husbands

A Novel
by Patricia O'Donnell

For information contact:
Unsolicited Press
Portland, Oregon
www.unsolicitedpress.com
orders@unsolicitedpress.com
619–354–8005

Front Cover Design: Kathryn Gerhardt
Cover Image: Jo Lynn Pinder
Editor: Summer Stewart

ISBN: 978-1-956692-83-9

For Michael, who knows that the much-repaired washing machine is the only detail in this book that came from our marriage.

Book One: Grief Wrongs Us So

Chapter One

Footsteps whisper on the marble floor and wooden pews creak, sounds wafting up and disappearing into the vaulted ceiling. The church slowly fills, grief thickening like a sauce. Abigail recognizes a senior editor from the publishing house where Douglas works, and the man's wife—Clara? They pause in front of the grey-streaked marble urn, shaped like a vase, resting on a pedestal in front of the altar. The woman touches it, long fingers stroking the smooth surface, then they take a seat not far from Doug and his daughter Phoebe. Abigail's eyes linger on Phoebe, on her slim, erect back in its dark suit jacket, on the shining fall of her hair. She imagines Phoebe washing her hair this morning, sudsing with eyes closed, needing to look good for her mother's funeral. Abigail wants to be next to her but sits a few rows back. James, beside her, straightens his back against the pew. Abigail adjusts her dark skirt over her tights.

Voices hush as a woman in a black dress steps to a music stand in a corner by the altar. Colored light falls on her from the stained-glass window. She lifts a violin to her shoulder and pauses, then slides the bow across the strings. The program, with Megan's photo on the cover, says it's "Air on the G String" by Bach. Abigail stares at Megan's face as she listens to the thin, slippery string of music. Megan is smiling as if she knows something about Abigail that she doesn't want to say.

Abigail folds her hands over the program and closes her eyes. Her hands are covered in warmth. She opens her eyes to see James' hand placed over hers. His head tilts toward her as he looks at her from above his glasses. She leans her head on his shoulder, briefly.

The ceremony will be short, without a full funeral mass. It's what she wanted, Douglas said; what Megan had asked for. As she listens to the music, Abigail is trying to remember if Megan ever said anything to her about what she wanted at her funeral. She can't think of anything; they talked about life, not death. Not what came after life. She looks down again at Megan's face on the program; taken ten or fifteen years ago, the wind is tossing her curls across her face. There is a glimpse of a grey ocean behind her.

A woman Abigail doesn't know steps up to read Biblical passages aloud. The one from Ecclesiastes, which always reminds her of the old song by the Byrds: "A time to be born, and a time to die; a time to plant, and a time to uproot the plant. A time to kill, and a time to heal; a time to tear down, and a time to build." Abigail knows this is true, but she can't help but think that it was too soon for Megan, too soon to have this life taken away from her.

The next reading is from the Old Testament. "Oh, would that my words were written down! Would that they were inscribed in a record: That with an iron chisel and with lead they were cut in the rock forever! But as for me, I know that my Vindicator lives, and that he will at last stand forth upon the dust."

After the readings, Douglas steps up. Rather than walking up steps to the pulpit as the readers did, he stands at the front of the church facing the congregation. He wears a navy linen sports coat and white shirt, and his light hair falls to one side of his forehead in a way that looks untended, but Abigail has seen him pushing mousse into it with his fingertips in front of his bathroom mirror. Tall and angular, Douglas can't help but command the room, even pale as he is now, even with dark circles under his eyes. From a jacket pocket he pulls something and holds it up. It is a silver cylinder, about six inches long. He moves it from one hand to the next, and from where she sits, Abigail can see that his fingers are trembling. She squeezes James' hand, grateful for his solid warmth.

"I hope you will forgive me for not having much to say today, but I wanted–I needed–to say something. My wife– Megan . . ." His voice catches on the name. He swallows, then goes on. "Megan deserves more than I can say about her. Her intelligence, her courage, and her kindness are–were–beyond compare." He looks down at the glinting cylinder, turning it in his fingers. "She saw beauty everywhere she looked." He holds the cylinder up, turning it in his fingers. "Megan kept this kaleidoscope in her bedside table, and I would sometimes come in her room to see her looking through it. Looking through this was just one of the ways she turned a plain world beautiful and prismatic."

Here Douglas lifts the cylinder, holding it against one eye as he looks around the room through it: at his daughter Phoebe, at others, at Abigail. He puts it down. "On the back of your program you'll find a poem by Douglas Dunn. When I found this poem, I knew I had to read it today. Not only because he and I share a first name," and here he gives a wry smile, the smile of a man fighting through his grief. "We shared more than that, as you will see."

He takes a folded piece of paper from his side pocket. Unfolding and opening it with shaky hands, he reads:

The Kaleidoscope, by Douglas Dunn

To climb these stairs again, bearing a tray
Might be to find you pillowed with your books
Your inventories listing gowns and frocks
As if preparing for a holiday.
Or, turning from the landing, I might find
My presence watched through your kaleidoscope,
A symmetry of husbands, each redesigned
In lovely forms of foresight, prayer and hope.
I climb these stairs a dozen times a day
And, by the open door, wait, looking in
At where you died. My hands become a tray
Offering me, my flesh, my soul, my skin.
Grief wrongs us so. I stand, and wait, and cry
For the absurd forgiveness, not knowing why.

At the last words, Douglas lets both hands drop by his sides. His eyes are wet and red-rimmed, his voice edged with hoarseness. "I wait for that absurd forgiveness and ask for it."

◆ ◆ ◆

They leave the church in silence, buttoning wool coats against a raw, wet wind. Abigail's mother comes up behind them and pulls her aside. The wind lifts her thin, dyed-brown hair above her head in a halo. "I don't want to go over to the house. I'm not up for it, and they don't need me there. Give Doug my sympathy, all right?" She pats her daughter's arm and makes her way down the sidewalk carefully.

In the car, James says, "What was that bit about forgiveness about?"

Abigail shakes her head. "No idea, really. He's distraught, maybe not knowing entirely what he's saying. Did you see his hands shaking?"

James nods, looking both ways before he pulls into traffic. "Of course she was sick, but still, it's a shock. He probably feels responsible, like any of us feel when a loved one dies."

"Right. We feel that our love should have kept them alive, somehow." Actually, Abigail knows that Douglas had real reasons to ask Megan's forgiveness, things Megan or James knew nothing of, but she is not going to mention them to her husband

Chapter Two

For the past six months, Abigail has stayed with her friend Megan for part of the day, five days a week. Though Megan was only in her early fifties, Multiple Sclerosis and repeated falls had made her rely on a wheelchair. Abigail helped Megan wash her hair, she prepared her lunch, she went with her to the local library. She fetched Megan's old dulcimer from the closet and put it on her lap and sang harmony with her to "I'll Fly Away," their voices blending like they had when they were young.

Mostly, though, they would talk. With Douglas at work, they had time and privacy to talk about whatever they wanted. They had been childhood best friends on the North Shore of Massachusetts. Megan was eloquent and graceful, remembering things Abigail had forgotten about their childhood. Abigail still saw in her the young girl she had played with in Beverly. Megan always said Abigail was the prettier one, the smarter one, but Abigail knew she was being nice, trying to soothe Abigail's insecurities. Abigail was simply facing reality when she said that Megan was smarter, more popular, and nicer than Abigail. People liked Megan. Megan didn't have to try so hard; life came more easily to her.

Abigail was the funny one, the sassy one. Later, she was the sexy one.

Abigail would stop at Megan's house every day on her way home from school. From the moment she walked through the door, Abigail felt the warmth of the household, the comfort in being there. The kitchen was full of color and light, with sun pouring through the large French doors that looked out onto a garden. The rooms were full of art, comfy furniture, bookshelves. Megan's father was a lawyer, and her mother was always home when they walked in. She would offer them homemade peanut butter cookies. Abigail watched and waited for the secrets Megan must be hiding about her family; there must be something dark behind all that niceness.

Some days she would still be there when Megan's father got home. She looked for the tension when he came in the door, hung up his coat, greeted Abigail, and ruffled Megan's hair. All she saw was Megan tossing her head away from his touch, with an irritation that was part affection, part full confidence of the way she was loved. His arrival was the signal for Abigail to go home.

She would put on her parka and walk the two blocks to her house slowly, stopping on the side streets to look for cars. Her parents lived in a two-story house in a neighborhood with small, scruffy lawns. If her mother were home from the nursing home where she worked, Abigail would hear the familiar sound of her sewing machine when she walked through the door. Sewing helped her relax, she said. When Abigail no longer wanted the skirts or homemade doll clothes, her mother would sell them at craft fairs. Her mother would take her foot off the sewing machine, swipe the pins from between her lips, say "Hi, sweetie.

Oh, I guess I better get dinner started." Abigail would pick her way through piles of cloth and sewing supplies on the floor, to lean over and give her a kiss on the cheek. Her father was a realtor, and they never knew what time he'd come home.

For two summers in middle school, Abigail went with Megan to her family's summer cottage on the Maine coast. It was an old rambling place that had been in her family for generations. They slept in an upstairs room with two beds under a sloping roof, and a window that looked across a lawn to the ocean. They walked along the beach, gathering shells, and making sandcastles as if they were still young children. She felt like a child there, a happy child in this dream of a place. In the evenings they played on the braided rug in front of the huge old fireplace, and sometimes her parents would join them in a game. Abigail felt, for that week, as if she'd stepped into the world of one of the books she liked to read, books describing a world she didn't think really existed.

When they entered high school, Megan no longer invited Abigail to Maine. She and Megan were no longer so close then. Maybe Megan's parents wouldn't have wanted to encourage their friendship. Abigail's parents hit a financial hard spot, something about some bad business deals her father had made, and they sold their house and moved to an apartment in Salem, where rents were cheaper. Abigail changed schools before her junior year. She told herself that she didn't care; she had better things to do with her summer than go to Maine. She still dreams about the cottage, though, waking with a sense that she has been somewhere beloved, distant, and lost.

◆ ◆ ◆

Cars line the curb of the stately Georgian house. They park two blocks away and walk through slush, Abigail holding James' arm to steady her in her high heels. A light, wet snow is falling. She pushes her loose curls down into her collar and holds her coat shut with her free hand. Her eyes feel heavy, as if there are more tears that need to come out. She thinks of Callie, her tawny cat, stretching out on the rug at home. She wishes she were home with her, sitting in the chair by the lamp, looking out the window at the falling snow. Or shopping at the Chestnut Hill mall, buying something outrageous and expensive and sexy, something that she doesn't need. Or at a restaurant, having a late, boozy lunch with a friend. She wants to be anywhere except here, about to enter this house she's entered so many times before, this time to mourn the passing of her best friend.

In the entry way she considers taking off her wet shoes but decides to leave them on. She wants to leave them on because they make her legs in her black tights look good, then is ashamed to be thinking that at a time like this. Frank, the old yellow dog, ambles over to sniff her legs, tail wagging in recognition. In his eyes as he looks up at her, Abigail imagines she sees loss. She rubs behind his ears. Then Phoebe is there, offering to take their coats, and the girl's face above her dark blue dress is so pale and so brave and trying so hard that Abigail can't bear it. She throws her arms around Phoebe and holds her tight, feeling the tense muscles in Phoebe's back, feeling the girl's arms hold her tightly. Abigail tries to keep her own tears in while offering what she hopes is comfort.

Finally she pulls away, straightens her dress, and wipes her eyes. Phoebe smiles at her, a slight trembling in her lips, her eyes shiny and damp. "You shouldn't have to do that," Abigail says, taking the coats Phoebe holds over her arm. "Let me do that. Go on." She shoos her away with a hand, as if shooing her off to play with her friends, something she remembers Megan doing when Phoebe was younger. Megan would wave her off, smiling, as if to assure her not to worry, waiting until her daughter was out of the door to turn to her friend and hold her elbows, hunch her back, let the smile drop from her face.

The large kitchen is filled with people Abigail doesn't recognize. She carries the coats to the guest bedroom upstairs. There she lays them across the satiny deep red bedcover, pausing to touch the smooth fabric.

The room that had been Megan's is at the top of the stairs. She stops in the door, frozen for a moment. It is as if she shouldn't just go on, shouldn't pass by the open door as if nothing had happened there. As if the bed had always been made so smoothly, the throw pillows arranged so artfully. As if it wasn't calling her to come in. The bedside table is cleared of bottles and tissues and books, polished and shiny, holding only a lamp and a clock. The lamp is turned on. She steps in, hesitantly, and smells it: Megan's smell, the flowery scent she wore. Under that, the lemony smell of cleanser, and under that the faint smell of body, of illness. Abigail turns away quickly.

As she walks down the stairs she is remembering dinner parties at this house long ago, before Megan became ill. Giddy voices, laughter, and Abigail holding on to this railing to keep from stumbling from too much wine. Phoebe a little dark-haired girl then, asleep upstairs, the child Abigail imagined she would have had, if she'd been able to have a child. Megan again the fortunate one, the one with the family Abigail wanted.

She sees Judith, the home health aide, sitting in a chair in the corner, sipping coffee from a cup. Judith stands and puts her cup on the side table. She stayed with Megan in the times when Abigail or Doug couldn't be there. Abigail looks into Judith's broad, compassionate face and feels comforted, and then is enfolded by her hug. She sees the glint of the tiny gold cross necklace Judith always wears.

James is in the living room by the bay window, in conversation with the wife of an editor from the publishing house where Douglas works. Actually, James is listening, nodding, while the woman—yes, she thinks her name is Clara—talks animatedly. The woman is thin and stylish, with grey-streaked blonde hair, and the way she moves her hands as she talks reminds Abigail that Clara and her husband were here, at one of those dinners. Abigail pushes next to James and takes his free hand in hers, holding it close to her side. His other hand holds an open bottle of beer. Abigail says hello to the woman, not by name—just in case she is wrong—and looks at the beer.

He glances at the other woman. "Clara was kind enough to bring me this."

"I think I'll have one, too." She makes her way to the table against the wall where she sees beer and opened bottles of wine next to cheese and crackers and fruit. Flowers in a glass vase. She pours herself a glass of wine, marveling at the ability of Douglas and Phoebe to pull this all together, in the midst of everything. How did they do it? Did someone help them? Megan's parents are gone, dead years now in an accident, and Abigail has never met Doug's mother. She thinks she lives in New York. Should Abigail have helped? She called yesterday, asking if there was anything she could do, and Phoebe assured her there wasn't. A friend of Doug's was helping. She did say Abigail could come over the day after the funeral, to help sort things.

She looks around the room of men and women in dark clothes, talking in murmuring voices. Any laughter that arises is quickly subdued. A woman in front of her steps aside, leaving a clear view of Douglas. On the other side of the room, by the arched doorway to the kitchen, he stands with one hand in his pocket, the other running his fingers through his hair in a distracted way. He is saying something, rapidly, to the woman next to him, a woman Abigail doesn't know. His eyes are closed as he speaks, shaking his head slightly, as if he can't bear to say what he is saying. He opens his eyes then, and looks at Abigail, who is looking at him.

Chapter Three

It was last Saturday night, a week ago, when Abigail got the call. She'd been asleep, turned on her side away from James in their dark bedroom, when the land line in the hallway rang. Or maybe she hadn't been asleep; maybe she'd been half-awake, half-dreaming that she was here in bed, about to receive a phone call. Maybe the phone rang several times before she was awake enough to realize that it was a real phone, not a dream phone, and she needed to get out of bed to answer it. She still wasn't quite awake when she said hello, feeling exposed and confused in the coolness of the dark hallway. The blue numbers of the clock said it was 1:10. Out the window to her left, a nearly full moon rose over the trees.

Doug's voice was husky, strained. "I can't wake her," he said. "Can you come over?"

"Of course," Abigail said, and it was only after she hung up that she wondered why he hadn't called the ambulance, why she hadn't told him to call the ambulance. James asked her the same thing, as she struggled into her jeans and sweater in the dark bedroom. "Why did he call you? What does he think you can do?"

"I don't know," she said. "I'll call him back."

"Why was he trying to wake her, anyway?" James asked as she left the room.

"Medicine time," Abigail called over her shoulder as she ran down the stairs. She waited until she was sitting behind the wheel of her car before calling Douglas back. There was no answer.

At their house, Abigail parked the car in the drive and ran to the front door. She rang the doorbell, then tried the door. It was unlocked. She ran up the stairs, feet pounding on the thick carpet. The light came from the open door at the top of the stairs, where Abigail saw Douglas. He was leaning over the prone figure of Megan on the bed. With both hands on her shoulders, he was shaking her. Abigail would remember always the sound of his voice as he called her name; it was full of a restrained fury, like there was an anger he was trying to suppress. *Megan! Megan! Wake up!* he called over and over again, as if she could hear him, but was willfully not answering. From the looseness of Megan's body as he shook her, and from the whiteness of her face, Abigail knew that was not the case. She saw her eyelids flutter, though, so she was alive. "Have you called the ambulance?" Abigail said, and when he didn't answer, shouted "The ambulance!" Douglas looked at her then, as if he didn't know who she was, or what she was doing there. "Have you called them?" she asked.

"No," he said, and Abigail didn't wait to ask why.

After calling 911, Abigail pulled Douglas away from his wife. She leaned down, putting her hand to Megan's throat to feel her pulse, then in front of her mouth. Megan's breathing was soft, very slow, but regular. "Sit down," she said, leading

Doug to the stuffed chair by the bed, the chair Abigail would sit in when she and Megan had their time together. "Sit." He finally sat, with a shuddering sigh that was like a collapse. Abigail sat on the edge of the bed, next to Megan. She smoothed Megan's soft brown hair back from her face, where it had fallen when Douglas was shaking her, and took her friend's hand. Megan remained still, with eyes closed, but breathing. Abigail hummed, then began to sing in a low voice the song they sometimes sang together: "Some bright morning when this life is over, I'll fly away . . ." She stopped, realizing what the lyrics were saying—how could they have sung that, all these years? She stroked Megan's hand, and sat humming instead, her voice finding any tune, any series of notes—*lullaby, and good night, oh my baby sleep tight*—just to make a sound for Megan, to let her know they were there. She glanced at Douglas, who sat slumped in the chair, holding a hand over his mouth.

She stopped humming when she heard voices from below, and quick footsteps on the stairs. Before they entered the room, Abigail leaned over and whispered in her friend's ear, "Don't fly away just yet, sweetheart."

They lifted Megan onto a stretcher and put straps around her, something Abigail had seen only in movies, or in glimpses as she drove by accidents on the highway. Doug followed down the stairs. "Call Phoebe, will you?" he said over his shoulder as he went out the door. His face was wild, the face of someone else, and Abigail didn't ask what she should tell Phoebe. She called Phoebe's number once and got no answer. She left a message, "Call me, please," and tried again ten minutes later. This time Phoebe picked up. Her voice hoarse, she asked what was wrong. "It's your mother," Abigail said. "I don't know what's wrong, but your father called an ambulance. They're on the way to the hospital now."

"Should I come? I'll come," Phoebe said. "I'll be there as quick as I can."

After telling her to drive carefully and saying goodbye, Abigail stood in the hallway. The lamp was on in Megan's bedroom, shining on the rumpled bed, the cluttered bedside table. She stood looking at the glass of water on the table, a crumpled tissue. A few scattered white pills. Abigail switched the light off and walked downstairs. Frank stood by the living room window, pushing his nose through the curtain to look at the road. She patted his head, saying, "It will be all right, Frankie." She left a lamp on.

At home, she lay on the couch under a blanket, staring up at the ceiling with her cell phone on the table beside her. Callie padded into the room and jumped on Abigail, turning until she found the right spot to settle on Abigail's abdomen. She stroked the cat's fur, seeing, over and over again, the strange stark color of Megan's skin. She thought the sound of her friend's breathing had begun to change as she was being carried down the stairs and was trying to remember what it sounded like. Rasping, sort of? She couldn't remember, it had been such a whirl. She kept hearing Phoebe's voice on the phone, hoarse and disoriented, as she said she would leave right away.

When the sky began to lighten through the white living room curtains, Abigail went upstairs to lie next to her husband. He didn't stir, and his quiet regular breathing in the dark calmed her. He was steadiness, her rock. When she woke hours later, the space next to her was empty. She opened the curtains, looking out to see the empty space in the driveway where he usually parked. On her phone, still on the coffee table, was a text from Doug. "She's gone," and next to it, a note on a scrap of paper from James. "I'm sorry." Sweet James; as if it were his fault, as if any of it were his fault.

◆ ◆ ◆

Abigail side-steps the people in the living room to reach Doug. She touches his arm, and he turns to her. Their arms rise at the same time to hold one another; she feels the warmth of his chest through his shirt, through her dress. She forces herself to hold on, to not let go too quickly; they are simply old friends, comforting one another. It's okay to hold on, no one will think anything of it. Then Doug turns to James, who has followed her, and they hug. Abigail wants to be in the middle of them, wants to feel both those bodies pressed against hers, wants that warmth. It's not an idle thought; she *wants* it, wants it so badly that she bites her lip and turns away. She looks up to see Phoebe watching her from a few feet away. The girl has a tender look on her face, a small rueful smile; she sees Abigail's distress, and attributes it to sadness over her mother's death. And it is, Abigail thinks; it is sadness, and grief, and love, and lust all messed up together within her.

Chapter Four

Abigail's life spooled away from Megan's before it slid back again. When she was a sophomore at UMass Amherst, the fabric of her inner life, never entirely sturdy, began to fray. She sat alone in her dorm room one night and wondered what it would be like to climb twelve stories up to the roof and jump off. She'd found a way to get up there, one drunk night—a door with a broken lock, allowing her to creep along a narrow tunnel to another, secret door, which opened on to a roof. She sat on the hard mattress of her single bed looking out the window at dusky clouds that floated by on a windy spring evening, grey shading to lavender and a sliced moon, and thought, rather dreamily, of how fun it would be to leap off that roof.

There wasn't anything in particular that made Abigail feel suicidal that night. Nothing more than the usual. Her parents' financial situation was a mess, but that wasn't exactly news. Her dad had made some questionable decisions that decimated their retirement, and they had to sell the house. No money to pay for Abigail's college expenses, of course. She paid it with loans and a part-time job.

And then there was romance; also, nothing that was big news. Abigail always had a crush on someone, and the more inaccessible he was, the better. The latest was a theatre major, a slight, intense young man who seemed to–for reasons that made no sense to her, no sense at all—prefer another theatre major, a young woman even more slight than he was, over Abigail. That was really no more than an irritation, though, a sense that the young man had made a mistake, shown himself to have poor judgement. It was puzzling that someone would choose another woman over her.

The urge to climb the stairs and creep up to the roof didn't have directly to do with him. As she sat at the window, thoughtfully chewing a fingernail, she thought it had to do with two things. One, the urge for glory, for that moment when she leaped—laughing—off that roof, the woosh, and how it would forever be emblazoned on the memory of that theatre major, and of last semester's political science major. And the art major before that. And two, the sense that it really, truly, did not matter whether she did that or not: whether she made the effort of climbing up and seizing her bright moment of glory, becoming one with the grey/lavender sky, or whether she continued to sit in front of her dorm window, chewing a finger which was now bleeding, seeing no sense in any of this. None of it mattered, any choice was as good or as meaningless as any other choice.

Remembering that her mother, at least, would prefer that she not jump, Abigail decided the safer choice was to drop out of school. She found herself a little studio apartment off campus on the ground floor of an old house. She took more hours at the pizza place where she worked downtown, switching to making pizzas instead of serving them, which appealed to her. She didn't have to smile at customers. She enjoyed teaching herself how to throw the balls of dough in the air, stretching and twirling them in her hands. Occasionally men made suggestive comments to her as they picked up their pizza *(Do you have an extra pillow on your bed?)*, and–because she wasn't working for tips–she didn't have to answer unless she wanted to.

Abigail visited Megan at Bard once during this time. Bard was very different from UMass: smaller, richer, with cuter guys. At a party in an old house Megan took her to, Abigail met a long-haired music major who reminded her of James Taylor. Thin, lanky, mysterious. The air was full of marijuana and cigarette smoke. Abigail shared a bowl with the music major, whose name she forgot, then followed him out a side door. On a bare mattress on a dark back porch, she let him pull down her jeans. Without asking, he pulled a condom from his back pocket, and rolled it over his erect penis. She didn't object. When he was done, they went back inside. No one but Megan noticed they had been gone.

The next night they heard classical music in a building that had giant pieces of curved and twisted metal surrounding it, as if it were messily wrapped in sheets of aluminum foil. It was designed by a famous architect, Megan said. They walked from the concert back to the dorm with Megan's friends, where they sat in a lounge drinking wine from plastic cups. After Megan went to bed, Abigail went with one of Megan's friends–a slight young man who reminded her of her theatre major–back to his room. He was more polite than the music major, kissing her gently and asking her what she wanted to do. In response, she tugged at his belt and unzipped his jeans. He was surprisingly large.

Since high school, Abigail and Megan had written letters to one another regularly, but after Abigail returned to Amherst, they lost touch. Abigail forgot to write for a while—she was distracted, her life suddenly pressing, with messy immediacy, around her—and it was months before she realized she hadn't heard from Megan. Abigail hated to talk on the phone, to be required to sound like the person someone on the other end of the line expected her to be. She wrote Megan a letter instead, describing the past months in a breezy, off-handed way, referring elliptically to intense relationships and a bout of depression. Her goal was to sound cocky and self-assured, letting her friend know she had experienced the depths of human experience more deeply than Megan had, and had learned how to handle them and rise above it all, her wit and charm only enhanced. To make herself a hero. To make Megan admire her, maybe even see some appeal in Abigail's life that hers, at the ritzy private school, didn't have. Megan's reply was sympathetic and graceful, but brief, and revealed nothing of her life. Abigail sensed a reserve, a drawing away. She never got around to answering Megan's note.

◆ ◆ ◆

People are saying goodbye, holding Doug and Phoebe in long hugs. Abigail watches a woman she doesn't know hug Phoebe, then hold her out at arm's length, looking intently into her face. Phoebe is trying to smile but looks desperately pale. Doug is slumped beside her in an armchair, holding out his hands to be enveloped in a double hand clasp by an older woman Abigail doesn't know. Abigail slides over to Phoebe's side and touches her arm, breaking her away from the other woman's beseeching gaze. "I will stop by tomorrow, okay?" she murmurs. Phoebe turns to her with a grateful smile.

"Thanks, Auntie Abby," she says, a nickname from years ago.

In the car, Abigail closes the door with a sigh. "Thank god that's over."

James buckles his seat belt slowly and then just sits for a moment, hands resting on the steering wheel, staring ahead. His face is slack, exhausted. Sad. Abigail remembers that he cared for Megan, too; she doesn't share this grief alone. She puts a hand on his arm, squeezes. "Yes," he says. He starts the car and pulls slowly onto the empty road.

Chapter Five

The next morning Abigail wakes up feeling every one of her fifty-four years. Her knees crack when she gets out of bed. Megan, you left in the nick of time, she says to her face in the mirror. You knew it would be downhill from here, didn't you? She splashes cold water on her cheeks.

James is having coffee at the table with the newspaper spread out in front of him. Abigail pulls the cereal box from the cupboard. "They're going after the immigrants," he notes darkly.

"It's what he said he'd do," Abigail said. "It will get worse." She couldn't believe her country had elected that man in November, whose name she didn't want to say, and she couldn't believe he would be allowed to remain in the White House. The House so recently inhabited by the principled, intelligent couple who urged their followers to "Go High" when others tried to drag them down. It hurts her to think of it, but she can't help checking the news cycle first thing every morning, to see what he is doing now, to see if there is some way he will be forced to leave office.

She has arranged to meet Phoebe at Douglas's house. Phoebe answers her knock and brings her into the kitchen.

Megan's wheelchair is parked by the door, as if waiting to go out. "Someone is picking that up today," Phoebe says. She wears leggings and a sweatshirt with the hood pulled over her head. Still pale, she looks a little more herself than she did the day before. She drove over from her apartment in Boston, where she is studying film. "Dad's at work," she says.

"Work?" Abigail looks quizzically at Phoebe, thinking, the day after his wife's funeral, and he goes to work?

Phoebe lifts her hands, drops them. "You know what a workaholic he is. It comforts him, I think, the regularity of it."

Abigail puts her bag on the floor and looks around. Yesterday's dishes are washed but the floor is dirty, and the large table is stacked with cards and covered dishes. She has always loved Megan and Doug's house; it is nearly 200 years old, with a kitchen looking out to a peaceful, landscaped lawn. Every time she sees it, Abigail thinks she should work on their own lawn. "And how about you?" she asks. "Are you missing classes?"

Phoebe shakes her head. "It's spring break week." She smiles weakly at Abigail. "Convenient, right? Mom was always considerate."

"Are you still seeing that guy? Jonathan?"

Phoebe shrugs one shoulder. "Sometimes."

"He seemed nice. What can I do to help here?"

Phoebe looks around. "Dad is taking care of the financial stuff, the legal stuff, and Jennifer will come to clean. He asked if we could go through her things here at home. You know, deciding what to do with them, her clothes, that kind of stuff."

"Oh! It's so soon, isn't it?"

Phoebe scratches her head under the hood, rubs her face. "I don't know. I don't know how these things go. Dad asked me to, so I thought . . . I mean, he and I will go through some things ourselves. I'll put some stuff aside for him and me to look at together. He just didn't want to tackle it all. Do you mind?" Phoebe looks at Abigail anxiously, two neat worry lines between her brows.

Abigail wants to smooth those lines out. "Of course, whatever you two want. I'm at your service."

Phoebe had been a toddler when Abigail and James moved back to the North Shore. She was a charming child, always smiling, laughing, learning new words precociously. She inspired Abigail to try to have a child, something James had been wanting. After several years, they were both tested, and were told there was something wrong with Abigail's cervical mucus. The doctor said her mucus was "hostile" to the egg. There were treatments they could try, but the idea of one of her own organs biologically hostile to new life in her body had convinced Abigail not to try them. It was as if her body were telling her, reaffirming something about herself that she'd always suspected; there was something deep within her, uncontrollable, that was hostile to life.

Yet being around Phoebe always warmed Abigail, cheered her. She loved the girl; she always had, from the moment she laid eyes on her. How could she be hostile to life, when she loved this bit of growing life so much?

In the bedroom they stand uncertainly, before Phoebe opens the door of the walk-in closet and switches on the light. "Guess we might as well start here," she says. One side of shelves and racks are filled with Doug's suits coats, pastel button-up shirts, jeans, and sweaters neatly folded. No shoes litter the floor, all lined up on a shoe rack.

The other side, by contrast, is a jumble of color and fabric. Patterned blouses hang half-off the hangers, voluminous skirts of the type Megan favoured falling on the floor, leggings and sweaters thrown onto shelves rather than folded, shoes scattered. Drawers hanging half-open, draped with unfolded items. Phoebe laughs. "Can you believe they stayed married as long as they did?"

"Well, it was love."

"First love–for Mom, at least, she told me, and it lasted twenty-eight years."

Abigail steps forward, lifting up the sleeve of a sweater hanging out of a drawer, and dropping it. "You should go through these things first, to see what you want to keep. She was close to your size."

Phoebe shakes her head. "I would rather do it together. I don't want to be in here alone."

Abigail realizes she'd been wanting to hear something like this; something that indicated that she, Abigail, is needed, not just as a pair of hands but as emotional support. She turns to the clothes. Phoebe told her she could take whatever she wanted, but it seems wrong, as if she's stealing, as if taking the clothes is a kind of schadenfreude. As if she is proclaiming herself the winner in some unstated battle, and to the victor go the spoils. She picks up a soft gray shawl; the label says it is hand-knit in Ireland. Holding it in her hands, she looks at Phoebe. "Take it," Phoebe says. "Mom would want you to."

Phoebe's taste in clothes runs toward the minimalist, while her mother's, especially after she became ill, was all exuberance and patterns. There are some older, more professional clothes from when she worked at the publishing house, but the more recent ones are colorful. Colors cheered her, Megan said. They fold items to take to the thrift store. Every now and then, Phoebe holds something up to herself, looking in the mirror; a silk blouse, a scarf. Every time, Abigail says, "Yes. It looks good on you." They all look good on Phoebe; everything looks good on Phoebe.

Phoebe's hand holding the scarf drops, and she looks at Abigail. Her face puckers. "I hate this," she says. "I really hate this."

Abigail is there, arms folded around her, letting Phoebe's head drop onto her shoulder. "I know. I know."

"The scarf..." Phoebe throws it to the floor. "I don't want the scarf. I want my mother."

"We don't have to do this now. Maybe it's too soon." She feels the girl's sorrow, and her own, and something else, something she can't look directly at, can't acknowledge: the small, gleeful thought that now, she can mother Phoebe.

◆ ◆ ◆

Douglas was Megan's first love, but Abigail doubted Megan was his first love. Abigail's first love lasted two years. She met Ryan at a pub in Amherst. Just off work as a pizza chef, she was sweaty, her clothes sauce-stained. He was at a stool leaning forward onto the bar, smoking a cigarette. Though the place was half-empty, she sat next to him. He turned to look at her, and she said, "You've really got that *Barfly* look going." When he continued to gaze blankly at her, she said, "You know, the film? Micky Rourke? Based on Charles Bukowski? Never mind." She took her wine to an empty table, and after a stunned minute, he followed. After several glasses, she invited him to her one-room apartment. As she unlocked the door, he lifted her hair and kissed the back of her neck in a way that sent shivers down to her legs.

He was older than Abigail, thirty to her twenty-one, but she sometimes felt older than him. They moved in together almost as soon as they met, a real apartment with a bedroom and a kitchen. Ryan had a job delivering furniture. In his free time he played the guitar and worked on a novel. And drank and got high. Abigail bought a little Ficus plant, put a retro flowered tablecloth over the Formica table with the metal legs, tried to learn how to cook something other than macaroni and cheese. Ryan kept the cupboard stocked with gin.

His friends treated her kindly, like a little sister they liked to corrupt. Abigail went from drinking on weekends to making gin and tonics after work every day. The freshness of the drink seemed sophisticated, mature, healthy; a tonic. Ryan would light up a joint in the morning, and she discovered being high made the walk to work pleasant, softened the colors of the pizza restaurant, made her co-workers funny instead of annoying.

She lost touch with Megan—forgot about her, sort of— and rarely was in touch with her own parents, though she didn't exactly forget about them. It was a long drive from Amherst to Beverly. After she'd been living with Ryan for a while, she got him to wear a long-sleeved shirt that covered most of his tattoos, and drive to her parents' apartment. Ryan was the first boyfriend she'd ever brought home. They made the trip there and back in a day to avoid spending the night.

She remembers that day, over a quarter of century later. Her mother, opening the door smiling and neat in her pastel outfit; her father standing tall and forbidding, shaking Ryan's hand without looking at his face. Abigail knew he would not approve of Ryan, and she tried not to care. Her parents' kitchen in the apartment smelled like the meatloaf her mother had cooked. She remembered the expression on her mother's face as Abigail told her, "Oh I'm sorry, we're vegetarians now. I thought I mentioned it." Ryan, in a rare moment of tact, decided to have some meatloaf when he saw Abigail's mother's face. He was rewarded with her mother's grateful smile as she cut him a thick slice. "That looks really good," he said. Abigail's father sat silent, all military bearing and dark looks.

After lunch, they brought coffee out on the little deck that overlooked a shared yard. Abigail's mother asked Ryan about his work, his music. Her father stared out into the yard, eyes following a cat slinking through the weeds growing against the fence. They could hear a baseball game from a radio inside a neighbor's apartment.

"Your mother's nice," Ryan said as they left. He sucked on his cigarette, which he'd somehow refrained from for two and a half hours. "But what's your dad's deal, anyway?"

Abigail shrugged. "No one is ever good enough for his little girl," she said, though that wasn't quite right. "He's always that way," which was more right. "Maybe he's jealous of you." This last comment was closer to the truth than she wanted to say.

THE SYMMETRY OF HUSBANDS

♦ ♦ ♦

Phoebe picks up the scarf and folds it carefully. "I don't know if I can do this right now."

"Let's leave it. We can come back to it."

Phoebe walks over to the bedside table and opens the top drawer, revealing neat rows of brown plastic medicine bottles. She takes one out and looks at it. "What are we to do with these?"

"I'll take them," Abigail says. "James knows where to take pills in order to get them disposed of properly."

"Thank goodness," Phoebe says, and hands Abigail the bottle. "I'll make us some lunch."

The table is a three-drawer marble-topped antique, one Abigail had always admired but never looked in. She wonders if the kaleidoscope Doug held at the ceremony is kept in this table, if that's why she'd never seen it before. Doug would prepare Megan's meds in the morning before Abigail arrived, setting them out on the kitchen counter. He lined them up in a little pill holder, a plastic container with separate sections for different times of the day. He left a printed note telling when and how to give Megan the pills in the first compartment, the second, the third. Abigail at first felt condescended to, treated like a teenage babysitter, but she appreciated the ease of following his directions. It had become hard for Megan to swallow; she coughed and choked, and it took a while to get things down, even when Abigail crushed the medicine and dissolved it in water. Abigail would put the pills with a cup of water on the table and sit with her as she slowly got them down.

Megan paid no attention to what medicine she was taking. She swallowed the pills, if she were able, and after coughing and choking, continued talking about what they'd been discussing before this matter of medication had so rudely interrupted. The pills were an annoyance that had nothing to do with who she was, or with what she was talking about, what was important to her. In her last years she suffered from back pain from falls, but Megan didn't want to talk about it; she would not be defined by her illness, or pain, or her failing body, or the things she needed to do to keep it alive.

Abigail takes out the brown plastic pill containers one by one, throwing the rattling containers into her large shoulder bag. Under them in the drawer are pencils and pens, and an unframed photo of baby Phoebe, grinning at the camera to show her one tooth. A photo of Megan and Doug, leaning into one another, smiling. Doug is wearing a light-colored suit and Megan a creamy, antique-looking dress with lace trim. She is holding a bouquet. They are outdoors, standing under a white tent. When they married, Abigail and Megan were out of touch, and she had not been invited to her wedding. In the photo Doug looks jubilant, as if he has won a prize, and Megan's face is hazed with sunlight. The light surrounding them, Abigail thinks, looks like happiness. She feels something familiar when she looks at the photo, at the joy on their faces; a painful twinge she doesn't want to probe too deeply. She doesn't see the kaleidoscope, but under the wedding photo is a flowered cloth-bound journal. She opens it gingerly to see Megan's neat handwriting. She raises her head and listens: a faint kitchen clatter, the banging of a pan. She closes the journal and slips it into her bag, along with the pills.

Chapter Six

Abigail tells herself she took the journal for Phoebe's sake. She wanted to read it through before she gave it to her, to make sure there is nothing there that will hurt her. The journal rests in the bottom of her bag, under the pills, under the shawl and a light jacket that smells like Megan's perfume. Maybe Megan wrote things in the journal that she wouldn't want her daughter to see. More truthfully, Abigail hopes there is nothing there that will make Phoebe think less of her, of Abigail. She had no doubt, when she took the journal, that it was something she had to do; that in some undefined way, it was the right thing to do.

When she lets herself into the house, Callie winds herself around her ankles. "Hello," she hears James call from his office. She picks up the cat and walks to the open office door to see him at his desk typing, papers spread on every surface. "Hi there," she says.

He looks up at her, bemused, distracted. His glasses are smudged. "How was it over there?"

Abigail shrugs, stroking Callie. "Okay. Phoebe was glad to have me there, I think."

James nods. "Emotional support." His eyes wander back to his laptop.

Abigail hangs the blouse in her closet, puts the shawl in a drawer, and takes her bag into her office. Her office is a former nursery next to the bedroom. From her desk pushed against the wall, she has a view into the back lawn. At one time she pictured a swing set in that open space, maybe a treehouse in the oak tree. A crib against the wall, next to her desk. She planted flowers where the swing set would have gone—tulips and daffodils in spring, roses and hydrangeas later. Now the bushes are bare, their branches damp and dark against a thin cover of snow, as if in a black and white photo.

The cover of the journal is thick and padded. Inside Megan has written *Megan Adams*, the script especially careful, as if she were signing a contract. Doug's handwriting, as Abigail recalls, is loose and large, angled to the right like a sailboat leaning into the wind, while James' is small and neat, like Megan's. Abigail's own handwriting is sloppy, slanting up and down, often illegible. She wonders if that means anything. Callie sits at her feet, looking up expectantly. She lifts the book so the cat can jump up, settling herself on Abigail's jeans. She reaches around the cat to put the book on the desk and turns the page.

The first entry is dated 1998, almost twenty years ago. Written on the title page: "Happy Boss's Day! You're great!" Apparently, it was a gift from Megan's administrative assistant at the publishing house. Abigail reads over the first page quickly. She expected notes about Megan's life, documenting Phoebe's growth, marital issues perhaps (she would love to read *those*), but finds notes instead, scribbled notes jotted across the page, sometimes slanting up and down; little sketches of a plant, a goofy cartoon-like dog, a face. The drawings show a skill Abigail had forgotten Megan had; now she remembers admiring her work in Art class when they were kids, and then again in high school. She remembers their classmates saw Megan as an artist. What are the notes? Bits of poems, perhaps? She can't tell; she makes out: *your face, laughing then still; your eyes, brown, looking, wondering, questioning . . . passed.* Doug's eyes were blue. Was she referring to someone who had died? A comprehensible, neatly written note: *Jenny gave me this journal for Boss's Day, and for her, I should use it to write beautiful things.* This is followed, the irony either intentional or unintentional, by a to-do list: *Monday, Dr. appt, 2:00. Pick Phoebe up 3:00; buy gift for Zane.* Abigail remembers Zane, one of Phoebe's friends, a round-eyed little boy.

The thought of Zane brings back a flood of memories. Abigail and James had just moved back to the area, as he began a tenure-track job at Salem State. Abigail had finally completed her Master's degree, and was teaching part-time: First-Year Writing in the fall, Introduction to Literature in the spring. Abigail and Megan picked up their friendship again, cautiously. Megan was friendly, but hesitant. Abigail scoured her memory to see how she had offended her. She knew she'd been reckless in years past, in so many ways; which of those ways had hurt her friend? She remembered visiting her at Bard, long ago. A few letters after that, and they'd fallen out of touch.

Their first meeting at Starbucks had been uncomfortable. Abigail, falling back into envy patterns from long ago, thought that Megan looked wonderful, her shoulder-length curls a natural mix of light and darker brown. Megan had the good job; Megan's family life was everything Abigail wanted. Rallying, she told Megan she loved teaching part-time because it gave her time to write and just live her life, so much that she would choose it over a full-time job; how she and James hadn't had a child but really, they enjoyed the freedom to pick up and go wherever they wanted—just last weekend they'd gone to New York, to hear jazz and see a Broadway play.

Was it that meeting, or a later date when they'd gone to a bar next door, where they'd had wine and more of the truth? The place had been shadowy after bright sunlight, nearly empty. The padded booth in the corner protected them, enclosing them, and Abigail remembers being tired of projecting her own perfect life. "We've had our ups and down," Abigail said of her marriage. "We both drank too much, and we would fight. We work hard to keep it in line, both of us."

"Ups and downs," Megan said. "Tell me about it." She'd nearly left Doug over an affair she'd discovered he was having. She took baby Phoebe with her and left. "Just picked up and left. I went to the cottage in Maine. Stayed there a couple of days, then went back."

"That must have been hard," Abigail murmured, staring at her friend. Megan's face in the dim light was narrow and expressive, framed by thick curls, her smile wry. It was hard for Abigail to believe that Megan's marriage wasn't perfect.

Megan said, "What was hard was to go back. To trust him that it was over...to believe it wouldn't happen again." Megan seemed to need someone she could confide in, someone she could trust. She looked at Abigail searchingly, as if to see if she was still that person. Abigail wanted to be that person.

Megan said, "I felt, in a way, as if I *should* have left him. Like if I'd been stronger, more true to myself, I would have." She looked at Abigail and shrugged. "But he's a good father to Phoebe, and she loves him, and . . . you know? I like our life."

"I know," Abigail said, but she didn't know if she did know, actually.

The couples started meeting occasionally for dinner. Abigail and Megan took Phoebe out to the park, to the Boston Children's Museum, to the Aquarium. Abigail, in love with the little girl, offered to babysit, and once in a while they took her up on it. She had put Phoebe to bed at Megan and Doug's house the night Doug came home from a business dinner, the night they first talked together alone.

◆ ◆ ◆

She puts the journal down to get ready for class. She is teaching Introduction to Literature at the university, meeting once a week. As she dresses, draping Megan's shawl over her dress, she thinks of the first time she met Doug. When they were introduced, Abigail felt an electrical shock, a jolt to her midsection. It was something she'd felt just a few times before in her life, something so rare that she thought it would be wrong, immoral in the large scheme of things, to ignore it. She knew, then, why his young co-worker had taken up with this married man. *Who wouldn't,* she'd thought.

The class meets in a basement room, painted bright green and lit by fluorescent overhead lights. She always flinches when she enters the room. Tonight they will discuss Raymond Carver's "Cathedral." The story's narrator, a non-communicative man who drinks and smokes steadily, is forced into hosting a blind man, a friend of his wife's. In the story's strange, transcendent ending, the narrator closes his eyes and, with the help of Robert, the blind man, sketches a cathedral, and has a brief, powerful moment of freedom. "These guys must be really drunk," a student says. "You see all the booze they pound down? And then they get stoned?"

"Yes, why?" Abigail asks. "Why does Carver have this guy drink so much? What does it show about the character?"
"He knows how to have a good time?" a young man suggests. The class laughs.

"He's unhappy unless he's drinking?" a young woman asks, twirling her hair around her finger.

"He's trying to connect," another says.

"Yes, Malik?" She calls on the dark young man at the back of the room, who has a hand half-raised.

"He's afraid he can't talk to anyone." Malik's voice is husky and slow, tinged with an accent. "He can't see any meaning in his life. He thinks the alcohol and weed will give him courage, will help him make sense of things."

"Yes." Abigail pauses, caught by the music of Malik's voice, his searching expression. "And does it help?" she asks. It seems a non-literary question, maybe not the best way to approach the text, but she wants to know what they think.

"He seems happier at the end," a young woman in the front row says in a hesitant voice.

Malik leans forward, long fingers supporting his chin. "He connects with the blind man," he says, "because they are drawing a cathedral together. They are communicating not because they are wasted, but because they are thinking of God." He says *wasted* as if it is a curse word and breathes out *God* like a mantra.

Abigail doesn't respond. She is remembering reading this story aloud to Megan, on a winter evening last winter. Megan had been feeling particularly unwell, and Doug had asked Abigail to stay with her. There was somewhere he had to go, Abigail doesn't remember where. Megan, resting in bed, asked Abigail to read to her. It was already dark outside as she sat in the lamp light next to where Megan lay propped up by pillows. After she read the final lines: "My eyes were still closed. I was in my house. I knew that. But I didn't feel like I was inside anything," there was a silence, and Abigail thought that Megan had fallen asleep. Then she'd opened her eyes, looked at Abigail, and smiled.

"I didn't feel like I was inside anything," she said softly. "Not even this wreck of a body, for a moment."

Abigail is looking at the students, who are looking at her, and she can't remember what they are talking about.

Chapter Seven

Abigail and Ryan did some hard drinking in the time they were together. She thinks back on that time fondly. If she forgets the hung-over mornings when she had to go to work; forgets hunger satisfied by booze because there was usually not enough food in the house; if she remembers instead the warmth of that first drink, with Ryan and his friends at their apartment, or a bar, or some party, and how her giddiness rose as the evening progressed, the giddiness seeming to be a part of the night and the experience, not even related to the gin or scotch she drank; how beautiful she felt; how she stopped worrying and set herself free; and the laughs she and Ryan had together before things turned sour, then it was a wonderful time, a hilarious, glamorous time. They were the Fitzgeralds without the money, the young Bob Dylan without the music, or Dylan Thomas himself, without the poems. How long was it before their lives together lost their sparkle, darkened and turned sad; two years? It was gradual, Abigail supposed, though in her memory it went from daylight and sunlight to something not dark as night but just grey, barren, a kind of bleakness that diminished her.

Leaving Ryan was the hardest thing she'd ever done. Yes, she'd been in love, but she moved in with him because it would save on rent, and would be fun, not because they were ready to commit to one another in the long term. At least that's how she'd felt.

She remembered coming back for the last of her stuff on a Sunday morning. Ryan was sitting in his wooden rocker drinking coffee, feet on the windowsill since she'd taken the coffee table for her new place. The winter sun poured into their small kitchen and living room, bare now without her things. Ryan was hungover as usual, with shadows under his eyes and a dark stubble on his cheeks. Standing by the doorway with a bag full of clothes and toiletries, she felt as if she were escaping a trap she'd accidentally walked into. She was longing to get away, to be done with him looking at her, to get on with her life. She could make something of herself, she thought. She saw her coffee maker on the counter behind him but didn't want to move over to pick it up. "Well, goodbye," she said. He didn't answer, just turned his head to look out the window.

Abigail got a waitress job at a restaurant where she earned good tips. Living by herself in a small studio apartment, she was able to save enough money to buy a car, and to start taking classes again at UMass Amherst. She didn't worry about earning a degree, and she didn't worry about pleasing her parents by choosing a major they wanted her to do, since she paid for classes herself. She took subjects that interested her: drawing, fiction writing, literature. She took a class in contemporary Irish literature taught by a young teaching assistant named James McDowell. He was of medium height, solidly built, with fair hair and a pale complexion. Abigail didn't often speak in class, but noticed that whenever she did raise her hand, however tentatively, the TA called on her. He never looked at her directly; in fact, he rarely looked any of the students in the eye. When discussing a poem or answering a question, he would instead gaze out the windows close to the ceiling. This gave the impression that he was staring up at the sky, at God perhaps, to gather his inspiration. Despite these eccentricities, or because of them, the students liked him, calling him Dr. Mac even though he told them he wasn't a doctor, yet.

Abigail didn't see the young TA again until she went to a fiction reading on campus the next year. She came in late, taking a seat near the back. Halfway through the reading, she glanced to her right, and it was him sitting next to her, their upper arms touching. "Oh!" she said, surprised. She saw by his embarrassed smile, by his eyes looking over her left shoulder instead of directly at her, that he'd recognized her.

◆ ◆ ◆

Abigail plans a lamb stew for dinner. It's a recipe she wanted to try but was reluctant to buy lamb. She has in her mind a living lamb, one she saw when she was a child. She remembers a round hill, green with spring grass, on a farm outside of town. Wind blowing, and a small white lamb running around the field, kicking its little heels before running to its mother. To cook the meat today, she has to get over the idea that the lamb was, to her, the perfect representation of young life, spring, beauty, and childhood, sunshine and a warm breeze carrying the smell of flowers after a long winter. The owner, an acquaintance of her father's, let her touch the lamb's round head, covered with curly fur. She loved it.

THE SYMMETRY OF HUSBANDS

On the way home, her father told her that the lamb would
not grow up; the people are raising it to be slaughtered. That
lamb would have its throat cut, he said. The lamb's white fur is
paired in her mind with the image of blood flowing over it,
innocence born to be consumed.

For a time, in Abigail's early adolescence, she became
enraptured with the idea of the blood of the lamb, the thought
of Jesus as the lamb of God, his sacrificial blood spilled for her.
She knelt by the side of the bed in the morning, wearing her
two-piece cotton pajamas and pondered, over prayers, a man as
innocent as the lamb. She thought she might become a nun.
She would spend her life thinking of that man of pure goodness
and become good herself in thinking of him. She pictured
herself wise and unsmiling, staring out in profile from a convent
window, wearing the nun's black veil and the white thing she
learned was called a wimple. She would keep that innocence
within herself, within her body, covered by the long black
gowns.

Later, laughing, she would recount to friends how she used
to want to be a nun. She smoked cigarettes with her high school
girlfriends just outside the school gates, daring someone to
catch them, daring someone to kick them out of school for their
ripped fishnet tights and low-cut tops. As they talked about
boys and sex and inhaled their cigarettes, their laughter was
bitter and raucous, pretending to a toughness it didn't yet own.

Megan was never part of that group. She and Abigail
remained friends even after Abigail had to change schools, but
their friendship was kept within their homes, with movies
watched and confidences shared in Megan's bedroom. When
they saw one another in public, they kept their distance. Abigail

saw her group of friends as brave, experimental and feminist, willing to create their own authority, their own rules to govern themselves. Some of them were good students, as she was; others received frequent suspensions and barely passed their classes. They all had a reckless, I-don't-give-a-fuck attitude that she found brave and compelling. They were united by a sense that the real world was elsewhere–in LA, in New York, in Seattle or London, in dark alleys and smoky city clubs, not here, on Massachusetts' sedate North Shore.

Megan's friends were people she met in track or her Honors classes or orchestra, where she played violin. They were good girls, who kept their legs together when they wore skirts, and at other times, Abigail presumed. Megan played music with them, she went out for ice cream after rehearsal with them, sat on the bus with them on the way home from track meets. She told Abigail about her friends' hidden eating disorders and fears, and Abigail told Megan about her friends, the ones who cut themselves, the ones who had abortions. They vowed one another to secrecy, and they kept those vows. If they passed one another surrounded by their respective groups, Abigail and Megan would share knowing looks, a smile.

She will buy lamb, she thinks, and she will cook it carefully, honouring it. Perhaps the sauce in the stew will soften, transform the violence in the meat into something life-giving and delicious.

Something about the lamb is right for the evening—a cold day with hunks of icy snow refusing to melt, a light sleet falling, the darkness after dinner. When Abigail finishes eating, she reaches over and takes James' hand. He squeezes in response, looking at her. "How are you doing?" he asks.

"All right." The stew makes her wish for a Mediterranean beach. "Phoebe texted today, asking for more help at her parents'—her dad's—house this weekend."

"Are you okay with that?"

"Sure." She thinks of the journal, tucked into her desk drawer, still unread. "I took a bag of pill boxes from their house. Megan's prescriptions. Don't you have somewhere to take unused medications, instead of just throwing them away?"

"The Police Station has a collection site. They want them in plastic bags, not the pill boxes. If you put them in bags, I can drop them off." He taps her hand with a finger. "Any good ones?"

"Probably. Don't be getting any ideas."

◆ ◆ ◆

Abigail kept seeing the young TA around campus. He would be in the snack bar when she stopped in for coffee on her way to class in the morning. He sat at a table in sight of the coffee bar, hands resting on the keyboard of his laptop. He didn't seem to be typing, and though he didn't look at her, she felt as if he were aware of her. She thought he was cute, in a smart, awkward kind of way, and there was something sexy about the idea of getting together with one of her professors. After a week of seeing him in the same spot, she took her coffee over to his table and sat down. "Do you mind?" she asked. The flush that suffused his cheeks gave him away.

"No, not at all." He moved papers aside for her to put her cup down. They chatted about her classes, about her job. She was about to ask him about his classes when he asked if she'd like to get a drink sometime.

"Well, sure," she said. "If you think that's legit." When he looked at her questioningly, she laughed and said, "Well, you *were* my professor."

"I'm not a professor," he said, with a smile. "I'm a student, like you are."

He kissed her good night on their first date. For their third date, he invited her to his studio apartment and made her spaghetti. The place was clean and Spartan, with framed posters on the walls, an Ansel Adams landscape, two botanical prints of birds. In the main room that served as living room and bedroom both, a couch and a bed. He was polite, shy in a professorial way, and his eyes kept pointedly turned away from the bed. She wanted to see what would happen in that bed, if he'd keep that reserve, if he'd ever look her directly in the eyes. After drinks, she pushed him gently towards it. "Are you sure this is okay?" he asked. His eyes met hers.

"Yes," she said. "Can't you tell?"

He kissed her. "Well, I am your professor . . ."

After that it was their recurring joke, their fantasy play, she the innocent schoolgirl and he the lecherous older professor. He was actually only two years older than Abigail, but–after a certain amount of inquiry–it became clear that she had more sexual experience than he did. She was gratified to see that his shyness, his reserve, fell away with a small amount of encouragement.

They moved to a larger apartment together. James was teaching classes and working on his dissertation. One day when he had a deadline to meet and was having trouble focusing, Abigail gave him an orange and white capsule. He felt as if the pill helped him work well that day, and occasionally he and Abigail would take one when they needed a boost. Abigail enjoyed the feeling she could get things done. She continued working at the restaurant, and taking classes, working slowly towards a Master's degree. She did well, and James' dissertation was moving along, helped by the orange and white pill.

They argued sometimes, usually when they were drinking. James stayed calm, but Abigail, infuriated by his insistence on a rationality that hid his emotions, would scream at him. Once or twice, wanting to shake him from his superior, insincere calm, she slapped him. She never achieved her goal from those moments, which—if she'd taken the time to articulate it—would have been to break down his icy reserve, to get him to be honest with her and himself, to admit to feeling the anger and pain his passivity was showing. Instead, over coffee the next morning, he would say that they should cut down on their drinking. She knew he meant that she should cut down on her drinking, but she took him at his word, and they both made an effort to cut back.

Later, when James was looking for a full-time job, they worked on being temperate. No more weed, just two or three glasses of wine at a time at most. No more Adderall. They didn't fight anymore. James got his job, and they got boring, Abigail would say, looking back wistfully on her earlier days.

◆ ◆ ◆

Abigail takes her bag into her office. She pulls out containers holding various amounts of pills, from just a few, to nearly full. She only gradually became aware that Megan was ill. Megan wasn't one to complain or over-share, as she called it. Her problems first became apparent to Abigail around ten years ago. Megan was working as Production Editor at the publishing house, a job she described as "a bit of everything, really." She worked half-time rather than full-time to spend more time with Phoebe. She worked more and more from home, and Abigail gradually became aware that Megan was truly ill, not just fragile. She learned she had Multiple Sclerosis not long before Megan had to completely quit her job.

To be sure, it wasn't easy to get Megan to talk about it: "I'm sick of talking about my body! It's boring. Tell me something interesting." Abigail learned to shift the subject to something else, anything else: a comment a student made in one of her classes, Phoebe's art lessons, a book she was reading. If nothing else worked, she brought up their childhood. This was to be saved as a last resort, however, to be used in only the most necessary moments, as it was a subject Abigail herself preferred to avoid.

After Megan retired from her job, the number of pill bottles on her counter increased. Now Abigail sets them on her desk in a row. Most of the names are unfamiliar, the elaborate names created by drug companies, but one catches her eyes. It is one-third full of round white pills. She recognizes the name; it's an opioid, a type of oxycodone, one of the drugs she and James had played with when they were younger. She didn't know that Megan had been prescribed opioids, or that she'd had the need for them.

Chapter Eight

"Do I really have to wear a blazer?" James asks, standing in front of the bedroom mirror. "For visiting high school students? On Saturday?"

"Yes," Abigail says, smoothing his lapel. "You look handsome."

He picks up his shoulder bag and kisses her, their lips touching briefly in a morning goodbye. The taste of coffee on his lips, eyes half closed, meeting hers briefly. A flash, something there.

Abigail picks up a slice of lemon cake from the coffee shop and takes it to the apartment in subsidized housing for seniors where her mother has lived alone since Abigail's father died. Her mother likes it there; she has a social life. She and her friends play cards in the lobby, watch tv together, and sit outside chatting on nice days. Now her mother holds the front door open, welcoming her into the kitchen. "Still in your robe?" Abigail says.

"Why not? Who do I have to worry about?" Her mother tightens the belt around her plump waist and pours coffee. She cuts into the lemon cake with pleasure. "I have my exercise class this afternoon. I'll work this off then." On the wall is a watercolor of a bouquet of lilies she painted in her art class. She can still spend an entire afternoon at the sewing machine, but she stays away from it for days at a time. She looks up now to see Abigail watching her and offers a bite of cake.

"No, thanks. I'm on my way over to help Phoebe with her mother's things." Her mother watches her, fork poised mid-air, and Abigail looks out the window. She's not sure what her mother's silence suggests. It may have something to do with her own father's death, the distance Abigail kept from her parents before the death, and the fact that she visited her mother regularly only after he died. On one of those visits, her mother tried to give Abigail some mementos–her father's zippo cigarette lighter with a map of South Vietnam engraved on it, for god's sake, as if she would want that. A pair of cuff links, a framed high school graduation photo. He was handsome, with a strong jaw and hair parted on the side. He gave the impression of a serious, principled young man, on his way to great things. Abigail turned those down but asked if she could have a wedding photo. Her father in a suit, her mother in a knee-length gown, both of them grinning and flushed.

Abigail thinks of buying flowers–she hasn't bought any yet, and it is traditional–but remembers the flowers crowding Doug's kitchen the last time she was there. She buys a box of chocolate truffles at the market instead. In the car she listens to classical music, soaring stringed instruments rising, then descending to a quiet piano. She takes the long way to Doug's house, a road that sweeps out into the country, past a small lake visible through flickering trees. The music reminds her of Megan's ceremony, the urn holding her ashes. She wishes she could have seen her friend's face once more. She imagines

Megan's head resting on the white satin of a coffin, hands folded on her lap. Her hair spread out, a peaceful look on her face . . . No, maybe it was best they didn't do that, create the artificial look of peace on her dead face. Instead she remembers Megan's face slack, unaware, her color off as Doug shook her. Is death peaceful, Abigail wonders? She doesn't think of it as peaceful, but as the end of strife, end of difficulty. Not the same thing as peace. Just . . . nothing.

She pulls up to the house, taking the bag with the truffles to the door. Doug opens before she rings the bell. He is wearing a wrinkled white shirt, perhaps the same one he wore to the funeral. He closes the door behind her, takes the truffles and puts them on a side table, uninterested. "Phoebe is delayed," he says. "Something about a broken pipe in her apartment, she had to wait for a plumber. She called just now, couldn't leave. She'll be here in an hour or so, maybe." The circles under his eyes are dark.

"How are you doing?" she asks, carefully.

"God," he says. "God, it's hard. I'm going insane, actually." He runs a hand through his hair and shakes his head. "I don't know what to do with myself."

Abigail can't help herself, she moves to give him a hug, to comfort. It feels so good; it's like that first drink, to feel his arms around her, to feel the warmth of his body. They stand like that, their arms moving gently on one another's backs, and he raises a hand to stroke her hair. His fingers massage the back of her head. Abigail thinks of nothing but his hand on her head, her face lifting to his. It's been so long. The roughness of his unshaven cheek against hers, the familiar aggressiveness of his kiss. His smell. The undeniable force and attraction of him, as he takes what is not his, what he knows will be given.

◆ ◆ ◆

An hour later, Abigail sits cross-legged on the floor of Megan's bedroom, sorting through a pile of clothes stacked on the floor. Phoebe has not yet arrived, may not be able to make it at all. Abigail thinks of nothing as she lifts dresses and blouses and sweaters, just the clothes in front of her. She checks them for holes or wear or stains, putting them in three piles: one for her (very small, just one sweater); one for Phoebe to look at; one for the thrift store. She focuses on the task at hand. Some of the items in the thrift store pile may not be acceptable to them, but she will let them make that determination. It would be rude to Megan, to her memory, to just throw this blouse with the underarm stains, these jeans with the worn knees, into the trash. Many of the clothes are from years ago, when Megan was active enough to wear holes in the knees of her pants. In her later years, she wore leggings under loose skirts, her thin legs dangling down to the footrests on the wheelchair.

Abigail doesn't want to think of what else might be rude to Megan's memory. Or—more pressing—rude to James, just now smiling and chatting with blank-faced high school students and their cheerful, nervous parents, as he tries to look them in the face rather than out the window. When Doug dressed and went downstairs earlier, he was cheerful, grateful, his cloud of anxiety lifted. With the warmth of his body, the force of his personality gone, Abigail lay on the bed in the guest bedroom quite still, eyes closed. She didn't want to open them, to see the

51

darkened room with shades pulled down. She didn't have the energy to get off the bed, to look at herself.

As she sits on the floor, she lifts a madras blouse to her face and catches a whiff of Megan; a flowery cologne, a scent she'd worn for years. She presses the blouse to her face, and lets the tears come. She'll take this one home. With her eyes closed and her face buried in Megan's blouse, Abigail pictures Megan as she was years ago, when they were teenagers. The image is so sharp that Abigail thinks it must be a photo somewhere; otherwise, how could she see it so clearly? Megan is leaning against a low slatted fence, green grass behind her and afternoon sunshine slanting across her face, which is pink and shiny with sweat. She wears a track tee shirt and shorts, and her hair is in a loose ponytail. There is no future illness for her; there is only this bright moment. She is laughing, joyous, and her face, looking at Abigail, is full of what can only be called love.

◆ ◆ ◆

The night visits began when Abigail was in sixth grade, around the time she began thinking she might become a nun. In the middle of the night, Abigail would wake to see his dark shadow beside her bed. The first time she thought it was an intruder, and was about to scream, when he touched her arm, whispering "Shh! Shh. It's me, Daddy."

"What?" she whispered. "What's wrong?"

"Nothing," he said, and got into her bed, laying his long body down beside her. She knew her mother was asleep, she slept through anything. "I just want to cuddle," he said.

Her father was not a cuddler, not affectionate. Her mother would give Abigail a good night kiss, but her father would just say "Good night," sometimes not even looking up from the tv. She lay rigid as he pressed himself against her. He smelled of beer and something else, smoke or whiskey, she didn't know. Sweat. She was afraid. Her stomach rose to her throat as he pushed up her pajama top, touched her small breasts. "Stop it," she said. She turned away, pulling her arms across her chest, but he pulled her back toward him. He chuckled, and whispered, "Little fried eggs." He pinched. It hurt. She thought she would vomit. She turned away from him again, trying to pull her pajama top back down.

He finally left her alone, but she was afraid it would happen again. It did.

She began thinking of a cloister, of her body safe inside locked stone walls, covered by long black gowns. Offering herself to God, who would not touch her body, only her heart. She shared this with Megan—not the night-time visits, of course, she couldn't tell anyone about those—but her desire to be a nun. She tried to talk her friend into entering the convent with her. Megan was reluctant. "They don't go outside the convent, then, right? And never get married, never have kids?"

They were sitting on the concrete of the public pool, leaning against the stone wall of the dressing rooms, their knees drawn up to their chests. Megan's thighs were skinnier than Abigail's, her chest flat under her one-piece. Abigail's two-piece suit had a bra to cover her breasts, which were sore from being pinched. "We could work with kids," Abigail said. "We could be teachers. Or wait—we could work in an orphanage. It would be like having kids, only we'd be helping kids who didn't have any parents."

Megan looked skeptical. "Do they even have orphanages anymore?"

"Whatever." She was distracted by Matt Rowe, a seventh grader who stood in front of them in his dark suit, dripping water. He played air guitar to "Born to Run" playing over the pool loudspeaker, showing off. "Really, Matt?" she said. Did he know how ridiculous he looked, his skinny chest like that of a little boy? "Who needs kids, anyway?" she said to Megan. "They just grow up to be like him." She nodded toward Matt.

Boys still seemed like children to Abigail in middle school. This perspective gave her a certain power, she discovered; she wasn't afraid of them. Even Alex, the track star all the girls had a crush on, seemed like a child to her. She felt free to tease him, to talk with him or not talk with him, as she pleased. He would laugh at her jokes, and tease her back, but he wasn't as good at teasing as she was, and sometimes a look would cross his face–a look of insecurity, of uncertainty, as if he weren't as confident as he seemed to be. She would pull back then, but she knew her power. He was a boy, like all the others. Her father was a boy too, a grown-up kid who liked to torment her. Megan asked Abigail about it once. "Alex is nice," she said. "He likes you. Why are you so mean to him?"

Abigail was lying on Megan's bed, playing with a large balloon. She'd brought it from a birthday party, where Megan had listened to Abigail tease Alex. They were spending the night at Megan's, her parents asleep in their room down the hall. As always, Abigail felt comfortable in Megan's room. "I don't know," she said, and tapped the balloon into the air. When it came down, she flicked it again, enjoying the way it returned. It reminded her of Alex, walking away from her into the kitchen when she called him a dork, then making his way back into the living room where she sat, paying him no attention. She'd finally given him a sideways smile that let him know she was teasing. "Because it's fun?" Megan had given her a look at that, a look of disappointment and judgement. There were boys who liked Megan, but she seemed not to notice. When Abigail pointed out that Todd Jordan kept looking at her, Megan became shy and couldn't talk to him.

Abigail sat up then, and let the balloon drop to the floor. "I guess I'm not very nice, huh?"

"Sometimes," Megan said, picking up the balloon and holding it carefully between her two hands. "You can be nice. But sometimes you're not."

Chapter Nine

Abigail knew that many prostitutes had been sexually abused as children. She knew about other issues that survivors encounter. Some of them sounded familiar to her own experience, but most didn't. She didn't think she had low self-esteem; she knew she was smart enough to do well in college and grad school, and for the most part she felt confident of her attractiveness. Sometimes she was down on herself, sometimes she hated herself, but who didn't?

Abigail did not want to be one of those women who railed against their parents, tearing them or their memory down, blaming them for their problems. Her parents were part of who she was, for better or for worse. Her mother was scattered and nervous, but she loved Abigail, and wanted her to be happy. Her father had been a good parent in some ways. No one was perfect. She wasn't going to be a whiner, and she wasn't going to tarnish his name by complaining about him. That wasn't a look she liked.

It wasn't until she had been with James for a few years that she thought there might have been something dangerous about her earlier promiscuity. It was living with James, seeing how he was affected when she flirted with another man, and seeing how she felt the rare times he flirted with another woman that changed her. She was faithful to him. She only flirted once in a while, and it never went anywhere. Not until she met Doug.

◆ ◆ ◆

This week, according to the syllabus, they were to discuss stories by Flannery O'Connor. In an impulsive act, Abigail changed the syllabus to include a story by Alice Munro called "Wild Swans." It is a subversive story, she thinks; a young girl is warned about the frightening things that can happen when she travels alone on a train. And sure enough, an older unattractive man, without looking at her, molests her under a newspaper with his hand. The subversive part, in Abigail's mind, is that the girl, frozen with fear, takes pleasure in the man's touch. Abigail loves the way the story doesn't follow expected paths, removes itself from didacticism or ideology.

Discussion is slow to start. One girl admits to confusion as to what actually happened. Is the girl, Rose, molested, or does she imagine it? It takes a good ten minutes of discussion to decide that yes, she was molested. "What was her reaction?" Abigail asks. She has pulled her hair on top of her head in a messy bun, and pushes her reading glasses down to look at the class. Stark silence greets her question. Then: "She's afraid," Sarah says, quietly.

"Yes," Abigail says. They find places in the text that show her fear. "What else does she feel?" she asks. "What happens at this moment?" She reads from the story. The girl is looking out the train window. "Such cunning antics now, such popular visions. The gates and towers of the Exhibition Grounds came into view, the painted domes and pillars painted marvellously against her eyelids' rosy sky. Then flew apart in celebration. You could have had such a flock of birds, wild swans, even, wakened under one big dome together, exploding from it, taking to the sky. She bit the edge of her tongue." Abigail puts the book down and looks around. "Well?"

"She sees beauty," Robert says, ever dutiful. Malik is silent, his head down, one long finger tracing a pattern on the desktop.

Morgan, the cocky girl with half of a shaved head and the rest of her hair dyed a different color every month, blurts out, "She gets off." In response to Abigail's look, Morgan clarifies, "She gets excited. She has an orgasm. She's enjoying it."

"Ew," Sarah says.

Morgan goes on. "See here it says, earlier, 'She opens her legs. Greedy assent.' She opens her legs! She's excited! Then she bites her tongue, to make herself be quiet. She gets off."

"All right, that's disgusting," Sarah says, and puts down her book. "I'm offended."

"Why is that bad?" Morgan asks.

"From that creep," Sarah says.

"She didn't ask for this," Morgan says, heated. "Why can't she take pleasure from it?"

Abigail can tell that some students are uncomfortable with the discussion. Two girls at the back sit with their heads down, sharing meaningful glances with one another. "Why do you think Munro gives us swans there, at this moment? And title the story 'Wild Swans'?" Abigail is thinking of the beauty of the swans, and the fact that they reflect some of the physical sensations Rose is feeling as the man's fingers touch her, finding beauty in imagining swans even in this situation, their beauty reflecting her body's sensations.

Malik finally speaks. "Swans mate for life," he says, in his husky, soft voice. A silence follows his comment, an emptiness that lingers, like a soap bubble, until discussion starts up again and sweeps it away.

◆ ◆ ◆

James sits in his armchair, reading *The Boston Globe*. Abigail, on the couch, is reading a novel, but she is thinking of her husband. After decades of marriage she is good at figuring out his moods, although she doesn't always know their causes, unless he decides to divulge them. Tonight he is quiet and moody, melancholy, and she doesn't know why. He's been that way often lately. She tells him about the discussion of the Munro story, and he says, "I could never have gone there with my class. It would be way too awkward."

"It's different for a man," Abigail concedes. "I think a woman can bring things up that a man can't. Especially if she has grey hair."

"You're not grey-haired," he says. "You have touches of grey."

He goes back to his newspaper. Abigail asks, "How was work?"

He looks up at her, taking a minute to focus. "Eh, all right. Department meeting sucked no more than usual. I doodled."

THE SYMMETRY OF HUSBANDS

Abigail has seen this, James looking as if he is taking dutiful notes while he creates small elaborate designs in his notebook. Some of her students do the same trick, though their doodles are mostly of eyes or manga faces or, sometimes, dogs. James' doodles are abstract, geometric. Whatever is troubling James is nothing he wants to talk about. She tells herself it can't be about her and Doug. It would be impossible for him to know. She goes back to her book, trying to ignore her uneasiness.

Chapter Ten

Her mother always told her marriages have rough spots. Abigail was not inclined to take marital advice from her mother, of course, given what she knew, and her mother didn't know about her father. What her mother knew about was bad enough: the reckless real estate deal, the lost savings. The first time Abigail thought of that trite phrase, "a rough spot," in relation to her own marriage was when they had been living in Salem for a couple of years.

Their first year there was filled with the excitement of a new home, a new job for James, finding work for Abigail. James was absorbed in his work, irritated when he thought Abigail didn't understand all he had to do. Abigail was hired for the second semester to teach literature and writing classes part-time, and though she was glad to have the work, she felt the offer was a bone thrown to her from the house of the master. She knew she wasn't justified in feeling this way: it had been her own choice not to go for a PhD. She would keep looking for something else, a full-time job that her master's degree would qualify her for.

During James' second year, the glow of the academic honeymoon wore off, and he worried about getting a book published. His interest in sex waned as he worked late nights and weekends. Then he was gone for a month, a summer residency in Vermont to work on his book. Abigail, home in Salem, at first enjoyed being alone–she could do whatever she wanted during the day! Pop a frozen dinner in the microwave, instead of cooking!—but she thought of James. When he didn't write or call every day, she worried. She told herself she was being silly, but when he came home, she couldn't stop herself from watching his face, his gestures, for signs of his feelings.

He was tired from the long drive and didn't have much to say. "Well, it was wonderful," he said to her questions. Did he get a lot done? Yes, though he wasn't sure how good it was. "I'm just really tired," he said. He leaned over to kiss her good night as she sat on the couch. She turned up her face, but he kissed the top of her head instead.

When James played music, he usually listened to classical, or jazz. After his return, she would see him in his chair in the living room, wine glass in hand, listening to moody, angsty songs sung by soft-voiced young women. Love songs, it occurred to her, and this, combined with his emotional distance, seemed strange and suspicious. He'd never sat around listening to music like that before.

She was sure he'd fallen in love with someone else when he was in Vermont, and the thought drove her insane. She had been faithful to him, and the thought that he might be–even emotionally–unfaithful made her wild. All that time she'd been so good! All those missed chances!

By the time the snow fell, James had stopped listening to angsty love songs, and was back to Bach or Miles Davis. Abigail, by then, could not stop thinking of Megan's husband. She meant it as a fun flirtation, to give herself a boost. Doug and she talked at dinners, flirting, but James and Megan talked too; it was harmless, part of the winey ambiance.

When Phoebe was there, all their attention focused on her. They were all in love with Phoebe. Abigail remembered one of their first evenings together, when the four adults pulled their chairs in a circle together on Megan's patio with an open space in the middle. The game was for little Phoebe, in the center, to try to break out of the circle. She hurled herself, laughing, from one side to another. An adult stopped her each time, always with a pat, a hug, a kiss. It was as if Phoebe was carrying the love to all of them, spreading it around.

The night Abigail found herself alone with Doug, Megan was spending the night with her parents. Doug had arrived home after Phoebe was asleep. They sat for hours on the couch, talking. Abigail loved to talk with him; the attention he gave to everything she said, and the way he looked at her, especially when they were alone, went to her head like cocaine. She felt particularly brilliant and witty talking with him, the attraction lighting everything up. He didn't touch her, and she didn't touch him. That happened later, after another–the worst–rough spot.

James finally got his book published. He earned tenure and was working on his second book. He was awarded another research fellowship, this one in Dublin. Years after her first miscarriage, when she had almost given up hoping, Abigail was pregnant again. She'd taken a test and it was positive, but she didn't tell James. She kissed him good-bye at the airport, hoping she would have a more fully developed secret to tell him on his return. If it didn't work out again this time, she couldn't bear to see his disappointment. She'd felt responsible the last time it happened, as if she could somehow change the receptiveness of her cervical mucus to a new life if she'd only tried harder. As if, if she were a kinder, more wholesome, more loving person, she could make her uterus more nurturing.

James had the semester off, but he would be in Dublin just half of the semester. Abigail began teaching her first-year writing course. She emailed her husband daily, not saying anything about the softness in her abdomen, the tender, growing fullness there, or her excitement at the new life, the raspberry-sized being which would become a child, now turning in the quiet liquid warmth. A week before his return, she felt a dull backache. She drank herb tea and sat quietly, reading. She tried to ignore it, tried to convince herself it wasn't happening again. She closed her eyes and held the being inside her in her thoughts, trying to protect it. The backache grew throughout the night until aspirin didn't affect it, and when she sat on the toilet in the dawn light staring at her bloody underwear, she couldn't deny that it was happening.

She cancelled class that day and spent the afternoon in bed. The cramping was severe, the bleeding heavy, with bits of tissue she flushed immediately, trying not to see. She cried. She was nearly 40 years old, and she had a feeling this would be the last time she was pregnant. And maybe that was all right; she didn't want to face this pain, this loss, again.

When James returned, she didn't tell him what had happened. She thought she would wait until she found the right moment, but as before, when he returned he was distracted, struggling with something inside of himself. He was back to not being able to look her in the face again. When he did look at her, it seemed as if he didn't like what he saw. She imagined that his eyes lingered on the new lines around her mouth, the dark shadows under her eyes.

She told herself she was being oversensitive. She dressed up for a dinner party, wearing a red clingy dress she'd bought before James left for Ireland. She came down the stairs, anxiously smoothing the skirt. James was walking through the kitchen carrying a full cup of coffee. He stopped and sipped, looking at her over the top of his cup. "What?" she asked. "Do I look all right?"

"It's fine," he said. "I didn't know we were dressing up. You look very stylish. A little tight, isn't it?"
Abigail turned away without saying anything, and walked upstairs, burning with anger. Did he think *he* was still a perfect young thing? He was softer around the waist, like she was. Upstairs in front of the full-length mirror, she turned side to side, looking at herself in the dress. Yes, she was no longer twenty years old, but she was an attractive, shapely woman, with the body of a healthy woman her age. She knew she was attractive. She would wear the dress, and carry herself proudly, and watch for that light in the eyes of the men she talked to.

Abigail sometimes hoped that he would reach out to her, try to draw her closer. Instead he retreated to his study or his office, into a silence that felt cold. Abigail, usually the one to break a silence, vowed–just this once–to let it be him. When he remained inexpressive and silent, her anger grew heavy within her. It would burst out sometimes, over things unpredictable: he didn't empty the garbage, he didn't comment on a new hairstyle. He was gone when she came home sometimes, without saying where he'd been when he returned.

He didn't have to teach until the following semester, so his time was his own. The last time he'd been in that position was when he was writing his dissertation, and had the assistance of pills, booze, and smoke. He stayed away from those now, except for wine at night. Her grief over her lost child was enormous, and the longer she went without telling him, the more impossible it became to say. There was no way he could share this even if she were to bring it up; every response he could have would be inadequate.

In the spring, they had a fight which Abigail started. She took responsibility for that. She wanted to see him angry, she wanted heat and noise and fire. It was over their summer plans, whether to spend an entire week visiting his mother in Baltimore or spend some time on the coast by themselves. "You see your mother twice a year," she said. "We haven't had a real vacation together in years." She accused him of not caring for her, of not caring for anyone but himself. He stuttered, he stumbled, he would not yell. "My mother is 70 years old and alone," he said. "Give me a break." He answered in tones meant to be reasonable and logical, and with every purposefully quiet word, Abigail grew angrier. "I feel like I'm alone too," she said, and started crying. Alone with her feelings, she meant to say; alone with her sadness that she could not share.

It was the next day, in front of the vending machine in the hallway at the university, that Abigail talked with Marisha. Marisha taught French part-time, and said she was planning to go to France for the late summer and fall. "My boyfriend is there," Marisha said.

"How wonderful," Abigail said, instantly jealous.

Marisha shrugged, in what Abigail thought of as a Gallic shrug. One shoulder shrugging up to meet her blonde hair, not quite dismissive but accepting whatever would happen. "We will see how it goes," she said. "First I need to find someone who can stay in my apartment and take care of my sweet dog."

It was all Abigail could think of. Living in an apartment for those months, with a dog; it would be her own little residency. Maybe she would begin a new writing project or make headway on that paper she started last year. Maybe she would take piano lessons, or paint. She could start a new life.

The day she told Marisha she would do it, she made a chocolate tart for dessert. She waited until she and James were at the table, well into their meal, before saying that she would be staying at Marisha's place starting in August. James stopped eating and went pale, sitting up straight at the table. At first he said nothing, then, "You want to get away that badly."

"It's available. She needs someone to watch her dog. I think it might do both of us, you and me, good to have some space." She chewed, avoiding his eyes.

"I'm sorry. I didn't know you were that unhappy."

"I'm not *that* unhappy," she said, finally looking at him. "It's just until the end of the year."

"What will you do then?" he asked. "Will you come back home?"

It was spring when they had this discussion, a clear, windy day. She couldn't imagine what she would be thinking in the middle of next winter. Would she come back to this house, move back into bed with James, cuddling against him for warmth as the winter storms blew outside? Only if things were very different than they were now.

"I don't know, I don't know," she said. "Let's see." They didn't talk much for the rest of the evening, but as days went by and the moving date approached, they loosened up. James was gentle. They were kinder to one another, a slightly formal kindness, like roommates. They'd been together for fifteen years. They didn't go to the coast that summer, and James went to Baltimore by himself.

◆ ◆ ◆

James helped Abigail move, carrying in boxes of books and clothes, bags of food from the grocery store. Alfie was waiting for them, an ancient yellow/brown mutt with a curling furry tail. James started to put food in the cupboards but Abigail stopped him, a hand on his forearm. "James. Thank you, but . . ."

He stopped. "Oh. Of course. Don't know what I was thinking." He grinned at her, sheepishly. He stood, hands in his pockets, while Abigail put her canned food and bread away, fruit in a bowl on the table, watching him from the corner of his eyes. She didn't know if she wanted him to leave or not. He seemed to feel the same.

She came into the small living room where James stood in front of the non-working fireplace with a dried plant arrangement in its open space. Marisha's abstract paintings were on the walls; the bay window overlooked the quiet street below where only the occasional car passed. "Nice place," he said.

Then awkwardly, "I hope you'll be happy here, but not too happy." He coughed. "I'll miss you."

They hugged. "Thank you," she said. Then she was alone with Alfie, who lay by the couch looking up at her. She put her books on the space Marisha had left for her on the bookcase, her clothes in the little painted dresser in the bedroom, her laptop on the desk in front of the window overlooking the back yard. She turned the radio Marisha had on the windowsill to a folk station and wondered what new adventure she would do first. But that evening, she just sat in Marisha's stuffed chair, looking at Alfie. "What's it all about, Alfie?" she murmured. He looked at her, then looked away, then looked back at her, as if he were as puzzled as she was, trying to find an answer to her question.

The apartment was on the upper floor, and the front window was shaded by leaf-heavy trees. She would use Marisha's dishes, she would sleep in Marisha's bed, sit on Marisha's couch. She felt like a young woman again, except she wasn't. She was alone, and as long as she fed and walked Alfie, she was responsible only to herself. She had a sensation familiar from when she was younger, as if her self were not formed. As if whoever or whatever she was, was as much a part of the air in the house, the sound of a car passing, the rustle of the leaves, the sensation of the chair against her bare legs, as it was anything inside herself. The feeling was pleasurable, then it was uncomfortable, then–as the air darkened in the room, and she didn't turn on the lamp, and Alfie gave a breathy, barely audible whine–it was frightening.

Chapter Eleven

Only one other person in the world knew what Abigail's father did, besides Abigail and her father, and that was Megan. For two years, from when she was eleven years old until she was thirteen, Abigail lived in dread of his night visits. Weekends were dangerous times. Her father often went out on weekends, meeting friends at the bar. His visits to her room were related to alcohol; she could smell it on him, could see his eyes half-closed in the shadowy room, hear his words slide together like he was drowsy. Not that he said much.

Abigail didn't want her mother to know. She thought her mother would divorce him and the two of them would live in a crummy apartment and be poor. She thought her mother would hate her and think she was dirty. She thought lots of things. And she didn't want to hurt her mother, to let her know that the man she was married to preferred her, twelve-year-old Abigail, to his mature, grown-up wife.

When her father came in her room and lay down beside her, when he touched her in places she didn't want to be touched and pushed himself against her, Abigail tried to pull herself away, tried to shield herself from him. He was stronger than she was, and it was easy for him to hold her tightly, whispering that he wouldn't hurt her, that it was natural for a man to want to touch a pretty girl. Whispering that she shouldn't tell anyone, that it wasn't such a big deal as people thought it was.

Abigail often stayed overnight at Megan's house on weekends, but she had never asked Megan to stay at her house. One Friday evening, Megan's mother called. Megan's grandmother had a heart attack; she and her husband had to drive into Boston and didn't know when they would return. Could Megan sleep at Abigail's house? Of course, her mother said.

Megan had dinner with Abigail and her mother. Her mother was nice to Megan, offering her seconds of spaghetti and garlic bread, telling her she had such pretty curly hair. Megan smiled at a phone call from her mother; Grandma was doing okay, she would be all right.

After dinner, they watched a tv movie about a woman who couldn't see or hear or talk. She was helped by another woman, who finally communicated with her by tapping onto the palm of her hand. When they went to bed, Megan fell asleep almost immediately, while Abigail stayed awake, watching her. Megan's mouth was slack, half-open, her cheeks perfectly round. Even asleep, Megan was pretty. Abigail heard her mother turn off lights, run water, flush the toilet. She heard the sound of her mother closing the bedroom door, downstairs on the other side of the house.

She imagined what it would be like, to not be able to see or speak or hear. To finally understand that certain taps on her hand meant words, like "water." What would life be like? She was dozing, half-dreaming of fingers tapping on her hand, the sense of meaning coming through, when the sound of the front door downstairs opening woke her. She lay still, holding her breath. His footsteps, stealthy, climbed the stairs and approached her door. This was the worst, the absolute worst thing that could happen. She had to stop him.

He was opening the door before she could think of what to do. She could tell by the way he stood, leaning slightly to one side, that he was drunk. He moved toward the bed. Abigail sat up. "No! she whispered. "Go away!"

He chuckled, approaching the bed. Reaching his hand out, he touched Megan's leg. He was still chuckling when she kicked and turned over. "What?" Megan said. "What is it?" Abigail's father stood up straight then, and they saw his dark outline frozen against the faint light coming through the curtains. Abigail could smell the whiskey and stale smoke on his breath.

He made a noise, a sort of angry exhalation, then turned and left without speaking. Abigail got up, closed the door tightly, and climbed back in bed next to her friend. "I'm sorry," she said in a strangled voice, and lay staring up at the ceiling.

"What was that about?" Megan's voice was sleepy, but alarmed.

Abigail didn't speak. She didn't know what to say. What were the words she would use?

"Was that weird?" Megan asked. "It seemed weird to me. It was creepy. He was scary."

"Yes," Abigail admitted. It was all she could say. Her father *was* creepy, and scary. Abigail tried not to let Megan know she was crying, tears running down the sides of her face into a pillow. She sniffled, and Megan turned to face her. "Abigail, talk to me."

Abigail didn't know what to say. "Does your father come in here often?" Megan whispered. Abigail nodded. "What does he do?"

Abigail just shook her head, slightly. "He's a jerk," she whispered. "I hate him." After a pause, she said, "I'm sorry," again. She *was* sorry, and she was, more than anything, embarrassed.

Megan sat up in bed. "*You* don't have to be sorry about anything," she said heatedly.

"Shh, shh."

"Okay," Megan whispered. "Whatever he's doing, it's not your fault, okay? It's his fault."

Then Abigail was crying, and Megan got up to get her a tissue from the bathroom. Beside her in the bed, Megan put her arms around Abigail and let her cry. It is a moment Abigail will always remember–the arms of her friend around her, Megan saying what he was doing was her father's fault, not her fault, and the relief, the wonderful release of tears.

◆ ◆ ◆

The next morning, Abigail woke before Megan. She had time to arrange her thoughts and find a magazine. When Megan opened her eyes, Abigail said, "You have to see this." It was *Sports Illustrated*, and on the cover was a dark-haired woman with her legs folded under her, sitting on the sand at the edge of the ocean. She wore a suit that was a scrap of red, barely covering her. The magazine was full of women in revealing swimsuits. "Look at this. It's Cheryl Tiegs," Abigail said, opening the magazine and pointing to a smiling young woman in a white one-piece bathing suit. She looked cheerful and pretty, a "nice" girl, but her suit was entirely see-through except for a white cover-up triangle between her legs.

"Oh my *god*," Megan murmured sleepily. "Why are you showing this to me?"

"Can you imagine *wearing* something like this? To the pool?" Cheryl Tiegs' nipples were large and surprisingly dark. "Can you imagine what Matt Rowe would think when he saw you in that?"

They had a bowl of Cheerios at the kitchen table, and then Megan went home. They didn't see Abigail's father that morning, and they didn't talk about what had happened the night before.

A few days later, Megan approached Abigail at her locker before school. "I have something for you," Megan said, and shoved a paper bag into Abigail's hands. She walked away then, looking over her shoulder at Abigail with a sly grin.

Abigail opened the bag partway and peeked in. A plastic package holding some kind of metal gadget. She lifted it partway out: it was a padlock and key, along with a metal strip. "Padlock and Hasp," the package read. She shoved it back in the bag, looking around to see if anyone had noticed.

That afternoon, Abigail sat on her bed and pried open the package. She saw how it would fit on her door. It came with screws and needed to be fastened to the wooden door from the inside. She put the bag with the lock in it inside a dresser drawer. She didn't think she could get away with putting it up. What would her father say? What would her mother think?

She avoided Megan after that. They had separate groups of friends at school, and it wasn't too hard to be looking the other way as they passed in the hall. Megan's mother usually picked Megan up after school, while Abigail took the bus. One day when she got off the bus close to her house, she was surprised to see Megan leaning against a tree. She wore the clothes she'd worn to school, a short plaid skirt and red tights, and her backpack. She fell in step beside Abigail. "Hey."

"Hey."

"I was wondering how that thing worked. Were you able to get it on?"

Abigail walked on, looking at the ground. "It's weird," she said, as if she didn't have any idea why Megan had given it to her. "But thanks."

"You're welcome. Want to come over to my house?"

"Sure, I guess." They sat on the old swing set outside Megan's house, then climbed her apple tree. Neither of them mentioned what had happened, or Megan's gift, again.

◆ ◆ ◆

For a time, Abigail's father left her alone. She lay awake weekend nights, listening for the front door opening, listening for his footsteps, coming up the stairs. Sometimes they would pause downstairs, and she would wait with eyes wide open, but they didn't come up. She started to sleep better, thinking maybe it was all over.

One Friday night, she jolted awake. What was that? She heard nothing, then a sound. Was it his footsteps, coming up? She thought it was, but they were quiet, for him. Still, her mother would never do that, would never creep upstairs when Abigail was in bed. Her door was closed, and she watched it open, slowly. Did he know–he must know–how frightened she was, how terrified? She closed her eyes tightly but could smell him.

Suddenly, without thinking, she was out of bed, pushing past him to the door. She had never done that before, and she caught him unawares. She heard him grunt, felt him reach out for her. He had her shoulder under his hand, but she jerked away and ran into the hallway, down the stairs. "Mom!" she said, pushing open the door of her parents' bedroom. "I had the worst dream ever!"

That was the only time she ever woke her mother up because of her father. She lay down beside her mother on the bed and made up a dream. "A bear was chasing me, and he turned into a man who wanted to kill me. He had a knife, a big knife. Oh, it was so scary."

Her mother, surprised and half-asleep, took her daughter's face between her two hands, a tender gesture Abigail couldn't remember her using before. "Think of something nice," she said. "Think of summer vacation. Or Christmas." Abigail, lying beside her mother with her face cradled, was ready at that moment to believe she'd had that bad dream, and if she just thought of Christmas, it would all go away and be well.

Abigail went back upstairs, walking past her father in the dark living room without looking at him. She was awake for a long time that night, long after she heard her father enter the downstairs bedroom and close the door. The next day was Saturday. Abigail slept late, and when she went downstairs her parents were nowhere to be seen, the car gone. She went into the garage and found what she needed on her father's tool bench. After much trial and error, she was able to push the screws through the holes in the hasp, into the wooden door, and secure them tightly. The piece was slightly crooked on the door, but never mind. She pushed the padlock in and locked it, and it worked.

She held the key in her hand, wondering what to do with it. Where to keep it, how to not lose it. How to hide it so no one would find it. Actually, she should hide the padlock too, she decided, or he might take it away. She thought of under the bed–too obvious–or in her backpack. She finally decided to put both the key and the padlock in a small pocket in an old pair of jeans. She buried the jeans at the bottom of a drawer in the dresser. Every night, even weeknights, she put the padlock on and clicked it shut. She left the key on the dresser at night and put both the key and the padlock away in the morning.

If her mother noticed the hasp on Abigail's bedroom door, she didn't mention it, and neither did her father. It was the following weekend when Abigail heard, through the closed and padlocked door, the sound of footsteps on the stairs. She held her breath as the footsteps approached the door, as she heard the doorknob turn. The door met the closed hasp with a *thunk,* followed by a whispered curse. He tried again; another *thunk.* Abigail prayed the latch would hold, the door not splinter apart, her father would go away. "Abigail!" her father said in a hoarse whisper. She shivered and pulled the covers over her head.

He said no more, just waited, then walked away. She heard the footsteps down the stairs. She pulled the covers from her head and stared up at the ceiling. After a moment her heart stopped pounding so hard. She took a deep breath and smiled.

Chapter Twelve

When she was at Marisha's and needed something from her house, Abigail would call or text James first, so her appearance wouldn't surprise him. She sometimes chose times when she knew he wouldn't be at home. On a Sunday morning in October, she felt a sudden yearning to see the leaves on the maple tree in their yard, turning color. She missed the grassy spot in her yard where she would read on warm days near the maple tree. She missed her cat. It was a sunny day, warm for October, the light flickering through gold leaves. She texted him she would stop by.

James' car was in the driveway and the front door was unlocked. She hadn't received an answer to her text. Had she missed him, too, she wondered, like she missed the leaves? She did, but it was the old James she missed when she had still lived at home, the James who would be interested in what she said. The James who found her fascinating and sexy.

The kitchen was empty, light shining through the windows onto the wooden floor. Her maple tree was as red as she remembered. As she stood looking out the window she heard James coming down the stairs. She turned to greet him with a smile. "I missed my tree!"

He stood awkwardly, hands shoved in the pockets of his khaki pants. She approached him, holding her arms out to the sides as if asking a question. He opened his own in response, and then they were hugging. She'd forgotten how tall he was. She'd forgotten how good his arms could feel around her.

◆ ◆ ◆

That evening, her cell phone, sitting on the table by the couch in Marisha's apartment, buzzed and lit up. "I heard you moved," Doug said. "I have a little housewarming present. May I stop by?" The nerve of him, the cheek! Alfie barked when the doorbell rang, and stood beside Abigail, tail wagging, as she opened the door. She laughed when she saw Doug standing in the hallway, holding a bashed-looking potted geranium. He held it out. "It got knocked about a bit. Sorry. Megan's better at these things than I am, but she's out on the town with Phoebe. Dinner and a play, whatever. Dad not invited."

He stepped inside, set the plant down, and walked around as if he were familiar with the place, comfortable. As if he had every right to be there. He looked into the narrow kitchen with the freshly painted white cupboards, peeked into the bedroom at the other side of the living room. "Nice," he proclaimed. "Looks like it has good light."

"Want something to drink?" she asked.

"No, no," he said. "I can't stay. I just wanted to say hello, see what you were up to." He gestured at the living room, the kitchen. "Whatever's going on with your life now, I wanted to wish you well."

"Thank you. Come by again," she said as she walked him to the door.

He stopped and looked at her. "I might do that."

The next time, he brought a bottle of gin and a bottle of Rose's lime juice. "A gimlet," he said. It felt easy and right that he was there. They were friends, after all. "Why do they call it a gimlet?" she asked, as he set the bottles on the small kitchen table and opened them. "Isn't that a tool of some kind?" She took wo of Marisha's cocktail glasses from the cupboard.

"I believe it is. It drills holes into wood." He poured gin over ice, with lime juice on top. He looked up at her and smiled. "Best not to think too much of that." He handed her a drink. "I think it's because they make you gimlet-eyed. Piercing." Cheers," he said, tapping her glass to hers. "To your new life." They sat at the little wooden table drinking, the gin's sour tang making the setting sun brighter, more golden. "So why are you here, if I may ask?" Doug said. "Why not at your own lovely home with your husband?"

Abigail was aware, as Doug looked at her, that she was dressed in her new mauve silk blouse, that she had carefully made up her eyes—smoky, but not overdone—and curled her hair. She shrugged. "My friend Marisha needed a house sitter. I thought it would be nice to have some time alone."

Doug sat, waiting. He leaned back in the kitchen chair, slim in his wrinkled dress shirt. "What does James think of this?"

"You could ask him that," she said, looking at Doug. "It was my idea, but he didn't protest much."

Doug leaned forward and poured them each another drink. "Well, I hope you both are happy. James is a good man. And if he knows what's good for him . . ." He leaned his glass against hers, in a toast that felt as if he were touching her skin, "he'll do anything he can to get you back."

After that the mood shifted. The gin made everything funny, the light warm and golden. It seemed then that Abigail was adventurous and daring, to be living in this apartment away from her marriage, to be choosing to spend time with this compelling, brilliant man. It felt wonderful to be admired again, to be desired. When she stood up to get a drink of water, she had trouble walking a straight line. The drinks were strong. Douglas stood up next to her, very close. He put his hands on the sides of her head and leaned in close, kissing. She didn't think of stopping him when he kissed her, or when he pushed her gently into the bedroom.

They fell on Marisha's bed in a tangle of limbs and laughter. Doug took a condom from his wallet and put it on without discussion. He seemed to have no guilt, no compunctions about sleeping with her. That made it easier. They were friends who were attracted to one another, and they were in another world, one that didn't exist outside Marisha's small, brightly painted apartment, the colors swirling around them like a kaleidoscope.

◆ ◆ ◆

There were times when the other world came uncomfortably close, when the two worlds were in danger of touching one another. Megan asked if she could see where Abigail was living. Abigail wanted to say no, but she could think of no legitimate reason to do so. Megan was part of the other life, the life where Abigail was married to James and Megan was married to Doug. "Of course, stop by any time," she said, but offered no specific date. When Megan did come to visit, she walked through the place like her husband had (and for that moment Abigail thought of that phrase, *her husband,* with a pang), touching the pathetic geranium and looking up at Abigail with a smile. "Poor little thing," she said, referring to the plant. She peeked into the bedroom, and Abigail couldn't look with her, knowing the things that had happened in that room.

Megan walked slowly, carefully, with a kind of a limp that Abigail hadn't noticed before. She touched the doorways when she walked through them, as if steadying herself. Abigail asked how she was doing. "Oh, fine," Megan said, and bent down to pet Alfie. "What a sweet dog."

The next time Doug came over, Abigail made herself ask. She waited until Doug was pulling his pants back on and buckling his belt. Lying on the bed with hands crossed behind her head, she asked, "How is Megan doing?"

"All right," Doug said, glancing at her then in the mirror as he put his tie back on. "Why?"

"She seems fragile, that's all. Has a kind of limp."

"She fell down and doesn't know why. She's getting things checked out." He leaned over the bed to kiss her, a gesture that seemed almost husbandly to Abigail, done as if it were a habit, without thought. His thoughts were elsewhere, not on her. On what was next.

◆ ◆ ◆

And then there was the day she took a walk with Megan and Phoebe in the Boston Commons. Megan had called to see if Abigail wanted to drive into the city with them "for an adventure." It had been a while since they'd been out together. Abigail hadn't called Megan, for obvious reasons. She didn't want to think too much about it; she just wanted to live her life, to take what happiness she could. Hurting Megan wasn't an intentional part of her plan.

Megan was still working part-time. On this day they walked slowly, Megan's steps sometimes awkward. Phoebe, thirteen years old, ran ahead to lean over a stone wall bridge, looking down at the ducks. The day was sunny but cold, tree branches mostly bare against the bright sky, leaves spotting the grass with color. They talked of Abigail's life in the apartment, and of how things were going with James. "We had dinner at the house together the other night," Abigail said. "Takeout. It was kind of fun, like a date. He actually talked to me." It had been a nice evening; she'd felt confident, her attractiveness reflected in James' eyes as he looked at her.

Megan stopped on the path to look at Abigail. "Oh, I'm glad to hear that. That's so good. He's a good man, I think, and you two need to be together." She put a hand on Abigail's arm to slow her steps on the path, to keep out of the range of Phoebe's hearing. "I have something to tell you," she said.

Abigail turned to her, face alight. "Oh, goodie," she said. "What is it?" She expected good news: a job promotion, a new house. Maybe even a pregnancy, who knew. Abigail would celebrate that with her, would share her friend's joy. She didn't want to take anything from her.

Megan's face told her something different, even before she spoke. "I guess I have this disease. I finally got it diagnosed." It had started with tingling and numbness in her limbs, she said, then weakness, and she didn't walk as well as she used to. "I fell down a few times. Dizzy. Other issues, too, that you don't want to hear about," she said, making a face. "So they finally decided it was MS."

Abigail, as if she hadn't really looked at her friend in a long time, saw her moving with difficulty, saw her tense when Phoebe ran up and threw an arm around her.

"I'm sorry," she said quietly after Phoebe turned away. She was sorry for Megan, and she felt something else, something she didn't remember feeling before. She'd always looked up to Megan but it seemed at this moment that Abigail was the strong one, looking down at a vulnerable Megan. It was up to her to take care of Megan, as if Abigail were responsible for her friend. They walked slowly, scuffing through the leaves at their feet, toward Phoebe on the bridge. Phoebe turned to them, her face bright and smiling in the sunshine.

Chapter Thirteen

A week before Thanksgiving, Abigail's mother woke to find Abigail's father unresponsive in bed next to her. Abigail was grinding coffee beans in Marisha's kitchen in her robe and answered the phone when the machine quit grinding. She heard her mother's breathless voice, stuttering slightly. "It's your father," she said. "I don't, I don't know . . ." Now Abigail was the daughter getting the phone call, racing to get dressed and meet her mother at the hospital.

By the time they were taken to his bedside in ER, her father was motionless, covered with a sheet on a bed. His eyes were closed, his mouth hung open. Abigail could tell he was gone. A doctor standing beside his bed looked at them, her face full of emotion. "I'm so sorry," she said. It was a brain aneurysm.

◆ ◆ ◆

Abigail locked her bedroom door until she and her parents moved to the apartment. Her father never tried it again. Once in the apartment she left it off, daring him to try. She wasn't a little girl any longer. She wondered if her mother ever noticed the lock on the door; if she did, she never said anything. Did she know what her husband was like, did she know what he was capable of? He could be a charming man. Abigail had often seen this side of him when she was a child, when they went somewhere as a family. His face was a different face then, full of light and humor, the creases at the side of his mouth attractive as he smiled. Her mother would be pink-cheeked and laughing at his jokes. At home, she never saw her father or mother smile when they talked with one another. She didn't hear them argue, but she didn't hear them laugh, either.

In high school, Abigail grew openly defiant toward him. There are scenes she can't forget: shouting at her father in the dining room, "You can't tell me what to do!" The color of his face rising as he struggled to maintain control over himself, if not of her. Always, the knowledge between them of what he had done, never mentioned. She refused to go on family outings unless she was forced, until her parents gave up and let her stay home. Her mother between them, trying to calm her father, trying unsuccessfully to support him and be stern with Abigail.

Her mother tried to talk to her. She came into Abigail's room after a fight between father and daughter. "Abby, what's wrong?" she asked. Abigail remembered her standing by the door, wearing the cotton pants and shirt she sewed for herself. So hopelessly out of fashion. "Is there anything you want to talk about?"

"No, Mom. No. Thanks, but . . . go away." She was well-intentioned, she loved her daughter; she was simply clueless, and had slept through it all. Her mother was collateral damage. Abigail felt sorry for her.

Abigail hadn't thought her father would die, not for a long, long time. He was powerful; he could be damaged but not seriously hurt. He was the monolith in her life she still fought against, in her thoughts if not face to face. When he died, she saw that she had shaped herself in reaction to him. With him gone, there was nothing to put herself in opposition to. She felt sometimes as if she would fall into pieces, dissipate and slip away like smoke.

At the hospital her mother surprised Abigail by finding the strength to do what she needed to do: she signed papers, made decisions as to what to do with her husband's body. They hadn't talked about it, she said, but she wanted him to be displayed in a coffin. It seemed the right thing to do. The thought of his face in a coffin horrified Abigail. She protested, but her mother said, "That's what we'll do," and didn't talk more about it.

At home her mother poured herself a glass of her husband's bourbon, something Abigail had never seen her do, and collapsed in the recliner. Abigail took a glass for herself upstairs.

Her bedroom in the apartment was just across the hall from her parents'—now her mother's—bedroom. It was smaller than her bedroom in their house had been. Her mother had taken down the posters Abigail had put up in high school and painted the walls pale yellow. The little desk her mother bought used and painted white for her was there, some of her favorite books still lined up on top. *Jane Eyre,* the *Little House on the Prairie* series from when she was younger, and *Poems Written Before Jumping Out of an 8-story Window* by Bukowski. When Abigail lived there she sometimes heard her father come home when she was in her bedroom with the lights off, and lay there waiting, daring him to open the door. *Come on, just you try. Just see what happens.* She almost wished he would, so she could let him have it. She would scream, she would make sure her mother knew. He never did.

She'd thought when he died, she would feel relief. She hadn't cared for him for years, was happy to get away from him, and this final departure could only make her life easier. So she thought. As she sat at her desk that night drinking bourbon, then refilling the glass, she remembered something she hadn't thought of for years. Her parents had taken her to an amusement park in New Hampshire one summer when she was a kid. She was small, the memory fuzzy, but it had been genuine magic. The Cinderella ride in the pumpkin-shaped coach, in which she felt like the true princess. Cotton candy, a ferris wheel, her father a big warm presence, his smells comforting. His touch welcome. It had all changed later, and she'd forgotten that father. Now it seemed, in the sleepy warmth of the bourbon, that he may have been the *real* father, the warm and loving one, inside the frightening, drunk imposter who used to come into her bedroom.

She heard slow footsteps on the stairs, a pause between each step. Her mother stopped in the doorway, looking at her daughter. "You okay?" she asked.

Abigail saw the dark circles under her eyes, the shoulders slumped with exhaustion. She stood up, wrapping her arms around her mother. Her mother bowed her head, resting it on her daughter's neck as if she were the child.

Abigail bought herself a black suit to wear to the funeral. She didn't care how much money she spent on it. The skirt was close-fitting, and she wore high heels. She wanted to look good at her father's funeral. The morning of the funeral, she put on sweatpants and took Alfie out for an early, long walk. The sun wasn't up yet and the sky was pearly, iridescent. When the sun came up above the houses, its brightness was some kind of incongruous promise. Alfie trotted along happily, tail waving as he jerked his body toward invisible scents. Sometimes he would stop motionless, tail up and eyes half-closed, just smelling the air.

Back at Marisha's apartment, she curled her hair and defiantly put on mascara, daring it to run. Tears were not in her plan. She was angry; she would show him. He was gone, but somehow this was her last chance to stand up to him, to get his attention. To show him who she was and what she was made of, to show her strength. She wasn't his little, helpless girl any longer.

Her mother wore her mauve tweed suit, her "good suit," she called it, that she'd owned for years. "I decided I didn't want to wear black. I don't have to, right? It's not my color." Abigail stopped at the apartment to pick her up, and from the passenger seat she looked at Abigail for approval. Abigail saw the dark circles covered with makeup, the hair blow-dried, and imagined her mother, alone now in the apartment, staring into the mirror.

"You can wear whatever you darn well want to wear. You look good."

They opened the heavy wooden doors of the old Catholic church and walked inside to the hushed quiet. Abigail hadn't been here in years. She felt like a child again. The ceiling stretched high above her head; the air scented with incense like it always had been. She walked toward the front with her mother. People were scattered throughout the pews, familiar faces from her parents' past, and unfamiliar. She tried not to look at the casket open at the front, but when she moved to go into the pew her mother pulled her towards the front. "Up here first," she whispered. Abigail had no choice but to stand there, looking down at the open casket next to her mother.

His face was waxy and severe against creamy satin. Who thought of this, Abigail wondered. Who thought of taking the blood out of a dead body, maybe taking the organs too—she didn't know—covering the face with makeup, and putting it in an expensive piece of furniture to be buried under the ground? The casket cost more than any piece of furniture in her mother's apartment, and it was made to be viewed for a day, then hidden away in the damp earth. Abigail's stomach felt like a musty cavern full of fluttering bats and dripping acid water, but she would not cry. His face looked as if it was carved out of some artificial material, his folded hands made from the same material. She found it hard to look away from those hands. He would never have folded his hands like that.

Abigail could feel her mother trembling beside her. Abigail turned to move toward their pew, when someone came up behind her, touching her shoulder, then embracing her in a tight hug. Abigail smelled the scent Megan wore, felt her feathery hairbrush against her cheek. Megan turned to Abigail's mother then, giving her the same tight warm hug, and Abigail saw her mother's face soften, her lips trembling in a smile. Doug was nowhere in sight. "Can you sit with us?" Abigail asked.

And then James was there, dear James, who did matter so much to her, after all. Who would show up when it mattered. His hug was warm and enveloping; she felt the bats fluttering in her stomach die down. His suit coat was scratchy and warm against her cheek, smelling faintly of smoke, and she didn't want to pull away from him. She loved him.

They moved into the front pew reserved for them. Her mother turned around and leaned into the pew behind them, clutching the hand offered by her friend Margaret. Abigail sat between James and Megan. Her mother, on the other side of James, squeezed a handkerchief in one hand and James' hand in the other.

Something in Abigail was moving, shifting away from the artificial thing in the casket and toward the warm, living things beside her. These things, these people, cared for her. Abigail felt responsible for them, in a way she couldn't articulate. She'd been wrong, done something wrong, but maybe she could still make it right. It was too late with her father, if there had been anything she could have done to make that relationship right. She couldn't imagine what it would have been. But James was beside her, taking her hand, and Megan was on the other side.

The priest stepped up to the altar, and the sounds in the church hushed. At that moment, in the pew at St. Mary's Star of the Sea, Abigail felt as if she'd lost something important, something she thought she didn't care about, and now had been on the verge of losing everything else she cared about. It was up to her to hold close things that mattered. She reached for Megan's hand and held James' hand tight.

◆ ◆ ◆

That night, she called James. "So Marisha will be back next month."

"Mmm."

"I'd like to move back home. If that is all right with you."
There was a pause; Abigail imagined the air between them,
vibrating with static. "Yes," he said. "That is certainly all right
with me."

Chapter Fourteen

Abigail gave Alfie a final walk on the day Marisha was to fly into Logan. She'd been cleaning for days, clearing out traces of her life there. Outside Alfie ambled along, sniffing at food wrappers and traces of other dogs. It was December, the ground covered with snow. He seemed uninterested in their outing, as if he knew something was up.

Abigail took her suitcases and boxes to the car. Alfie observed her from his spot on the carpet. She refilled his water bowl and squatted down to hold out a treat. Marisha had told her she didn't need to stay; her parents were picking her up from the airport, and she would be back in her apartment before dark. Alfie walked closer, sniffed the treat she held out, then slowly lowered his body to the ground. He ignored the treat and sat looking at her, reproachfully. Abigail stroked his rough fur, scratched him behind the ears. "You've been a good boy." He tilted his head to the side, modestly. "Marisha," Abigail said. He lifted his eyes, looked to the door. "Marisha will be here soon. Very soon. She's on her way." Finally he took the biscuit between his teeth, delicately, and set it on the carpet in front of him. "You've been a good dog," she told him again. He gave her a look, then returned to the biscuit.

It was late afternoon, the ground barren and the sky grey and heavy. Snow was forecast. At their house, James came out to greet her. He stood in the driveway looking at her for a moment, and she looked at him. "Well," she said. "Here I am."

"Here you are." He took her two suitcases and carried them in. He had a fire going in the fireplace, and the tables had been cleared off and shone as if they'd recently been dusted. Callie jumped up on the couch and looked at her.

Abigail set her bag down on the floor. "Callie, you look angry," she said, and picked her up. Callie twisted away from her.

"It may take some time," James said. "But she'll come around."

After eating the dinner James cooked, Abigail helped him clean the kitchen. It felt comfortable to be with him, drying dishes, putting them back in their familiar places. In the wine cupboard, she found an unopened bottle of zinfandel, her favorite. James never drank zinfandel. She held it up. "Did you buy this for me?" He shrugged. She poured herself a glass and sat on the couch.

James brought a glass over and sat next to her. "Cheers," she said, tapping her glass to his.

"Sláinte. I'm glad you're home. I missed you."

"I missed you, too." She looked around the house, through the door into the kitchen, the polished wood of the living room floor, the fireplace in front of them where low flames flickered. "The house looks beautiful. I feel like I belong here. With you." She sat back and put her feet on the coffee table. It was her table; she could do that. No Alfie sitting on the floor next to her, just a cat, roaming suspiciously, and a man who was still her husband sitting next to her. She had put her clothes back in her dresser upstairs, her toiletries in the bathroom. She took a breath, and said, "There is something I need to talk with you about."

He looked immediately uncomfortable, then tried to appear as if he wasn't. "All right."

Abigail looked down at her wedding ring on the hand circling the stem of the wine glass. This was hard. Remember, she told herself: it's for the sake of your marriage. You need to. She had still never told James about her father's night visits to her room, and she had no plan to. "When you were in Ireland . . ." She took a deep breath, watched the consternation cover James' face. Did he think she was going to say she had an affair? No, she was in the business of saving her marriage now, not wrecking it.

"When you were gone, I had another miscarriage. I was pregnant with our child, and I lost it." Saying the words brought it back again, brought the fresh upsurge of pain and loss, and with them the tears.

James looked stricken. "Why didn't you tell me?" he asked.

She waited until she could speak. "I was waiting until you got back, and then . . ." She shook her head. James didn't ask more. He moved closer to her and folded her in his arms.

"I'm sorry," he said.

They were tender in bed with one another, shy as if it were the first time. Abigail, remembering James' comments from before he left, was slow to undress. Perhaps he remembered, too, as he told her she was beautiful, her body perfect. It was very different from being with Douglas—better, more loving. But she wouldn't think of that.

After, as she lay on her side and he spooned behind her, she wondered what it was she was feeling. She'd felt love for her husband before, but this was something new. It was a sense of him, or their relationship, as something valuable and fragile. Something they needed to protect and take care of, as they would a child.

◆ ◆ ◆

"So what was it like, living at Marisha's?"

Abigail turned her head to look at James. They were on a Caribbean island, a fact she reminded herself of every morning when she awoke. It was beautiful and warm, the sunshine endless. The trip was James' idea. He lay beside her on his beach towel now, face up to the sun, eyes closed. His hands rested on his naked chest, fingertips lightly stroking the fair hairs there. She'd been nearly asleep, the sand smooth beneath her towel. The only sounds were faint cries of children playing in the water, and the regular rush of the surf. Earlier they had snorkelled, following colourful fish through the sun-filled water.

"I enjoyed it, for a while." She put a hand on his bicep, letting it rest there. "It was like playing house, being a single young woman again. Only a single not-so-young woman."

"Did you really enjoy it? Did you really feel that way?" His face was still turned to the sun, eyes closed.

Abigail thought she knew what he was asking. He had never asked her whether she saw anyone when she was away from him, whether she remained faithful to him. She squeezed the warm flesh of his arm. "I wanted to feel that way," she said. "But I also always felt like it was play-acting." That was true. She wanted to be as truthful as she could in answer to his question, to catch the essence of her experience without saying anything that would hurt him or anyone else. "I always felt like I was on vacation, and one of the things I feel when I'm on vacation is I kind of want to be back home."

He turned his head then, squinting one eye to see her. A breeze shook the palm branches above their head. "I missed you," she said. "And then when Dad died, at the funeral . . ." Abigail sat up on her towel, arms crossed across her raised knees. She'd taken a chance and worn her bikini and tried not to think now of how her stomach folded when she sat like this. It didn't matter; her husband loved her. "I just realized that you were the most important thing in my life." She felt her voice quaver and let it. "The rest was just play-acting." That was true, and she hoped he wouldn't ask anything more. "How about you? What was it like for you, living alone again?"

"Well, I did that in Ireland, too."

Abigail looked at the water, the sun glinting on the blue. She waited to hear what else he would say. "Played like you were single, you mean?"

"I mean I lived alone." He picked up her hand and placed it against his warm belly. "I enjoyed being in Ireland. It's so different from America, more humane and livable somehow. I wasn't thinking of whether I was single or married. I knew I was married, just living alone. It was exhilarating, and I enjoyed it then, yeah. But when I came home and you left, then I really felt single." He paused, and they listened to the surf roar. The air was a little cooler now, the water closer to their feet as the sun sank lower in the sky.

"Did you enjoy that?"

He looked at her again, a half-smile on his face. "Abigail." He sat up and moved closer, putting an arm around her shoulder. "The truth is, I hated it. I was miserable. I just wanted you back home again. I hated waking up alone in an empty bed, I hated coming home to an empty house." He brushed sand from her back. "And I hate to cook all the time. I'm a terrible cook."

She rested her forehead against his chest. "So you wanted me to come back so I would cook dinner."

"Yes," he said. "And talk to me at night, let me tell you about my day. No one else is interested in how my day went."

Then they were quiet, until Abigail said, "Speaking of dinner . . ." They stood, shook their towels out and brushed sand off their legs. She looked forward to a shower, and wine before dinner, and eating freshly caught fish in a café by the water with this man she didn't deserve, but who somehow remained her husband nonetheless.

Chapter Fifteen

In January 2008, Abigail watched as President Obama spoke in his inaugural address of the responsibility of shaping the country, of "giving our all to a difficult task." In the following years she wondered, sometimes, what "difficult task" she might be giving herself to. Her marriage was one, she guessed. Being a responsible person, a good person. Not wrecking her life, or her marriage, or someone else's life.

She hadn't talked to Doug alone since she'd moved back home. There was no goodbye, just a return to their former lives. His absence at her father's funeral was a message to Abigail. She'd received a sympathy card from him, with a "So sorry, dear Abigail" scrawled across it, but he didn't call. She called Megan, and Megan called her, and they made plans together, without husbands. On the rare times when she saw Megan and Doug together, it was all as it was before, only without a certain tension, a fizzle, that had been there. If Abigail's eyes met Doug's, she kept them friendly and calm, one-dimensional, and turned away.

With her revised relationship with James—she thought of it as redecorated, like a house—Doug wasn't hard to forget. It was only occasionally, only at certain moments, that she thought of the times he would visit her in Marisha's apartment, and it would seem like that was another world, a world not only of irresponsibility and danger, but of reckless possibility and excitement.

◆ ◆ ◆

The episode with Doug after Megan's funeral was a lapse—a regrettable incident, fuelled by her own grief and Doug's, and the misbegotten idea that she could comfort him. Or the idea that it was, somehow, her duty as a friend to comfort him. That Megan would want her to, even.

Abigail knows this is insane. She also knows it will never happen again.

She makes one more visit to Doug's house, arranging to meet Phoebe when Doug will be at work. She and Phoebe take a last box of clothes to the thrift store, and Abigail takes a box of Megan's books.

At home, she fits the books on the shelves in her office. Some of them are from the publishing house, some are from Megan's college years, poetry and anthologies with margins full of notes. Phoebe picked up a book of poetry, one filled more than others with Megan's marginal notes. "I'll take this, but I can't take any more. No room in my apartment. No room in here." She put a hand on her chest. "Too much feeling already. I'm not able to look at them."

"Later you will be. They are yours whenever you want them," Abigail said. She opens one now, sees lines underlined and a faint note from years ago: *Never a child have I borne/Though Myrtle and Holly and Pine Trees have grown.* And this, underlined in ink that looks fresh, as if she just marked it the other day: *Poor ghost, old love, speak/with your old voice/of flaming insight/that kept us awake all night.*

Seeing Megan's handwriting reminds Abigail of the journal, still hidden in her desk drawer. She never finished reading it. It is late afternoon in a March that doesn't seem to end. On Twitter Trump is accusing Obama, with no evidence, of having wire-tapped him. She looks out the window to the grey sky, pale light falling on wet lawns and clumps of dirty snow. The beach in St. John, and her time before that in the apartment, were eight years ago, distant as another life. She takes the journal from the drawer, settling in her chair.

After a shopping list, there are pages of drawings. Partially completed sketches of a man, reading by lamplight; Abigail recognizes Doug's slightly arched nose, his hair, falling over his forehead. Words, phrases here and there that don't make coherent sense: *Wash behind your ears (why?), my mother's rum trifle.* The words *JA tomorrow* arched around a sketch of a rising (setting?) sun. And on a page to itself, a drawing of a young child, naked, curled up in a "c" shape inside a circle. The drawing is fully realized and beautiful; in a corner, a word written in small calligraphy, the name Abigail doesn't need in order to recognize her: *phoebe.*

◆ ◆ ◆

When Abigail and Megan were children, before Abigail had ambitions of being a nun, they determined they would move to a city together. They sat in the apple tree in Megan's yard, pretending that the upper branch was Megan's apartment, and the lower branch, Abigail's. Abigail would have a yellow convertible to drive them around the city. She pictured the two of them, collapsing with laughter on the front seat of the convertible, with the top down. She didn't know how to drive yet, which must be why she imagined the car stopped, and neither of them paying attention to the wheel or the other things that make a car move. They were just laughing with hysterical abandon. That's how much fun she thought they would be having, young adult women without parents around, grown up and on their own to do what they wished.

Abigail slices eggplant, tomato, and green peppers for dinner. She is remembering that desire for utter abandonment. It's like the feeling of getting high: the desire for *fun,* for giddiness, for abandon. For intensity. Who wouldn't choose that? Megan, she thinks. Megan didn't choose that.

She remembers a time sitting with Megan during her illness. Megan was in the stuffed chair in the living room, bundled up in a sweater, a pillow behind her head. They each had a glass of wine in their hands —why were they doing that? Drinking wasn't something Megan normally did, in the evening or in the middle of the afternoon, as it was then. They were celebrating something. New Year's Eve, that was it. She and James were going out that evening to a party, and she and Megan were having a glass now. Doug was gone somewhere, as he always was when Abigail was there. Abigail was a nanny, of sorts. "Cheers," Abigail said, and drank.

Megan took a sip, then set the glass down. "You never drank much, did you," Abigail said. "Why not?"

"It never appealed to me. That woozy feeling–it made me feel stupid." She smiled wryly, then took another sip.

"Funny," Abigail said. "It always made me feel smart. For a while, anyway. Until the next morning."

"Exactly." Megan looked out the window at snow beginning to fall.

Abigail felt a little irritated at this. "What *does* appeal to you, then?" Abigail softened her tone. "I mean, what would you be doing now, if you could be doing anything you wanted?"

"Anything at all?"

"Anything."

Megan smiled, looking up toward the ceiling. Abigail waited to hear what Megan was thinking of, what gave her face that softness. As if remembering she needed to answer, Megan finally said, "Talking with someone I love, I guess. Late into the night."

After a moment's thought, Abigail asked, "Anyone in particular?"

"My husband, of course," Megan said, laughing. "Who else?"

Slightly discomforted, Abigail raised her glass. "Well, here's to marital love, then."

"To marital love in the new year!"

There are things about her friend that will always remain a mystery. Thinking of this conversation, Abigail goes back to Megan's journal after dinner. After the drawing of little Phoebe, there are more lines of poems. Is that all she wrote, lines of poems that other people wrote? Well, she was a reader and an editor. *April is the cruellest month, breeding/lilacs out of the dead land, mixing/memory and desire, stirring/dull roots with spring rain.* Following those lines, Abigail finally finds words by Megan that seem to be her own. Starting at the top of the page, her neat script filling half the page–not veering from its straight path, though the pages have no lines–Megan wrote: *April may be cruel, but it has its own harsh beauty. I will always remember his face, as we walked along the shore. At least I hope I will always remember it: I am writing this, I guess, to guarantee that I will. When I was younger, I could not have appreciated this moment in the same way. We wouldn't have been able to have that conversation when I was younger; we would have been too stupid, too tongue-tied. We could not have had the honesty, the openness, with nothing held back. And it is knowing that my days will not last forever—I mean KNOWING like I do, feeling it like I do— that gives these moments their added sweetness.*

It was April, and the wind blew wet sleet into our faces, and our shoes were soaked through our socks, and everything was perfect.

Wow, Abigail thinks, laying the book in her lap. It is hard for her to imagine that this was written about Doug. She and Doug would have been married for some time when that was written. Phoebe was a young child when Megan first got the journal, and it doesn't sound to her like Megan was writing about a conversation with a long-married spouse.

She turns through the next few pages. More sketches, random notes, phone numbers. She closes the book. She can't read anymore; she feels she is invading her friend's privacy in a new way, now that it seems perhaps Megan actually had something she needed to be private about. Haven't you don't enough damage, a small voice inside her says.

Chapter Sixteen

Abigail wonders, sometimes, what there is that is good about her as a person. She has too much free time, perhaps, without Megan to help take care of, and these thoughts rise up, doubts she thought she had left behind long ago. If there is something good, how would she know? If she had a child, she could see herself reflected in the child's eyes, and know whether she was succeeding or failing at life. Her husband reflects her, but the image is so mixed up over the years that she doesn't know what it is. His love for her is partly his need for her. And she can't trust that reflection; she knows what he doesn't know about Abigail.

Saturday morning, she sits across from her mother at the small pine table in her apartment. Her mother settles into her coffee and lemon cake, moving unopened mail and flyers aside. She cuts off a corner with her fork and eats it with pure pleasure.

"How are you doing?" Abigail asks. "Your hair looks nice." Her mother has stopped dying her hair.

"Does it? Doesn't make me look too old?" She touches the gray strands with her fingers. "Your father wouldn't have liked it."

"Not at all. I love it. The grey actually is softer, prettier."

"Thank you. I'm fine. I made dinner for Margaret this week. Chicken cacciatore. It turned out very good."

She wonders if her mother ever questions herself in the way Abigail does. She is a regular attendee of Catholic Mass on Sunday mornings. Abigail sips her coffee, hesitating, until her mother asks, "So, what's up with you?"

"Umm . . . I was just thinking."

"Yes?"

"I was just wondering how someone knows if they're a good person."

Her mother looks at her. "What do you mean?"

"Okay, I mean, we all think we're good people, but how do we *know* we are?"

Her mother finishes up the lemon cake and sits back in her chair. "Well, no one's perfect. I don't think much about it. Most people I know are good, good enough anyway."

"Good enough?"

"Good enough not to mess up too bad."

"Is that it? Is that all we have to try for? What about heaven and hell? What about God? What about fulfilling our purpose on earth?"

"Ah." Her mother flaps a hand. "I don't think about that. Hell is a concept made up to frighten people. God is loving. He knows we all need forgiveness, we are all trying." Her mother eyes her. "So what's going on with you, anyway? Why are you thinking about this?"

Abigail lifts her hands, lets them drop. "No reason, don't worry. I just thought, since you're a churchgoer, you might have some insights into what makes a good person."

Her mother puts down the fork, her plate empty. "It's not that hard, really. You know. Basic stuff, Ten Commandments." Yes, Abigail supposes she does know, and that is what's troubling her.

◆ ◆ ◆

On Monday she stops by James' office, catching him between classes. She sits in the chair where students sit when they come to his office hours. His desk, scattered with books and papers and his computer and keyboard, is in front of a wall of books, next to a window overlooking the courtyard. She hands him the sandwich she picked up downtown. "Vegetarian Rueben, right?"

"Right, thanks." James, leaning forward to eat over the desk, tells her between bites about his morning class. A student had taken offense at something another student said in discussing a poem, saying it was a sexist comment. "What was it?" she asks. "What did he say?"

"He said love is more important to women than men. That women want to be in love before they have sex, they care about those things more than men do. The other student, the young woman, said he was just wrong. She was incensed about it."

"What did you do?"

James shrugs. "She clearly wanted to let the class know her sexual history, that *she* didn't need to be in love to have sex. She said the same is true for other women she knows and started to say how emotionally needy men are. I interrupted, brought the conversation back to a different aspect of the poem."

"What do you think?" Abigail asks. "Was he right?"

"It wasn't relevant in relation to—"

"No," she says. "I mean in general. Is love more important to women than to men?"

"I used to think it was." He wipes his mouth with a paper napkin. "In general, no. Different at different ages, I guess. When I was twenty, maybe it wasn't so important as it is now."

"Right," she says. "And for different people."

"Oh, yes. Doug, for example . . ." He shakes his head.

"What about him?"

"Well, he seems the type to me to not be too particular about love."

Abigail chews her sandwich, taking her time to reply. "What makes you think he's that way?" she asks. *Why bring him up,* she wonders.

"Just things I've heard, things I've observed over the years. You know he wasn't true to Megan."

Abigail hopes he can't hear the pounding of her heart. "She said something about that, but it was a long time ago . . ."
James leans back in his chair, looking out the window. "He's dealing with a lot, I know, with Megan's death, and with her illness before that. But if we're talking about men not caring whether love is involved with sex or not, he's an example to me of someone who doesn't seem to care all that much."

"What have you heard?" Abigail asks. "What do you know?" She tries to keep her voice calm, tries to act like a wife interested in talking with her husband about a mutual friend, not a former lover trying to find out about her lover's other dalliances.

James looks at her then, his expression mild. "I don't like to gossip . . . I've just heard things over the years. I saw him the other day, by the way. Having lunch downtown."

"How did he seem?" Abigail picks crumbs from her lap, glancing out the window.

"Good. Better than the last time I saw him. He was with someone I didn't know. A young woman; he introduced us, but I didn't catch her name."

◆ ◆ ◆

Abigail sits in her school office, staring at her computer. She shares an office with other part-time faculty, so the room is barren of anything personal, the only decorations a stack of paper boxes in the corner and a row of literature textbooks on the shelf. She has just come from her lunch with James and is staring at the screen unseeing. It would be hypocritical for her to think less of Doug for becoming involved with someone so soon after his wife's death; of course she knows that. No one can judge him, no one can know what he's going through. And her husband's words shouldn't surprise her. Megan told her that Doug had affairs; she told her about one, at any rate, the one that drove her away from him for a time when Phoebe was a baby. And Abigail knows he had at least one other one, having taken part in it herself. Why would she think there weren't more? The question she has now, though, is how many more? And when? And how does James know of them, and why does he choose this moment—no earlier—to mention it to her?

110

Abigail hears a tap and looks up to see a student standing at her door. Chelsea, from Introduction to Literature. "Come in! How are you?"

"Fine," Chelsea says. "Fine." She is a plump young woman, with long shiny brown hair. Very quiet. She tosses the hair to one side now, and says, "I wanted to talk with you about the stories you assign."

"Yes?" Abigail says, instantly wary.

"Oh, I like them," Chelsea says. "They are all good. But some of them are . . . hard to take, you know?"

"Yes, they are," Abigail agrees.

"I, and some of the other students I've talked to, would appreciate a warning. You know, let us know in advance if there is something that could be upsetting. Then we're prepared. That story last week, for example . . ."

"Wild Swans," Abigail says. "Right?"

"Right, that's the one. About the man on the bus." Chelsea shivers. "That's hard for some of us. We need trigger warnings." Abigail thinks trigger warnings go against the idea of literature and of art itself, which is to shock, to jar the reader or viewer, take them to an unexpected and intense place. However, she knows better than to make that argument with a traumatized student, one who will fill out an evaluation form at the end of the semester for a part-time, untenured professor. "Of course," she says. "I will try to do that." She makes a note on a piece of paper. *Trigger warnings.* "I understand. I'm sorry if it was upsetting to you."

"Thank you," Chelsea says. She looks relieved.

"How are you doing otherwise?" Abigail asks. "Is everything okay?"

"Fine, yes."

"Good," Abigail says. "See you in class, then." As Chelsea stands up, Abigail wonders what she would say if her professor told her that she, too, is among the ranks of those who have suffered sexual abuse, and relies on literature to take her places she is uncomfortable to go. Young people today, Abigail thinks–aware that, if she said this aloud, she would sound like a cranky grandma–are elaborately careful of themselves, of their feelings. Toughen up, she wants to tell them. Life is hard. Get used to it.

◆ ◆ ◆

Abigail has promised herself she will finish Megan's journal. In an odd way, it feels as if reading the journal is not something that she wants to do, but something that she must do; a duty, a job she must accomplish for the sake of some greater good, though she isn't clear on what that good might be. Understanding, perhaps. Knowledge. Maybe she will give it to Phoebe when she's done, saying it was at the bottom of one of the boxes of books.

After the passage about the walk in April with an unidentified person, there are more lines of poetry. She recognizes Yeats: *When you are old and grey, and full of sleep/and nodding by the fire, take down this book.* And the short poem by Robert Frost: *Nature's first green is gold,/her hardest hue to hold./Her early leaf's a flower;/But only so an hour./Then leaf subsides to leaf./So Eden sank to grief,/So dawn goes down to day./Nothing gold can stay.* Lines about time passing, about growing old, about loss.

She reads a passage about Phoebe. *Today was her fourteenth birthday. When she was asleep tonight after the family party, I went into her bedroom and sat carefully on the chair, so as not to wake her. I watched her sleep—if that's invasive and strange, I apologize now. (Thinking of A. here, of the night at her house, her father, when we were younger than Phoebe is now. All I forgave her for what I saw that night.) I thought of all Phoebe has given to my life, and all she will continue to give, until I no longer exist. Dear girl, with her humor, her adult insight, her surprising love. I will never stop being amazed by her.*

Abigail reads that over again. *A . . . her father. . . all I forgave later for what I saw then.* Clearly she must be "A," and what Megan saw was Abigail's father coming in her room. But, "forgave?" Where did that come from? She doesn't remember Megan forgiving her for anything. Discomfited, she turns the page.

More sketches of Phoebe, plants, unidentifiable people. A few lines of poetry Abigail doesn't recognize. *Somewhere unturned behind a silky leaf/ is the pleading trick of creation that would explode/ to make a world that turned with all of us on it/ in love/ and you especially, you saint/ hidden under the sky.* Abigail wonders if Megan wrote those words, and if so, who that "saint hidden under the sky" is.

A few more passages toward the end of the journal. Scribbled notes that Abigail finds hard to decipher; she will come back to them later. Watercolor paints used here and there, lovely touches of color. One of the sketches looks remarkably like James, just a face with shadows behind it. One could possibly be Abigail herself, a quick sketch of a figure in a doorway.

Who knew her friend had this talent? (And what, oh what, did Megan need to forgive her for?)

Book Two: A Symmetry of Husbands

Chapter One

Megan suspected from the moment she met Douglas Adams that he was not the kind of man who would be faithful. That's what she told herself later, at any rate, when the suspicion—if indeed she'd had one—had been confirmed.

Or maybe her suspicion was actually only in retrospect, when she told herself she *should* have suspected. All that personal charm, she thought later, could not be limited to, not be wasted on, one person. From the time Megan met Doug, when he called her into his office for the interview, she saw him as a larger-than-life person, one out of the ordinary, so it would follow that his passions and affairs would be larger-than-life also.

Thinking back, it seems that this was the time she began seeing herself as small, a sensation that has persisted.

She was already impressed and disoriented before she met him that day. From the outside, the building was huge: granite, distinguished in an old-Boston way. Inside, the lobby was all glass and metal and futuristic. Her low heels tapped on a floor polished to a high sheen, as spotless as if she were the first person to walk on it. A receptionist made a phone call and Doug came out to meet her—of course, she thought, her potential boss would be young and slim and handsome and charming. Was she in a movie? He took her down a hallway lined with book covers of their more successful books. Megan was too nervous to look closely. Suddenly seized by the idea that she was going to slip and fall down, she focused on her feet on the shiny floor, taking care to position each foot before moving on to the next one. When he seated himself in front of windows with a view of the city, and she sat across from him, she was embarrassed to find herself laughing.

He cocked his head. "Is something funny?"

Megan tried to control herself, to be professional, but it was too late for that. "It's just that this is all so . . . so *perfect.*" She motioned to the office, the desk, the windows—and Douglas himself. "The view, I mean," she said, trying for composure. He gave her a half-smile, taking her in.

She was twenty-two years old, just graduated from Bard College with a major in English, a wide-eyed wispy young woman with curly hair she couldn't control. Her professor told her the internship was just pro forma, unless she really messed it up. Douglas walked her to the front door when the interview was done. He shook her hand, giving a half-salute, half-wave, and Megan thought *Well, that's it. I set a new standard for fucking up an interview.*

She was assigned a cubicle of her own, with a desk and chair. She stood on a chair to tack up a poster of an abstract Kandinsky composition that filled up most of one wall. She worried over putting it up: what did it say about her, about her tastes? Too big, too wild, not intellectual enough? Did it in some way reveal her youth? She finally put it up anyway, because looking at it made it feel as if something inside her were expanding, opening up to a bright sky.

When she finished, she climbed down and stood looking at it for a moment. She turned to see a young man just outside her door. "It looks great," he said, and smiled. He reached out a hand. "Ben. I guess we're neighbors." He gestured to the cubicle next to hers. "I'm an intern, working under Katherine Reed."

"Megan Nielson." She shook his hand. The gesture still felt odd to her; formal and adult. She was in the world now where women wore heels to their office, and men wore ties, and everyone shook hands instead of nodding and saying *hey*. This man, however, wasn't wearing a tie; he wore a striped button-up shirt, pulled out over dark jeans in what Megan knew was a fashion. She didn't think it was a wise choice for this office. Ben looked no older than she was; nice-looking, she guessed, with attractively rumpled hair and dark glasses, but he seemed so young. "I'm an intern too, working with Douglas Adams." It was a pleasure to say his name.

Ben's eyes lit up with recognition, and something else; a look crossed his face. He looked around, at the empty hallway. "Watch out for him," he whispered.

"What?" Megan asked. "Why?"

"Ah, nothing," Ben said. "He's a single guy, that's all. You know how guys are." He laughed. "It's nice to meet you, Megan. Let me know if I can be helpful." He gave her a little wave and disappeared into his cubicle.

Her work at first consisted of photocopying and errands inside the building: some copy-editing, ferrying proofing sheets around from office to office. She loved it when she would get sent to the public library to look something up and could spend time in the reading room. She started fact-checking a nonfiction book about the history of Harlem Douglas—Doug—was working on. At those moments she thought she had the perfect job, poring over books and journals in the huge room, with the high ceiling arching over her, and with an intriguing boss.

Of course it wasn't technically a job, just an internship that paid her, but not enough to live on. Her parents paid rent for her to stay with a friend in Somerville, a short train ride away from the office. It was "just until you get on your feet," her father assured her.

◆ ◆ ◆

On the day that the Harlem book was finally done, Megan looked up from her desk to see Douglas, standing just inside the cubicle door. He had his jacket over his arm. "We need to celebrate," he said. "C'mon, I'll buy you a drink."

She looked at the clock on the wall. "That sounds delightful, but I'm supposed to work another hour."

"Megan," he said, shaking his head slowly. "You don't get it. I'm your boss. This is work." He smiled. "I'll wait for you downstairs."

When Megan left, she glanced at Ben's door to see if he'd overheard their exchange, but luckily, he wasn't there.

The bar was dark after the sunlight outside. She made out just a few people sitting at the bar, and one couple in a corner. Douglas led the way to a table in the back. He ordered a

Manhattan. "I'll have the same," Megan said. When the bartender left, she confessed, "I've never had one before."

Doug smiled at her. "I hope you like it. I'll feel responsible if you don't." He could be so kind, his face radiating warmth and a kind of approval that made her feel confident. When the drink came, she discovered that she actually didn't like the taste. She meant not to tell Doug, but her face must have revealed it. "Let me order you something else," he said, but she wouldn't let him.

"I think it's an acquired taste," she said. "And I want to acquire it." To help this process along, he said, Doug ordered her another Manhattan when she was halfway through her first.

As she sipped the second drink, Megan felt worldly, grown up, and so interested in the man sitting across from her. She couldn't stop looking at him over the flickering candle. She felt an embarrassed smile cross her face.

"What is it?" he said.

She shook her head and laughed lightly. "I just appreciate . . . how patient you've been with me, as I learn things. So kind." It's true, he had been. She'd been uncertain many times, had asked so many questions that she felt were stupid, and he always answered her thoughtfully, as if it were something he'd never really considered before. She felt her eyes become, most embarrassingly, damp. To change the mood, she lifted her glass. A tiny bit slipped over the side. "Oops. Here's to my slow acquisition of skills. And taste." She sipped.

He said, "It's nothing but a pleasure to work with you." The way he said the words made Megan feel warm inside. "How's that taste acquisition coming along?" he asked.

"Wonderfully," she said. She needed to take care to pronounce her words carefully. "I am loving it." The drink reminded her of Douglas Adams himself: sophisticated, heady, with a sharp edge of danger.

As Douglas drank his second Manhattan, Megan chatted away, more loquacious than she'd been before with him. She was grateful when Douglas ordered a plate of nachos and invited her to share. She told him about growing up on the North Shore, about her attorney father and stay-at-home mother, about their summer house in Maine. He told her about growing up in Manhattan. His father had died when he was eight years old and he grew up in a condo in the city with his mother. He was older than her, by nine years; "That's not very much!" Megan said, as if answering a question, and was immediately embarrassed.

After a while, their conversation slowed. He leaned back against the cushioned booth and looked at her, arms crossed. His look asked her, dared her, to keep looking at him, and she did. He didn't touch her—no hand snaking across the table for hers, no brushing his shoulder against hers. He didn't need to. She could feel his presence, his closeness, as if they were touching. He had lines on the side of his mouth that deepened when he smiled or, as now, in a thoughtful quiet moment. Megan imagined his face growing older, those lines surrounded by others, and she wished she could be there to see that.

When they left, they walked down the sidewalk slowly. It had become dark, the night shiny and black around them. They stopped at the corner where Megan would turn right to catch the train. "I live this way," Doug said, pointing left. They turned to look at one another. With a slight movement of

121

Douglas's head, and a questioning look, it was decided. They turned left.

Chapter Two

It was strange to be in the office with Doug after that. Megan had to pretend they didn't spend many nights together; she had to pretend she hadn't watched him put on that tie that morning or made coffee in his kitchen. She had to not think about how he'd come up behind her as she stood in the kitchen, wrapping his arms around her tightly and pressing his face in her neck. And those other things, the things that happened the night before, that she tried to keep from thinking of. Of course they had to keep it secret, and act professional. Office politics, Doug said. He could lose his job. It went without saying that they wouldn't be able to continue with their relationship if it became public in the office.

Ben and Megan chatted in the copy room and the hallway and became friends of a sort. He suggested going out for lunch, but she always made sure to bring a sandwich with her to work so she had an excuse. He sometimes wandered into her cubicle just to chat. "I'm so sick of photocopying," he said. "I have to take a break sometimes. How's it going with Adams?"

"Pretty good," she said. "He's not bad to work with." She looked at her watch, trying to ignore Ben's assessing look.

When Megan told Doug that it was difficult to continue working with him and seeing him also, he suggested that she ask for another position, with another supervisor. Then if it came out that they were dating, he wouldn't be in such trouble. She agreed that was a good idea. She framed her application to another position by saying she really wanted to find out more about the job of Production Editor, rather than Doug's position of Editor. In truth, the work that Doug did was her first interest, but the sacrifice of that internship was worth it for a relationship with Douglas Adams. It was worth it, it was all worth it, for the giddy rush of seeing him smile at her, touch her cheek. Feeling loved by him. She accepted a different internship, in another part of the building.

Ben asked to take her out for a drink, to celebrate, he said. And to say goodbye. "I'll miss working next to you," he said. "I'll miss you turning down my offers for lunch."

"I'm sorry," Megan said. "The truth is, I have a boyfriend."

"Really? We could still have a drink. I promise not to steal you away from him."

She smiled and shook her head. She let herself say "You're so handsome, Ben, I don't think I could help myself. I wouldn't be responsible for what happened." She enjoyed watching the red creep across Ben's face.

After she stopped working with Doug, she wondered when they would stop hiding their relationship. The secrecy was fun at first, and necessary when she worked with him, but the fun was wearing off. Doug said he wanted to still keep it secret. "It's too soon," he said. *Too soon?* Megan wondered. They were sleeping together but didn't go out together in public.

Doug was interested in Megan's family's second home in Maine, calling it her family's "camp." "Well, it's actually a house," she said. "Near the ocean. Not much insulation, but it does have heat, and plumbing, and all that." She got the keys from her parents and they drove to Maine on a warm and sunny fall weekend. Megan had a plan.

After they parked on the gravel drive Megan pointed out the glint of the ocean through the trees, but she didn't need to: Douglas was taking it all in. She unlocked the door, and the smell of the house, with all its summers and sounds of seagulls and smell of salt air, hit her.

Megan started a fire in the stone fireplace, stacking up small sticks of wood over balled-up newspaper. She nursed the flame, and when the sticks caught fire, she put another log on top. Doug stood beside her, hands in his pockets. "Amazing," he said. "You're the fire goddess, what's her name—Vesta? It's you." With the fire crackling, they sat on the couch, looking at the ocean through the trees. She made coffee in the old percolator, and Doug poured whiskey in his. "My god, this place," he said, looking at her over his drink.

"Not too rustic for you?" Megan asked. The house, built by her great-grandfather in the early 1900's, had been updated with heating and plumbing, but left alone in the important ways. The wood floors were scratched, and the old rugs covering them, though beautiful, were thin and threadbare, the rockers on the wrap-around porch creaky and ancient. Not wanting to turn the heat on, they piled old quilts in the bedroom downstairs to keep warm at night when the fire went out.

"No, it's just right. Have your parents ever thought of selling? This must be worth a bundle."

"No, never. They want it to stay in the family for their grandchildren and great-grandchildren."

The next morning after breakfast they went for a walk, following a narrow path through the woods that led to the shore. The wind was strong, blowing away clouds. Megan led the way, turning to look over her shoulder at Doug. He was grinning in the sun, above his zipped-up fleece jacket. It was time, she thought. She pushed branches out of the way and stopped on a bare spot with an overlook. Doug stepped up beside her, putting a hand on her back.

She turned to him, then turned to look at the water. She folded her arms across her chest. It was hard for her to bring this up. She liked to be in agreement on things; she saw herself as supportive and easy, un-demanding, the farthest thing from a prima donna. She took a breath. "I'm tired of pretending we're not having a relationship," she said. "I'm tired of hiding. We're not doing anything wrong." Doug dropped his hand from her back. "I feel like I'm your illegitimate mistress or prostitute, or something."

He put his hands in his pockets, looked down at the dirt, then out at the ocean. "Since we're still working at the same company, and you used to be my assistant, they'll think I took advantage of you. Even if they don't do anything, they'll disapprove. My reputation will be damaged."

She grabbed a pine branch by her side, twisted it impatiently in front of her. "I'm beginning to think you like it like this," she said. It was true. There was no downside to him in continuing this way. She saw a look cross his face; he'd been caught out. Dark waves glittered in the early sunshine, and when they crashed on the rocks below them, spray misted their faces.

That evening, over a dinner of fried fish next to the big kitchen windows, he said, "Well, if you were working for another company, there would be no problem."

◆ ◆ ◆

A month later, Megan landed a job as Editorial Assistant at a different publishing house. It was a real, full-time position, not an internship. Doug had helped her apply but said he didn't pull any strings. She wasn't sure of that but was happy to have a paying job in publishing so soon out of college.

And so their relationship became public, and progressed, with visits to parents. They met Megan's parents at a restaurant in Beverly. Megan was anxious, both for what her parents would think of Doug, and what he would think of them. Doug wore a suit and tie and treated her parents as if they were the most important people he'd ever met. Megan's mother was charmed. She drank an extra glass of wine and was flushed and laughing by the end of the meal. Her father was polite as always, but Megan could not tell what he really thought. When her father liked someone, it was easy to tell, in the openness of his smile, in his manner. In his conversation with Doug, her father was reserved and serious. In quiet moments between conversations, he sometimes sat back and observed Doug with glances that left Megan uncertain. Over dessert her father saw Megan watching him, and smiled at her with affection, and what she thought was a trace of pity.

Doug took Megan to visit his mother in her upper East Side condo. "They bought the condo before I was born," he said, as they drove along the Merritt Parkway in Connecticut. "He was in business. She worked at an art gallery, then was a receptionist for a law firm. She's an artist," he said. "You'll see her work. Quite good, I think."

"What do you remember of your father?" Megan asked.

Doug shrugged one shoulder, keeping his eyes on the road. "Tall guy, deep voice. Suit pants and shiny brown shoes. I don't remember much except for the shock when he was gone. Just— boom. One day, no dad. Hit by a car crossing an intersection. He was rushing and wasn't in the crosswalk where he should have been." He glanced over her and smiled. "This is why I'm always careful about crosswalks."

"I'm sorry," Megan said. "It must have been awful. Your life is so much more interesting than mine. My childhood was nice, but . . . boring."

He took his eyes off the road, then, to fix her with a look, one eyebrow slightly raised. "I would have happily settled for boring."

They took the stairs to his mother's apartment on the third floor of a large stone building on the west side. Megan thought of Doug, running up and down these stairs as a child, a city boy used to street life and the subway. She imagined him as a teenager striding down this street, passing teenage girls whose eyes followed him longingly. Her own teen years in Beverly seemed unbearably wholesome and bland by comparison.

Doug's mother opened the door and spread her arms wide. Megan felt herself wrapped in scented elegance, colorful flowing silks, soft touches on the arm. Amy was an attractive, fluttery woman in her late fifties, with grey-streaked hair that swooped over one eye. Doug leaned in for his hug, a long, warm one, before Amy turned to Megan. "I'm *so* glad to meet you," Amy said.

"And I you," Megan said, flustered. Amy held her at arm's length, smiling, before letting her go. Behind the swoop of pale hair, smiles, and mascara, Megan felt that Amy observed her shrewdly.

The apartment was comfortable and bright, but tiny, with two bedrooms each barely able to fit a double bed. Megan admired a painting on the wall behind Amy–bursts of color creating a barely identifiable landscape, a country lane between houses, light and dark crashing against one another. Amy dismissed Megan's praise. "It's just something I do to pass the time. What else can an old woman like myself do? Here, come in, sit down. I'll make us some drinks. Do you like gin, Megan? I have good gin, but it's the tonic that makes it: quinine from Africa, ginger from India." Amy had finished her drink and was halfway through another before Megan finished hers.

After dinner, Amy offered martinis. When Doug and Megan turned her down, she made herself one. Megan cleared and Doug loaded the dishwasher. "Leave it," Amy said, waving her arms. "I'll have to redo it all anyway, you know that."

"I don't do it right, apparently," Doug said. They went into the other room. Amy sat in a wingback chair, letting her head drift from side to side, as if listening to music no one else could hear, as she looked at her son. "What a boy he was," she said dreamily. Douglas scoffed. He turned his head to the window, to the row of lighted windows in the building across the street. "No, I mean it!" his mother protested. "All the women were after him." He rolled his eyes.

She reached down to her purse, pulling out a pack of cigarettes and a book of matches. "Do you mind if I smoke?" she asked, lighting as she asked. She inhaled, looking at her son. "All the women. Whether it was wildly inappropriate, or just inappropriate."

"Mother," Doug said, leaning forward with his elbows on his knees. "My girlfriend doesn't really want to hear my mother's version of my romantic history with other women."

"Oh, but of course I do," Megan protested, laughing, pleased to hear him call her his girlfriend. "That is, if she wants to tell. We are her guests, after all."

Amy looked at Megan approvingly. "That's right." She smiled through the veil of smoke, then leaned toward Megan and said, "Tell me about yourself," and Megan saw that there were to be no stories that night of women throwing themselves at Douglas.

◆ ◆ ◆

It was on the drive home the next day, windshield wipers flapping and jazz playing low above the sound of tires on wet pavement, that Doug told her about one of those women. His aunt, Amy's sister Clarice, younger than Amy by eight years. But still twenty years older than Doug. When she was in her thirties and Doug was in his teens. "Apparently she found me irresistible," he said. He kept his voice jaunty, trying to keep it light. Megan reached across the seat to take his hand. She

squeezed, and waited, looking at him. "She was married to a musician. He taught at the Manhattan School of Music."
"So what happened?" Megan finally asked. "Did she act on that attraction?"

With a glance at her, then back at the road, he nodded. "Yes, she did. It went on for nearly a year."

Clarice had lived in the city, not far from where Doug lived with his mother, and would often stop by. When he was in high school he would sometimes be home alone in the afternoon, and that's when it started. "I simply couldn't believe it," he said. "Sometimes I felt like the luckiest guy on earth, to have this older experienced woman teaching me how to please a woman. I mean, she was beautiful, an artist like my mother, and I was a hormone-crazed kid. You know how I can get." He looked at her, eyes wide; she did know. His passion could be intense, their sex acrobatic. "Other times, it was a nightmare. It threw me into shock. I was in a state of shock for two formative years of my life. How does someone handle that?" She saw the intensity of the experience still thrumming through him. His hands on the wheel trembled, just slightly.

"What happened?" Megan asked. "How did it end?" She paused, then, "I assume it ended."

He was silent for a moment. A small muscle twitched below his eye. "My mother found out. She confronted Clarice, and eventually her husband found out too. He left her. They divorced, and she moved across the country. She lives in San Francisco."

"Oh, my god."

"I felt responsible for breaking up their marriage. A teenaged kid. It fulfilled all my fantasies about myself, good and bad." He raised his voice, to be heard over the rain. "Just to be clear, I wouldn't wish that on my worst enemy."

"I'm sorry that happened to you," Megan said, her voice soft. Doug lifted her hand to his mouth for a quick kiss before letting go.

Chapter Three

Megan wondered if there was something odd in the fact that two people she was close to had both been sexually assaulted by family members in their childhood. Either she drew people like that to her, or she was attracted to them, or family sexual assault was everywhere. She did some research and decided there was more of it than she had thought there was. It made her grateful for her parents: their protectiveness, their normal, healthy affection. It also made her think of her old friend Abigail.

She hadn't seen or spoken with Abigail since their college days. There had been a few letters, nothing more. When Abigail visited Megan at Bard, she left a trail of stories behind her. Megan supposed Abigail had been going through a hard time– dropped out of college, working at a pizza parlor, trying to figure things out. Not that Abigail would ever let herself be vulnerable enough to say that she was confused or trying to figure things out. She always acted tough, as if nothing really troubled or frightened her. Megan had seen her cry only once, that awful, telling night so long ago. At the time she visited Megan at Bard, Abigail drank a lot and smoked a lot of weed and took whatever anyone offered her and seemed to have sex with anyone who wanted to, also.

Will had been his name. Another person would have been called Bill, or Billy, but Will was exactly right for him. He was a music major at Bard, and Megan could think of nothing but him. As Megan was a literature major and art minor, their circles didn't overlap as much as she would like; it took some effort. She went to musical events on campus, sitting in the back of the room and looking for the scraggly curls hanging down on his neck. She took up smoking just so she could stand outside at intermission, watching for him to come out and light up. She hated the taste of the smoke and the way it made her head feel, dizzy and slightly sick, but she pretended to need and enjoy it. She cultivated the friendship of a girl who had gone to high school with Will and got invited to parties where he might be.

When Abigail visited, Megan took her to a concert on campus. She couldn't tell Abigail about her feelings for Will; she was afraid of what Abigail would say, what she might do. Megan wouldn't cheapen her feelings by talking about them. After the concert, Megan did get the chance to say hi to him on the courtyard outside the concert hall. "Hey," he said, puffing on a cigarette. His eyes rested on her in a way that made her feel warm. Megan introduced him to Abigail. "This is my childhood best friend." He shook Abigail's, hand, his eyes bright under the curls.

It was Abigail who thought to invite him over. "We have lots of wine," she said. "Want to come over to Megan's dorm and have some?" It was so easy, Megan marvelled; why hadn't she thought of something so simple?

He nodded. "That sounds cool," he said. "I have to do something first, though. Promised my home skillet." He motioned toward his friend, leaning against the wall. "I'll come by later.

Back in the dorm, Megan drank wine in the lounge with Abigail and some friends. "You won't get into trouble for this?" Abigail asked.

"Not here," Megan said. "As long as one of us is over 21." Megan's friend Alice waved her hand above her head. "Thank you, Alice."

Megan kept her eye on the door. People stepped in and out, but no sign of Will. She and Abigail had stayed up late the night before, and her head felt fuzzy from the wine and from sleepiness. Abigail was looking through the box of cassette tapes someone had brought, asking about Cyndi Lauper and Dire Straits. Abigail could stay up endlessly once she got going. After a couple of hours, Megan gave up hoping Will would show, and went to bed. Sometime later, she heard Abigail open the door to Megan's single room and settle herself in her sleeping bag on the floor.

Their conversation the next morning lingers in her mind with painful clarity. Megan stepped over Abigail to use the bathroom, trying to be quiet. When she came back to the room, Abigail was lying on her side, her eyes open. Her cheeks were flushed in the bars of morning sun coming through the partly opened curtains, her lips red. She looked pretty, Megan thought. Abigail *was* pretty, with long curls, a curvy body, and an unself-conscious sexiness. She turned over on the floor and stretched, groaning, her breasts pushing against the long tee shirt. "You know that feeling," she said, "the morning after you have sex?"

"What?" Megan said. "What are you talking about? No, in fact, I don't know that feeling."

"That feeling like you're sore but happy?" She touched her pink cheek with her palm. "You know, your face is sore from rubbing against a man's bristly face?" She ran her hand down her body, to between her legs. "You're sore here too, but it feels kind of good? You know. I love that feeling."

Megan felt heat rise within her, outrage. She sat down on her desk chair. "What on earth happened after I went to bed?"

Abigail turned back on her side facing Megan, a little smile on her face. "Your friends showed up."

Megan couldn't talk to Abigail anymore, couldn't ask what friends, or who she had sex with. She just said, "I'm taking a shower," and left the room. In the shared bathroom, she let hot water run over her until she felt calmer. When she stepped out of the stall, wearing her short terry robe with her hair in a towel, her sometime friend Marie was standing in front of the mirrors, brushing her teeth. Marie was a round-faced, sardonic girl who wore expensive cashmere sweaters that Megan envied. She looked sideways at Megan, and spit into the sink. "What?" Megan said. "What did that look mean?"

"Oh, nothing. It's just that your friend disappeared with Will somewhere last night." Marie packed her toothbrush and toothpaste carefully into the designer bag she carried. "That girl doesn't waste any time, does she?"

Abigail didn't know of Megan's feelings for Will. Still, Megan couldn't think of her friend in the same way after that. She felt tainted, as if the reputation Abigail had gathered during her short visit would spill over onto her. Abigail wasn't the kind of person Megan wanted to be. Abigail left later that morning, and Megan forced herself to smile and act sad as they hugged in the parking lot by Abigail's car.

After that she remained polite but distanced herself from her friend until they fell out of touch. And she knew she could never talk with Will again without picturing him with Abigail, making her sore.

Chapter Four

Megan never doubted Doug's love. When she first discovered him with another woman after they had been living together for just a month, his shame and sorrow for her pain were clear, and undeniably real.

She found out by accident in a way that could not be argued with, could not be denied. She was on her way to a meeting in the Back Bay. It was a sunny day in early spring, and she gave herself extra time on the way to the meeting to walk slowly, to enjoy the air. She lifted her face to the sky, skirt swinging in a breeze. A man looked at her as he passed, and she felt young and pretty. Passing the glass window of a café, she glanced at it to check her appearance. Through her reflection in the glass she saw, on the other side of the room, a man in semi-profile who reminded her of Doug. His back was angled so he was facing diagonally away from her, but she could see his face. He leaned toward a woman across the table; the intensity of his posture would have caught her attention even if he hadn't looked like Doug. Megan slowed her walk, looking down at her shoes. She lifted a foot and played with the strap, pretending something was wrong with it as she leaned against a railing, looking sideways into the window. It was actually Doug, wearing the lilac-colored shirt he had left the apartment in that morning. He reached across the table to put a hand against the woman's cheek, caressing. The woman leaned down into his hand and looked into his eyes, a sweet, ardent expression on her face. Neither of them were aware of the curly-haired woman at the window, now just standing and gaping.

Megan didn't know what to do. She didn't know how to play the role of cheated-on girlfriend. It had never happened to her before; it wasn't a role she'd auditioned for. She went to her meeting, got through it somehow, and walked back to the office. She took the same route, so she could look in the window again, where she saw the table empty.

At work, she told her co-workers she was struck by a sudden illness. She put her hand on her stomach. "Food poisoning, I'm guessing." At home, she *did* feel ill, and lay on the couch with her eyes closed.

When Doug came home, she was up and preparing dinner. He kissed her cheek, breathing in the scent of her hair. "You smell so good," he said. He smelled like himself, with a slight smell of perspiration, not unusual after taking the train home. He changed from his lilac-colored shirt to a tee shirt and jeans, and came rattling down the stairs, cheerful. Megan absorbed herself making a meal he liked, seared scallops over spinach with a cream sauce. Seated at the table, she asked how his day was. He complained about a difficult author he was working with, a woman named Caroline who had a list of complaints. "Did she come to your office?" Megan asked, innocently.

"No, we talked over the phone." He looked up from his plate. "Why? How was your day?"

"Oh, fine. I just wondered if you met your difficult clients for lunch, or if it's easier to talk in your office."

"Sometimes I do, but I had lunch today at my desk. Too much to do. I got a sandwich from the deli." He spooned more sauce over the scallops. "This is delicious, by the way. Thank you for making it."

Megan put her fork and napkin down. She sat motionless. Her mouth opened, closed, opened again, trying to get words out. She stared at Doug, then back down at the scallops. "At your desk," she finally said. Her lips couldn't control themselves; her face twitched in a humiliating way.

Doug put down his fork and stared, concerned. "What? What's the matter?"

She finally stuttered, "I s-saw you. At lunch." She thought his face paled, something she hadn't seen before. "I was on my way to a meeting in the Back Bay." She opened her hands, holding them out to her sides like a helpless child. "There you were."

To his credit, Doug didn't deny it. He didn't continue to lie. Stricken, he said, "I'm so sorry." Megan was grateful to hear the words, to know she didn't have to argue with him about the truth of what she saw. "I'm so stupid. Can you ever forgive me?" It was just a stupid flirtation, he said; a woman from another agency had been flirting with him. She called him, he'd given in to her invitation for lunch, he never should have. It hadn't gone farther than what Megan saw, he said. He vowed never to see the woman again, he vowed to be true to Megan. Megan wanted to believe him and believed half of what he said. "What was her name?" Megan asked, wiping a cheek.

"Her name?"

"Yes. Can't you tell me her name? You know it, don't you?"

"It's Anna. Anna Boyle." Megan filed that away; she wouldn't forget.

"You mean more to me than anything," he'd said later, gathering her in his arms. "I'm so very sorry." When she saw his tears, she couldn't pull away. She'd never seen a man cry. He looked helpless, vulnerable, like an out-of-control, beautiful child. In the midst of her anger, she overflowed with love for him. She had never felt so much before, so many conflicting emotions. It made her want to hit him and hurt him, then fall down with him on the couch, put her hands on his bare back under his shirt, and not think about who else may have touched that body today.

A few days later, Megan was on the couch, reading a newspaper. It was Saturday, late afternoon, and the sun poured through the window of their fourth-floor apartment. Doug had gone out. She heard him come in the front door and into the living room, where he stood awkwardly in front of her, still wearing his wool jacket. He cleared his throat dramatically and pulled something from the pocket of his jacket. A small white box, with a pink silk bow wrapped around it. "Um . . . here." That's all he said, standing in front of her awkwardly. His face— was he blushing? Yes, flaming red.

It was, of course, a diamond ring. Up until now, one diamond ring had looked much like another to Megan, and none of them were anything she particularly longed for. But the ring Doug had chosen was simple and brilliant, and she wanted it, with a sudden desire she didn't think she'd feel.

The ring looked good on her hand. "How did you get the right size?"

"I guessed. The store clerk helped."

She turned her hand, looking at it, then pulled it off. "It's really pretty. But what does it mean?" If this meant they were to be engaged, she wasn't sure of it. "I'm just twenty-three," she said. "I don't think I'm ready." She didn't put into words what didn't need to be said, that it was him she was unsure of.

"It's all right," he said. He held her hand, the one with the ring, in both of his, covering it warmly. "Just wear the ring, if you want. We don't have to call it anything. It's just a piece of jewelry, a gift to you. We're not married until you get the other piece, right? Isn't that how it goes?"

"I guess," she murmured, looking down at the ring.

Doug leaned his forehead against hers. "I do want to be married to you, though," he said softly.

Megan lifted her head and took his two hands in hers. They were square, solid hands, long fingers with neatly trimmed nails. "This ring identifies me as belonging to you," she said earnestly. "You own me. But nothing identifies you as being loved by me, being owned by me. I can't own you."

He looked at her, and she saw the light moving in his pale eyes as it sometimes did. "Would you like me to be identified?" he said and smiled. "You can tattoo me. Your name, in a heart on my bicep."

In the end she wore the ring, trying to see it as a piece of jewelry, but of course she couldn't. People noted it, exclaimed over it, and she didn't deny that she was engaged. Her mother was delighted; her father asked if she was sure it was what she wanted. "Yes, I'm sure," she said. Her father looked at her face searchingly. The idea of being married brought her a mixture of joy and fear, but it seemed inevitable. She didn't want to let him go. They were already living together; it was the next step.

Megan bought Doug a silver ring with a black onyx stone. It looked striking on his hand, though she didn't think anyone would know by looking at it that he was engaged. But Doug was her fiancé. He remained faithful, as far as she knew, and he was charming, kind, loving. He did the right things. They planned a wedding. After living together for a year, they bought a big old house in Salem, and they both took the commuter train in every morning. It was a house for a family. Megan had her own small room, an office where she wrote and thought and sketched. She loved her house. The wedding took place, with joy and fear, and love bubbling like champagne. Then, she got pregnant.

Life happened, along with its accoutrements: a house, a child, love, pain. A marriage.

Chapter Five

Is it possible to have a good marriage when one partner is habitually unfaithful? Megan would have said no. Is it possible to love someone who is habitually unfaithful? Megan would have said clearly yes. Was her husband, Douglas Adams, habitually unfaithful? This was the question Megan was faced with when, again, she found he was involved with another woman.

From the time Phoebe was born Megan would read aloud to her, holding her on her lap with the book in front of them. It was a pleasure to revisit the old classics, and to see the beautiful, inventive new picture books. Megan came to be considered the resident expert among the editors she worked with on books for children and young adults. A woman named Lucy moved into Megan's old position in adult fiction. Though Lucy was younger than Megan, she had a graduate degree in literature as well as experience at another publishing house, which was more than Megan had when she began working at the firm. Megan could hear her in conversation in her office a few doors away; she had a booming laugh, and a confidence Megan envied. She was a different person, however, when Megan stepped in to say hi. She was quiet then, watchful, with a tentative smile in response to Megan's cheery comments. Thinking they needed to get to know one another, Megan asked Lucy to join her for a drink after work.

Megan made arrangements for the nanny to stay late. She pumped her breasts in the bathroom, putting the filled bottle in the office refrigerator to take home. Megan was back to working nearly full-time, and it was getting harder and harder to keep nursing, though she desperately wanted to. It was hard to stay away from Phoebe so long. Megan had asked the nanny to bring Phoebe in at lunch time today, so they could nurse and have a few moments of closeness.

Over the first glass of wine, they covered Lucy's life. She lived alone, had a long-term, long-distance boyfriend in New York that she saw frequently. "But we're happy not to live together," she said. "At least, I'm happy. I like my privacy. I like to set my own hours."

"And when you see one another . . ." Megan traced a path through the condensation on the outside of her wine glass with a finger.

"It's special. It's hot." Lucy raised an eyebrow. Megan was beginning to enjoy this girl, or maybe it was the wine. She rarely had it these days. Lucy's cheeks were flushed and black curls fell around her face. "So how is the beautiful Phoebe?" Lucy asked. She'd seen her photo on Megan's desk.

"She's wonderful," Megan said, wistfully. "It's hard to be away from her," she confessed. "Oh, I love my job, but I'm missing all these baby milestones. You know, blowing bubbles. Turning over. Crawling. At least I heard her say her first word."

"Which was?"

145

"Mama. Thank god it wasn't Dada, or worse yet, Emmy, her nanny's name. Douglas doesn't mind being apart from Phoebe as much as I do, of course. A man/female thing, I guess. Our baby never lived inside his body."

Lucy was silent for a moment, sipping from her glass. Then she said, "Actually, I met your husband."

"Really."

"He visited our offices once or twice. One of my colleagues used to work with him. Eileen. Do you know her?" Lucy glanced at Megan, then away.

"No, I don't."

"He seems a very nice man, your husband."

"Yes, he is." Megan waited, quietly, to see if Lucy had anything more to say about Eileen. "Truthfully," she said, "I do know who Eileen is." This was not true. She knew no one named Eileen, did not remember ever hearing the name mentioned. "Douglas and I have discussed her." She waited, watching the anxiety flit across Lucy's face. "I think they were close." She said this just to see what Lucy would say, to see the surprise on her face, to see the truth revealed there. Megan ventured further: "I didn't want to say it unless you knew." Megan had never seen herself as a good liar, but she was amazed now at her ability to lie, and to continue to lie to get at the truth.

"Yes," Lucy said. She looked relieved. "I'm glad you said that. I was afraid I'd stuck my foot in my mouth. I have a habit of doing that. And they are still . . . close?" she said, with another sideways glance. The way she asked let Megan know that Lucy knew the answer to her question.

Megan shrugged noncommittally. "It's hard to talk about. You understand," she said, tilting her head toward Lucy confidentially. "We're working things through. But no, you didn't say anything wrong." Later, she marveled at herself: a regular Meryl Streep, she was.

Lucy nodded. "Thank god. I can imagine it's difficult." She leaned back in the booth, resting her head on the padding, and sighed deeply. "I don't know what David does during the week, who he sees. As long as I have him on the weekend, and as long as he doesn't give me any diseases, that's all I ask. For now."

◆ ◆ ◆

Emmy was bathing Phoebe in the bathtub, holding the baby's middle as she bounced on her chubby legs. Phoebe, ten months old, shrieked and babbled when she saw her mother. "Mama, mama." Emma and Megan laughed. Megan's joy and relief on seeing the baby was enormous. Why was she gone from her so much?

She paid Emmy her week's salary and finished getting Phoebe ready for bed. She played with the child vigorously to keep her awake, dancing around the room to Paul Simon, putting off nursing as long as she could so she could spend this awake time with her daughter. When Phoebe was pulling at her blouse and Megan's breasts were full and aching, she finally sat in the rocker and unbuttoned. She felt the tingling rush of her milk letting down, heard Phoebe's contented sounds. The child was a soft warmth in her arms, against her chest. Phoebe had a habit of patting her mother's breast with her little open palm as she nursed. It was the sweetest gesture Megan had ever seen. Megan moved her to the other breast, watching the baby nurse until her eyes closed.

This was how Doug found them in the darkened living room when he returned; Phoebe sleeping with her mother's nipple still in her slack mouth, milk dribbling on her cheek, her open palm resting on Megan's breast.

Megan had been nearly asleep, also. She opened her eyes to see Douglas, standing inside the door watching them. He still held the key in his hand, his face full of affection. "What a scene," he said. "Worthy of Michelangelo."

Megan took a deep breath and said one word: "Eileen," sending the name in a rush of air into the room. She watched how it changed her husband's face, made everything electric and humming.

Megan stood up very carefully and lay Phoebe in her crib. The baby sighed but stayed asleep. She turned the monitor on and closed the door. When she returned to the living room, Douglas had switched on a lamp and was sitting on the couch. Long, elegant legs crossed at the knee, one arm thrown over the back of the couch, he sat poised and waiting for what was to come. Lines furrowed around his mouth in a way that made him look sad. Megan stood in front of him, buttoning her blouse. "Why?" she asked.

He jerked slightly, as if surprised. He probably wanted to ask how she found out, what she knew, but he knew that would be cheap, turning it into a game. She wondered if the game wasn't what he liked, if the thrill of the game wasn't the answer to her question. She knew she'd been tired lately, motherhood

148

and work not leaving much time for togetherness. Still, their sex life had been good, when they found the time; he loved the fullness of her nursing breasts and was as attentive and loving as ever.

Doug sagged back onto the couch. "I can't help it," he said softly, not looking at her.

Megan perched on her rocker, hands folded in her lap. "Were you with her tonight?" The look he gave her answered her question.

"Is it me?" she asked. "Is it something I'm doing or not doing?" She put a hand to her hair; she needed a cut, she hadn't been spending enough time on her appearance lately. "I can't be perfect. I have so much to do, and I'm human."

"Oh, no." Douglas looked genuinely pained by this, which gratified her. She wanted at this moment to pain him much, much more than that. "It's not you, you're perfect, you are. It's me, I can't help myself. I just feel . . . dead inside, sometimes." He put an open palm on his chest.

She waited for him to say more. His head turned away from her, he said, "I'm like a kid, an impatient kid. I have to do something, I have to stir things up, or I'll go crazy. I have to create trouble like that so I don't create a much greater trouble, so that I don't do something totally insane. You know?" He looked at her then.

He was like that exactly; an impatient child, who loved her and could be filled with genuine tenderness but had the need to be reckless, to cause damage. To hurt her. Teenagers drove too fast or drank or took drugs. The trouble Douglas needed to cause was suited to his temperament, to his skills. To who he was.

He said what she was thinking, then. "I suppose this has to do with my aunt. She fucked me up." He rested his head back on the couch and looked up at the ceiling. "Thanks, Clarice." He'd told Megan he hadn't met with or talked with his aunt since he was a teenager. His mother forbade any further contact between them when they found out, although she still spoke with her sister. Clarice still lived in San Francisco. In the way he spoke to the ceiling now, Megan wondered if he didn't have continued conversations with her in his head. Or perhaps real conversations with her? Late-night phone calls?

Megan said, "That doesn't excuse anything. You can't blame her for your failures. You're hurting me, and you will hurt Phoebe. You will destroy our family." She sounded prissy to her own ears, an outraged librarian. But she *was* outraged. "It's wrong," she said quietly as she stood up. She wasn't saying anything he didn't know. He didn't answer.

Chapter Six

Saturday, Megan was awake early. She'd lain on the futon in Phoebe's room for hours, watching the rabbit-shaped nightlight glow, the origami mobile above Phoebe's crib move in air currents she couldn't feel. Sometime in the middle of the night she knew what she had to do.

In the morning Doug came into the room while she was filling a suitcase with baby clothes, books, and diapers. He stood there in boxers, sleepy and befuddled, rubbing a hand through his hair. "What are you doing?" he asked, his voice hoarse.

"We're going to Maine," Megan said. She picked up a small sweater and folded it into the suitcase, then two fleece footed pajamas.

"It's terrible out there," Doug said. "Don't go. Stay." It was snowing, a light, fluffy snow falling on ground already covered. "It's worse in Maine. The camp will be so cold."

"I have snow tires." She didn't look at him but threw books into the suitcase. *Goodnight Moon, Oh the Places You'll Go, Baby's Book of Lullabies & Cradle Songs.* She'd decided that she'd be better off going to the camp than to her parents' house, where she'd have to talk, have to explain. She had a set of keys.

151

The camp would be chilly inside, but there was running water, and she could warm it up.

After a moment, Doug turned and left.

Megan drove slowly through snow-covered streets, past the cemetery, onto the highway. The traffic was light, people driving slowly with headlights on. Phoebe, in her car seat in the front beside her, kicked her feet and chewed a teething ring. Megan knew the car seat should be in the back, but she couldn't bear to have her back there, where she couldn't see her. What if the baby was choking and couldn't make a sound? She couldn't see her without turning around, couldn't reach her if she were back there. Their SUV was solid and big, and she would drive very slowly, very carefully.

The snow was heavier in Maine, the wind on the coast stronger. She felt the car buffeted on 95, and when she got off the turnpike she took corners toward their house very slowly. The road to their house had been plowed recently, only the driveway white and thick with snow. She parked at the end of the drive and left Phoebe in the car while she carried their bags, glad she'd worn her warm boots. The snow was piling up, nearly a foot deep. She set the bags down on the covered porch to fumble with the keys. All she could think of was Phoebe, in the car alone. At last she got the door open, brought the bags in, turned the thermostat up. Later she would start a fire in the fireplace. She turned on some lights and went back outside.

As she approached the car, she heard Phoebe's wail. Of course, she was crying at being left alone; who wouldn't? Megan unhooked her from the car seat, wiping her tears and wrapping her in a blanket. She held her tightly as she walked to the house, stepping her feet in the boot-shaped spaces she'd walked in before. Funny, she thought, how everything changes when one holds a child. The smallest moment is charged with significance, with responsibility, with danger. She mustn't fall.

She hadn't thought to bring any food from home or stop to buy some, and the refrigerator was empty but for half-used bottles of condiments and a gallon of water. After unpacking, she again she put on her coat, boots, and mittens, wrapped Phoebe in her snow suit, and took her out into the weather. She drove to the little grocery shop a couple of miles away, where she bought pasta, frozen dinners, cereal, juice, milk. And jars of baby food for Phoebe; not the good kind she got at home, but it would do. Phoebe sat in the cart, her feet in their little boots sticking through the slats in front. She rubbed her face with her little hands, then suddenly grinned at her mother: a bright, damp baby grin that lit Megan up like someone had switched on a light.

Megan had texted her boss that she wasn't feeling well and would probably have to miss Monday. She could miss Tuesday too, but after that, she really needed to be back to work one way or the other. When they returned to the house, it was warmer, nearly comfortable. Having food in the cupboard made things look better. She held Phoebe on her lap and fed her mashed peas and potatoes, while taking bites from a peanut butter sandwich.

It was late afternoon by then. The snow had nearly stopped, and the pale light through the windows was brighter. Phoebe crawled around on the rug while Megan brought in kindling and wood from the shed and attempted to build a fire. She didn't have enough kindling, and the fire seemed to be crackling away, then was dead the next time she looked. This happened several times. Finally she stuffed bunches of paper underneath the half-charred wood, brought in large handfuls of kindling, and fed the damn thing matches until it was roaring.

After she put Phoebe to bed in the ancient crib on the second floor, Megan fell asleep on the couch, exhausted. She woke, startled, in the middle of the night to a dead fire, and to the thought of the too-wide slats in the crib upstairs. Alone up there, the baby could have wedged her head in between those slats, her face pressed against the mattress. Megan wouldn't have heard her cries. She raced up the stairs, heart thumping, to see Phoebe sleeping peacefully on her back in the middle of the crib.

She put Phoebe in the double bed next to her, and piled blankets on both of them. She nursed and soothed the baby until she fell asleep again, then lay curled on her side in the dark, listening to Phoebe's even, whispering breaths.

She couldn't stay here. She could find an apartment, she supposed. The thought of moving with Phoebe filled her with anxiety. If this were to be something permanent, shouldn't she ask Doug to leave? Could she do that? Would she have to get a lawyer? It seemed wrong to say he had to leave his house, the home they made together. She didn't want to be a single mother living in an apartment; she loved her house, which had been decorated and planned by her in every corner. She even still loved her husband. Except for this one thing, their lives had been happy together.

Of course, thinking of *this one thing* kept her awake. Megan wondered if he was with her, with this Eileen, at that very moment. Was Eileen sleeping in their king-sized bed, cuddled up next to Megan's husband? She should have kicked

Doug out. She didn't know how to be a wronged woman; she was weak, she didn't even know how to be properly angry. She lay awake again for hours, her thoughts circling around, finding new corners, new alleyways. They often landed on the fifteen-year-old Doug. She pictured knobbly knees, thin white chest, his alarm and yearning, the energy of his teenage desire. She saw that teenager sometimes in him as they made love, the teenage passion and insecurity in the confident, successful man. She tried not to think of that, tried not to feel the desire for him it brought to her.

At 4:45 she opened her eyes to her daughter's hands, patting her face: her mouth, her cheeks, her eyes. "Mama!" The baby's face alight, delighted to see her mother lying next to her.

Downstairs, she heated water for oatmeal, holding Phoebe on her hip. The sky over the ocean was dark, but she could see a thin strip of light on the horizon. She watched it brighten, become tinged with orange, clouds left over from yesterday's storm streaking across in long grey lines. She didn't know how she would get through this day, without any sleep. The hours until night stretched out in front of her. She could rest when Phoebe napped, but that wouldn't be nearly enough. She picked up her cell phone and clicked it on to see a list of texts from her husband: *Did you make it? Please call. Everything okay? I'm worried about you two.*

After the sun came up and the room was filled with light, she put Phoebe down and texted back. *We made it, everything is okay.* In the early afternoon, she was not surprised to look out the kitchen window and see Doug's Camry parked beside the SUV. There was a knock, then she heard the mudroom door pushed open. "Hello?" Footsteps into the living room, where

Phoebe was playing, then Megan heard "Da? Dada!" A first, Phoebe had never said that before.

She came into the living room to see Doug holding Phoebe, squeezing her. His face was red, and he wiped his eyes. "I missed you guys," he said, turning to Megan.

"I want to take a nap," she said.

◆ ◆ ◆

They talked later. Megan sat wrapped up in a throw blanket on the chair in front of the fire, Phoebe playing on the floor between them. The sky was nearly clear, and sun brightened the water, the trees making shadows on new snow. "Give me another chance," Doug said. He sat on the couch, leaning forward with his elbows on his thighs, looking and sounding for all the world, Megan thought, like a TV husband. It felt strange to have him pleading with her; it gave her a rare power. She didn't think that power would last.

Megan said she didn't know, she would think about it. She knew that she didn't have the energy or anger it would take to kick him out, or to move out. Not now; maybe next time. He told her he'd ended it with Eileen. He pulled his phone from his pocket, tapped it, and leaned it toward her; "Here," he said. "I'll show you the text."

"No!" Megan turned her head away, as if he were trying to show her a dirty picture. She pictured him on a messy single bed in a dim apartment, energetically fucking a young girl.

Megan pulled the throw more tightly around her. "I want to cut back to half time," she said. "If they don't like that, I'll quit."

Douglas sat back down. "Okay," he said, eyeing her. "We can get by." He was wondering, no doubt, if these were terms she was laying down. If so, fine; she had no problem with him seeing it that way.

"And," she said, "you need counselling. You, or us, if you think we need couple counselling. One or the other. Otherwise, we won't come back. I'll get an apartment for me and Phoebe."

"Right," he said. "You're right, I probably need it. I'll go by myself. Like I said, the problem is in me, not you."

"Good," she said. "I can get some recommendations for you." Phoebe pulled herself up onto his leg and held out an arm to him. "Da!" She'd said it half a dozen times since he came in, as if to stress his role, as if to help persuade her parents to make this work. "And we should probably have dinner more often together, don't you think? If we're going to be married, we should act like it."

Later, as she cleaned up after their dinners of frozen food, she wondered how many times a conversation like this played out: how many times other women had said the same things to their wandering husbands, were saying them at this moment. Except maybe for half-time work; she knew she was fortunate to be able to say that part. *If we're going to be married, we should act like it.* She stared at her reflection in the kitchen window, looking at herself over the darkness outside. Her hair curled in a messy halo around her head, lit by the lights behind her, and her eyes looked shadowed, haunted. She wasn't exactly choosing security and financial well-being over happiness–not exactly, as she loved Doug, and did want their marriage to work. But it would feel so good to sleep in her own comfortable bed again, in their warm house.

Chapter Seven

On a sunny, windy day in June of 1998, Megan and Abigail walked an old railway bed made into a walking and biking path. They both wore workout clothing, and Abigail held small weights in her hands as they walked briskly. Often, however, the pace would slow as the conversation deepened, sometimes stopping altogether as they talked.

Megan had forgotten how much fun Abigail could be, and how good it was to talk with an old friend you shared history with. She was congratulating Abigail on earning her Master's degree.

"I'm glad to be done with it," Abigail said.

"Are you still thinking of going for the PhD?"

"I thought I would, but I'm not feeling it. I'm teaching First-Year Writing this fall at Salem State."

"You'll do well with that." Abigail would charm her students. She charmed everyone. Abigail wasn't perfectly beautiful–her nose had an arched bump that she saw as an imperfection, but that Megan thought gave her an imperious beauty. She had an enormous smile, an unaffected laugh, and charisma. Lingering from her youth was her habit of saying the unexpected. People were drawn to her; Megan was drawn to her, in the way she always had been, even when Abigail made her angry.

"I'll try to fake it, to not let them know I'm not smart enough to teach college. You've always been the smart one." Abigail pumped her arms with the three-pound weights as they walked. "You were always in another class. Literally and figuratively."

"That's not true. You thought I was smarter than you, but I wasn't." Abigail had always felt this way. Neither of her parents had gone to college, while Megan's had.

Abigail was talking about her grades in high school. "They were barely high enough for me to be accepted to UMass."

"You read as much as I did, or more," Megan said. "Heavy duty books too, classics. You just didn't like to do schoolwork."

"That's true," Abigail said. "So much of it was bullshit." She shook back her thick hair. "It wasn't until I went back to college after I dropped out that it started to make sense to me."

"I was just polite in school because I didn't want to offend. I put up with the bullshit because I didn't want to make waves."

"It worked out for you," Abigail said. "Great job, great family. Good life."

"You've got a good life, too. James is wonderful." Megan had recently met Abigail's husband. A tall, soft-spoken man, James looked at Megan when they were introduced and shook her hand, then looked away. He looked slightly to the side when she talked, but she could tell he was listening to what she said, nodding his head in rhythm to her words. Megan and Douglas had gone over to their house for dinner, and Abigail had been nervous, taking their jackets, setting out toys for Phoebe, apologizing for the dinner they were about to have, putting forth a wild, restless energy in every direction. James went over and stood by his wife, resting an arm lightly across her shoulders, and Megan saw how Abigail stilled, calmed, leaning against him. He was what she needed.

Megan was having a hard time keeping up with Abigail's pace on the trail. Abigail kept walking ahead of her, talking over her shoulder, and Megan would have to speed up. She felt breathless. Abigail said, "My main desire when I was a teenager was to make my parents miserable."

"Like all teenagers," Megan said.

"I was good at it. I tried harder than some." The thought of Abigail's father hung between them. They had never spoken about it since the day Megan had given Abigail the padlock.

Megan had told Abigail about Doug's former affairs, but she didn't tell her that she still wondered, that she found it hard to trust him when he said he was just taking a walk or had a late meeting. She didn't know if she could ever trust him. Now Abigail was talking about her husband, about their sex life. "It's good," she said. "It's fine . . ."

"But?" Megan said.

"But it's hard, having sex with just the same person all the time, isn't it? We lay on the same side of the bed, say the same things, do the same things . . ." She walked on, letting her sentence trail off.

"I don't feel that way," Megan said. "There's enough variety for me. Actually, I kind of like the familiarity of having sex with the same person in the same way. Doug may feel more like you do, tired of the sameness, but I find it reliable.

Comforting." She paused, watching the wind shake the trees by the path. A bicyclist passed them. She wondered how much to say. "If there's something that bothers me about our sex life, it's that I sometimes think about the other women he's been with. That gets in the way."

"Can't you put those thoughts aside? I mean, for your happiness, not his. Your satisfaction."

Her thoughts got in the way of her going to bed with Doug, but once there, he was always attentive. Sometimes there was a war within herself, as she wanted the experience but also wanted to hold back, to punish Doug. To show him that she still remembered and didn't trust him. "Don't you think that would diminish it, though?" she asked Abigail. "Diminish the full experience? I mean, shouldn't I be there emotionally as well as physically?"

Abigail stopped on the trail and adjusted her bra, looking at her friend. "No," she said. "No, I don't. You're thinking that you have to love him fully and all that to have sex?"

"Well, yeah. Right? Shouldn't it be that way?"

Abigail shrugged, and they started walking again. "I don't think so. Sex can be better when it's sex for sex's sake. Or at least as good. It's the excitement of the no-strings-attached thing." She looked at the trees, the sky, as she said this. "It can be exciting, to just fuck. Even if it's with your husband." She gave Megan a sly, sideways smile.

◆ ◆ ◆

This conversation was on Megan's mind that night. With Phoebe in bed, Doug came to her in the kitchen, embraced her, kissed her. She put her arms around his neck, as his hands wandered down her back. This was the moment when Megan's thoughts would veer to Eileen, to the other woman –Anna–in the restaurant. When she would wonder if he used to stand in some other woman's kitchen, clutching her bottom. Or even if recently . . . *No,* she told herself. *No strings; sex for sex's sake. For myself. For me.* She thought of Doug in bed and pushed against him, kissing him back. Maybe she, Megan, was that unnamed woman in the kitchen, taking something she wanted.

Chapter Eight

Megan thought it would be a matter of time until it happened again. She put it out of her mind–there were plenty of things to think about. Half-time work was more like three-fourths work, and being a mother was more challenging than she'd ever thought it would be. She had thought she and Doug would be better parents than her own, who were so unimaginative, so repressive, but now she just hoped she could be as good as they were. Her parents were always there, always loving and cheerful–it was incredible, how did they do it?

For Phoebe's tenth birthday in August, they reserved a picnic area at a park in a gazebo by the ocean. Megan put cake, sandwiches, and potato salad out on picnic tables. Doug's mother, who rarely left the city, didn't come, but they invited Megan's parents, a few of Phoebe's friends, and their own–Abigail and James, Doug's friend Richard. Doug and Richard had gone to college together, and now were both senior editors. Richard was handsome and assured, with curly grey-streaked hair, his stomach pushing out the front of his short-sleeved linen shirt. His wife, Clara, was thin and elegant as always, wearing an artfully designed loose dress in an unusual chartreuse color. She was an artist of some kind, working with clay, Megan thought. Their daughter Alexandra was a year younger than Phoebe. The girl, dressed up in a satin dress with a bow, shyly handed Phoebe a beautifully wrapped present. Didn't her parents know it was a *picnic?* Alexandra stood watching while the other girls threw a ball around, but she dashed off with them to the swings.

Megan's parents set gifts on the table and pulled lawn chairs from the trunk of their car. Megan's mother had recently stopped dyeing her hair and the bottom half, below her ears, was light brown, the top half a streaked grey. She sat in a light wind breaker and shorts, touching her hair self-consciously. Megan's father sat next to her, wearing baggy khaki shorts, one stout, hairy calf crossed over the other. Abigail leaned down to give Megan's mother a hug, then reached over to shake her father's hand. She pulled another lawn chair up to sit next to them. "Your granddaughter is the most remarkable child," she said.

"Oh, don't we know," Megan's mother said. "How are your parents doing?" she asked Abigail. "I never see them anymore."

Abigail shrugged. "Same, same. Fine, I guess." She gestured to the children, not interested in talking about her parents. "Look how they follow Phoebe wherever she goes. It's always that way, not just on her birthday. She's a natural leader." Abigail was as proud as if Phoebe were her own child.

People scattered for walks on trails along the shore. Megan took the little girls to a high rock by the water where they posed for a photo. "Be goofy, now! But careful!" The girls spread arms wide, made silly faces. The sun came out through fat white clouds, then was hidden again. They ran ahead of her to the picnic tables, where they ate tuna salad sandwiches.

Doug and his friends had disappeared down the shore. James offered to stay with the girls while Megan went for a walk with her parents. Megan and her parents made their way to the water and walked along the shore, watching the rocks, the waves rushing close to their sneakers and sandals. "Abigail found a good one there," her mother said, referring to James. "They don't have any children?"

"Not now. She wants one, though, so who knows. She sure loves Phoebe."

"And who wouldn't," her mother said.

Her mother needed to use the restroom. Megan pointed to a path that led to the public restrooms. Her father walked up with her, while Megan continued walking along the shore by herself. She passed teenagers sitting on the sand, children making a sandcastle, then she continued onto a narrow rocky shore where the woods pressed close. Clouds covered the sun, then parted, letting it beat down on the rocks, the sand, her shoulders. She felt warm and turned off where she knew there was a narrow, hidden trail through the woods. She and Doug had found it years ago, before they married.

She ducked under trees, twisting around corners into the sudden coolness. She paused, listening to how the woods muted the sounds of the surf. She remembered walking here with Doug, laughing at something. The words to a half-forgotten song twisted through her head: *Marcie in a coat of flowers, steps inside a candy store.* She stopped, looking at a fern spotlighted by a shaft of light. The leaves were darker around the edges, bright in the center. She imagined painting it.

She heard voices. Looking up, she saw movement in the distance, a flash through the trees. Someone was running, ducking. She followed the figure with her eyes as he ran. It was her husband; she recognized him from his dark shirt, his streaked brown hair, from the way he moved his shoulders. She smiled. What was he doing, playing in the woods like a child? He moved out of her sight.

She took a few steps, looking around, then saw him again. He was chasing someone. A flash of chartreuse. Megan saw him grab the other person's body, pull it close to him. Through leaves and branches she caught glimpses of a woman's hands, running through his hair; his head, turning into her neck as if to consume her. Clara. Their actions were familiar, easy; they had done this before. Megan was unable to look away. She stood motionless until they turned and moved slowly from her sight, together. They held each other closely, as if they couldn't bear to let go. She saw their arms drop from one another before they came into the open; saw them assume again their regular personalities. They never looked back in her direction to see Doug's wife motionless, stricken, in the woods.

◆ ◆ ◆

After a time, Megan picked her way back to the shore. What could she do but return to the birthday party, to her family. Her child, her parents. Her husband. She walked slowly along the narrow shore, her legs uncertain and trembling beneath her. Her hands quivered, her stomach still aching from when she had leaned down, retching in the woods. She felt weak as she made her way carefully between families on blankets on the

167

beach, children running and shouting around her. The sounds and light hurt her eyes; everything hurt. She wanted to lie down and close her eyes. She was unable to handle this life.

She saw a man on the beach walking towards her, hands in the pockets of his cargo shorts. James. He was looking at her steadily, with a faint smile. She must look terrible, she thought. As she drew closer she saw his eyes narrow in concern. She stepped around someone's feet on a beach towel and wobbled, nearly falling down. His hands were there, reaching out to steady her. "Are you all right? Megan?"

They walked to the edge of the sand, next to the trees. He sat down with her in the shade. "I don't feel well," she said.

"That's clear," he said. Then, embarrassed, "I mean, you look pale. Can I get you something?"

"It feels good just to sit down." She leaned against his shoulder. James lifted his arm and put it slowly around her shoulders. She saw him glance around, surreptitiously. "It's okay," she said. "If we see someone, I'll tell them I'm sick. Which is the truth." She did feel ill, as if the shock of seeing Doug with Clara had stirred something latent in her. Her thoughts seemed to shift with the waves. What she really wanted to do was to lie down. She moved away from James and spread herself out on the ground, her head resting on James' thigh, her bare legs below her cotton skirt on the rough rocky sand. James fanned her face with a piece of paper he took from his pocket. "I threw up in the woods."

"I can go get Douglas," James said. "If you want."

"I do not want," Megan said, her voice stronger. "I do not want you to find Douglas. I don't want to see his face. That's the problem," she went on, as if talking to herself. "His face…is the problem." Realizing how confused she must sound, she sighed deeply, and closed her eyes. "I just want to rest here a moment, if that's all right."

"It's fine," James said, his voice deep and soothing.

What a good man he is, Megan, thought, and let the words come out. "You're a good man." She rested there, feeling light and insubstantial on the sand, as if she were a piece of cloth, nothing left inside. But soft, his hip comforting to rest her head on, the little breeze created by the paper cooling her. She heard the sounds of children playing, the rushing sounds of the water and the caw of seagulls, and they were part of the breeze washing over her.

Chapter Nine

She opened her eye to see James' face, looking down at her. It was softened by her sleepy eyes, a blurry white glow around it.

There was tenderness in his expression. "You fell asleep."

"I did." She sat up, slowly. The light was different, the beach quieter. "How long did I sleep?"

"Just a few minutes." She looked at him, and he smiled. "Maybe half an hour."

"Phoebe," she said, remembering. "It's her party."

"Abigail is there, leading them in a game. The scavenger hunt she planned."

"Wonderful Abigail."

"And your parents are there, too. And probably Doug and the others by now, also."

"Ugh." She sat up, then stood up. The dizziness came back, but she felt stronger than she had. She was thirsty. "Can I take your arm?" she asked. "It would feel good to move."

"Do you want to go in the shade?" James asked, motioning to the trees. "There's a path in there."

"No." She never wanted to go there again. And it was cooler now, a breeze off the water making her shiver slightly.

They walked slowly, Megan holding on to his arm. "It's Douglas," she said. Her voice, the words, surprised her. But why not tell this kind man? "I saw him with that woman. With Clara. In the woods." She shivered, involuntarily, at the memory of Clara's hands in her husband's hair, her chartreuse dress.

"I'm sorry," James said, after a moment.

Megan looked up at him, searchingly. "You don't sound surprised."

James shook his head. "I know nothing about Douglas. I just know how people—how men—can be. So, no, it doesn't really *surprise* me. But I'm sorry, for your sake."

She believed him, she guessed, when he said he had heard nothing about her husband. Maybe Doug's infidelity didn't surprise him because he had taken the measure of the man. She had married a man with a weakness, she'd been a bad judge of character. She felt a sob rise up in her at the thought, but a little cough swallowed it down. She must look a mess, her hair wild, her face smeared. She rubbed a hand across her eyes. "What will they think when we go back? I look awful."

"You look fine." He stopped, turned her shoulders to him, looking at her face. Again she saw the surprising tenderness on his face. "You look more than fine. But here." He pulled a comb from his back pocket and handed it to her

"How old-fashioned of you." She pulled it through her hair, working it through the tangles, and handed it back to him. "I don't know what to tell them."

"You took ill on your walk. I found you, you rested." He put the comb back in his pocket.

"It's true. All that is true."

"They will be concerned, they won't ask questions. Doug will be concerned. He does love you, you know."

She walked on slowly, looking at their feet, hers in her leather sandals, his in his sneakers, step by step on the rocks.

"That's love?"

"I can tell by the way he looks at you. He loves you, he respects you. He has his flaws."

"Yes, he does."

When they walked back, the others were gathered around the picnic tables. A thin layer of clouds covered the sun, and the children were tired and sweaty. The cake was half-gone. Megan let go of James' arm well before they came in sight, so when her parents and Abigail and Douglas turned their heads to watch them approach, they saw James walking slowly, hands in pockets, next to Megan, who had her arms wrapped around her middle.

James told the group that he found Megan walking on the sand. "She's not feeling well," he said. "She needed to rest a bit before she walked on." She must have looked the part, as everyone—Doug, her parents, Abigail, even Richard—even Clara—looked solicitous and worried. "I'm fine, I'm fine," she said, waving them off and sitting down on the bench. "Phoebe, come here." Phoebe sat down and leaned against her mother, who put an arm around her shoulder. "Are you having a nice time?"

Phoebe nodded. "Are you all right?" she asked. She looked worried, the sweet child.

"I'm fine. Don't worry, it's your birthday." Megan brushed hair off the girl's cheek.

"We did the cake already, and the presents. Daddy said we didn't need to wait."
"He was right."

"Look!" She held up her wrist, a silver charm bracelet dangling. "And I got what I most wanted." She reached to the table to pick up a digital camera, turning it over in her lap.

"That's from me and your father. Do you like it?"
"It's the one I wanted. Thank you, Mommy."

The flurry of departures, the hugs from her parents and from Abigail, Richard's bluff, cheery good-bye. Clara stepping close—a whiff of perfume—taking one of Megan's hands between her own and pressing it. Clara's hands cool and dry on hers, Megan felt captured, imprisoned. "Thanks so much for having us. Feel better soon, okay?" All Megan could do was look at Clara's face, at the wide expressive eyes. She was close enough to see they were outlined in thin black, to see the fine lines at their corners, a red spot, a blemish at the edge of a nostril. It made her feel queasy again. She nodded, managed to say, "Thank you."

And James, his solid presence a moment of sanity, of grace. A hand on her shoulder. Warm, steadying. His glance into her face, that warmed her. "Take care, now. We'll be in touch."

Then cars were driving away and Douglas was packing up presents and leftover sandwiches, putting the plastic lid over the cake. Megan sat listlessly in a lawn chair. She wondered briefly if she should help. He paused, standing up to look at her. "Are you all right?" She watched his face, wondering if his concern was real, was actually for her. Who could tell? And if his concern for her was genuine, then why . . . He was so handsome, with his hair falling loosely to the side, his white shirt flattened against him in the wind. "You can go rest in the car if you want," he said. "I'll pick up here. Phoebe will help, won't you, girl? She's ten years old now."

So Megan stood, letting them finish, and sat by herself in the front seat of the Prius. She watched the wind catch pieces of paper and blow them around the grass; she watched Phoebe show her father something on the camera; she watched whitecaps form on the darkening ocean. Their voices were muted in the wind, through windshield glass. She leaned her head back and closed her eyes, remembering James' voice, and his hand on her shoulder.

Chapter Ten

Megan often thought of how James had looked when she'd opened her eyes on the beach to see his face. His expression had been unguarded and open, his eyes resting on hers. There had been a sadness in his face, and she wondered if it was for her, or for something in him, if it was his own sadness. Until that moment she hadn't seen how kind he was, how decent. She felt she could trust him with her life.

She took Monday off with a headache but went back to work on Tuesday. Confronting Doug about Clara was a task she didn't feel up to. And she didn't have to, if she didn't want to, she told herself. She didn't feel like talking to him. He was cautious around her; solicitous but careful, as if something was up, as if he knew she knew something. Their wedding anniversary was the following month. They had already arranged to spend it at her family's house in Maine, while Phoebe spent the weekend with her grandparents. Megan dreaded it.

The weather that weekend was distressingly beautiful. Warm for September, sunny, with a slight breeze that shook the leaves just beginning to turn color. Their first night they ate dinner at a restaurant on the wharf, sitting by a window watching boats in the harbor bob on the waves. Megan had never been adept at eating lobster from the shell. Doug tied the ridiculous plastic bib around his neck and told her she should do the same. "Then you won't worry about greasy splatters." The dead lobster's eyes were like small, dull black marbles. Demonstrating, Doug picked up his lobster in two hands. He twisted the body, breaking it in half, so the white meat and soft greenish center spilled out. He then twisted the claws, pulling them off the body. He squeezed the claws until she heard a cracking noise, then pulled them open to pick the meat out. He continued plucking the legs off, using a nutcracker to break what he called the "knuckle shell" and pulling out the white and pink meat. It looked easy when he did it. Done with that, he forced the creature's central body apart. More cracking, and the greenish stuff in the center was revealed. Megan watched, fascinated and a bit repulsed. The couple at the table next to them were watching also. They were older than Megan and Douglas, but had a sleek, well-groomed look, and the woman was attractive. Douglas picked up some of the soft green stuff in his fingertips. "You surely aren't going to eat that," she said. He put it into his mouth, licking his fingers.

"Delicious."

"Oh." She dropped the napkin in her lap and leaned back. "Disgusting."

"No, it's good. Try it," he said, holding some out in his fingers and grinning. She thought he was acting, hamming for the woman at the table next to them.

"No, thank you," she said coolly, looking to the side.

She worked on her lobster for a bit. Eventually, she gave up and passed it to Doug, who finished it for her, sucking the meat out of the thin claws. He wiped his wet lips with the white linen napkin.

After dinner, they walked along the narrow shore in front of the house. The sun had set and the air was cool, but the sand held the sun's warmth. Megan took off her sandals and held them in one hand, while Doug reached out and took her other hand.

"How are you feeling?" he asked. "Headache all gone?"

"Yes," she said. "That's fine. Just a little queasy." She put the hand with the sandals on her stomach, briefly. Her body, she thought, was reflecting her emotions. She'd managed to avoid talking with her husband much the past few weeks, retreating to their room to read when he came home, but it was hard here, with just the two of them. It was less than a month ago that she had walked on another beach, holding someone else's arm.

Then he asked, "Is anything else bothering you?" His voice was quiet, subdued; she could almost claim to have not heard him, above the sounds of the surf.

She walked along silently, scuffing her bare feet in the sand. She saw no reason to lie, but she didn't want to say her name, *Clara,* to hear his apologies and explanations and vows to renounce her and be faithful. She didn't have the stomach for that. He was still seeing the therapist, twice a month. He claimed it was helping, but Megan didn't want to get into it. So she remained silent, looking down; then she looked up at his face, and he must have seen what she knew.

It occurred to her that this was another moment when she would decide whether or not her marriage would survive. She had forgiven Doug and taken him back before, hoping that he would change and be faithful. She now knew that could not happen. He would not change. They walked back up the hill to the house without saying anything more. As she pulled her nightgown and robe from the suitcase, she wondered if maybe Doug was telling her—by his actions—that their marriage no longer worked for him. Maybe she was just too stubborn to listen.

He sat on the edge of the bed, watching her. It was an old iron bedstead, covered with a quilt and throw pillows. "Are you going to bed?" he asked.

She shook her head. "Just getting comfortable." She tied her robe around her waist, then sat down beside him. "So," she said.

"So." He reached over to take her hand, tangling her fingers between his. "So, should we talk about something?" "You tell me," she said. It came out more challenging than she'd meant it to be. But why put the burden of initiating discussion on her? She wasn't the one who'd been unfaithful.

He lifted his shoulders, looking baffled. He wasn't going to say anything until she did. "Okay," Megan said, and took a breath. "Do you want to stay married? Do you want to stay married to *me*?" She squeezed his hand, hard, looking into his face, hoping for what, she didn't know. Hoping for the truth, whatever it was. Hoping for his honesty. Hoping for something more, something he couldn't give her.

"Yes," he said.

"Truthfully?"

"Yes, yes, yes, yes, yes, yes. I want to stay married to you always, as long as we live." He squeezed his lips together in an odd way and blinked. "I love you. I respect you. I love our lives together. I love Phoebe."

"Then why . . ." She couldn't finish, she didn't want to finish. He knew what she meant.

"I have my failings. I know I do. I'm working on them, believe me." Then, as if realizing this was an admission, he hurried on: "I will try to be a better husband, a better father. I'd be lost without you." He looked at her, waiting for a response. There was none. "Megan." He put his arms around her and she leaned into him, reluctantly. He stroked her hair, held her head still next to his. "I'm sorry," he murmured low against her ear.

◆ ◆ ◆

They slept turned away from one another, but the bed was smaller than their bed at home, and their bodies touched. She felt his warmth against her back, and knew he lay awake as she did. Once his arm brushed hers, and she reached out and touched him, needing the familiar warmth of his skin. He turned, took her hand in his and brought it to his lips, then dropped his hand by his side, still holding hers. After that she heard his breathing slow, until it was quiet and regular. She lay awake, staring into the dark, weighing the pain of remaining with him to the pain of being alone.

◆ ◆ ◆

The next morning, they sat on the upper deck of a ferry boat. They'd bought tickets for a trip around the harbor. Looking out toward the open water, Megan was cold even in her fleece jacket. Doug sat close to her, wrapping a long arm around her for extra warmth. As the boat swung around the wind decreased, and Doug reached into the side pocket of his jacket. He pulled out a small, wrapped box. "Happy anniversary," he said.

She opened it to find a silver ring, with an unusual dark glittering stone surrounded by two diamonds. "Black opal," he said. "I thought it was pretty. It reminded me of you somehow. Full of unexpected color and light, if you look into it. See?" He held it up, then put it on the finger of her right hand, where it fit. Doug had always been good at buying gifts. "The woman selling it to me told me it had powers that became stronger when worn." He smiled crookedly at her, and Megan made a conscious decision not to imagine the pretty woman behind the counter, selling her husband this ring. "I always suspected you had witchy powers."

"Thank you," she said. "So pretty." And so, without speaking more of it, the decision was made. At least for now, they would remain married.

Megan thought of the phrase "the institution of marriage," and it seemed appropriate to her. Her marriage, their marriage, was an institution that surrounded them and supported them, like a large office building bustling with activity. Like other institutions, it was created to make things work. Phoebe, the flower it was all built around, continued to grow happily, seemingly unaware of rifts between her beloved parents. Their retirement fund grew. And if, at the core of the institution, there was a certain heartlessness; if the passion didn't burn as hot as she would have hoped it would, wasn't that, also, like an institution? Perhaps there was no place for passion within an institution; perhaps it would be destructive. Turning her black opal to catch the light, Megan considered the idea that passion is best left outside the institution, to grow like St. John's wort, like witch hazel, like spiderwort or periwinkle or larkspur, outside the walls, gathered at night and sprinkled into a candle flame, for healing.

Chapter Eleven

Megan worked from home more and more, on the computer or the phone. Some days she didn't go in to work at all, though she didn't want to do that too often. Office power dynamics can shift, and though Megan didn't see herself as ambitious and on a career rise, she did want to keep working there, and continue being respected. So most days she dressed up in her dark dresses with tight boots, or pin-striped pantsuit, or—if she was feeling flamboyant—her short skirt and lacy blouse, and took the commuter train into Boston, where she walked to Faneuil Hall. Being in the city gave her energy, made her feel charged up, and some days—depending on how her male co-workers spoke to her—made her feel attractive, desired. That was not a bad feeling, though Megan tried not to seek it out. It was a road she didn't want to travel down: cuckolded wife (can that term apply to women, she wondered?) takes lovers in revenge on her cheating husband. It simply felt nice to see admiration in a man's eyes when he looked at her.

And it gave her pleasure to send, and receive, emails from James. His emails were letters, lengthy and written with care. She'd received the first one just after returning from Maine. He said he was checking in to see how she was doing. He'd gathered from Abigail that Megan was feeling better and hoped that was true. Megan wondered if they discussed what she'd been upset about; she wondered if James had told his wife about Doug and Clara. Megan imagined the two of them huddled together on a couch discussing her, their voices full of sympathy, with an underlying tone of self-congratulation for avoiding her fate, for their faithful marriage.

She thought about his email for a day or two before answering. She worked up her courage and wrote: *As I told Abigail, I am feeling better, physically. Emotionally also; if time doesn't necessarily heal all wounds, it does create scar tissue. I didn't mention what I'd seen in the woods to Abigail and, as she hasn't mentioned it, perhaps she doesn't know?*

James's response came that same afternoon. *No, I didn't mention that to Abigail. I thought that was between you and Douglas, or you and Abigail, if you felt like telling her.* Megan's relief was overwhelming. She didn't like to think of him telling Abigail how upset she was, how he had to comfort her. That moment was something that remained between her and James.

Megan wanted to talk with him. She needed to. She wasn't sure how, or what they would talk about, but she thought she could gain something from him that would help her figure out how to get through things.

He mentioned that he was planning a visit to a museum at a nearby college to see a display of contemporary Irish art. Sitting in her small office at work, she read his email, then looked out the narrow window to the clear slice of sky above the building next door. She heard the murmur of office noise behind her through the open door, indistinguishable voices. It was nearly 2:00, the time she normally left the office. Phoebe had track after school and would be picked up by a friend's mother. She tapped her fingers on the keys, paused, then wrote to ask if she could meet him at the museum.

She found him at the entry desk, looking at the museum brochure. "I didn't know there *were* contemporary Irish artists," she said, smiling.

"Oh, there are many," he said. "Overshadowed by their English bully of a big brother, I suppose." He smiled back at her. "How are you, Megan."

"I'm doing well." Something more seemed appropriate. She thought of giving him a hug, but it seemed wrong. She wanted to too much, so instead she patted his upper arm, watching his face as he looked down at her. "Thank you for letting me intrude on your visit."

"It's wonderful to see you." They wandered down an empty hallway, looking at a series of photographs posted on the wall. "I wanted to see this exhibit because it featured women. And the work . . ." He stopped in front of a large photograph of a woman. Looking to one side with a calm, impassive expression on her face, she wore a necklace of bloody hearts around her neck.

"Oh my god," Megan said. "Horrible."

"And this." He gestured toward another photograph, this one of the same woman wearing a thick necklace of something dark and organic-looking. "Lambs' tongues," he said, leaning over to read the description on the wall.

"Real lambs' tongues." The photos repulsed and attracted Megan equally. Some of the work was beautiful, but it was another one by the same artist—Alice Maher was her name—

that she couldn't stop looking at. The woman in the photograph wore a high collar of stiff twigs around her neck, rising up over her face, covering her mouth. The twigs were dark, metallic-looking green, and above the woman's pale green dress, she saw that their stems left red marks on the white skin of the woman's shoulders.

They wandered up to a rooftop deck, where they sat on a wooden bench, looking down at a grassy lawn and rooftops beyond the trees. The leaves were bright fall colors under a sky darkening with clouds. "Powerful stuff," James said, referring to the photographs. "Not the stained-glass windows that other Irish women artists have been known for."

Megan agreed and felt suddenly tired. Why was she here with him, talking about art? Pretending she knew anything about Irish art by women, anything except how that image of the woman cut into her like the collar did into the woman's neck? What was she doing? She looked down at her thighs, their thinness widened against the wooden slats in her black pants. Despite the message she tried to send with her professional-looking pants, she felt acutely female, human, vulnerable.

"I needed to talk with you again, after what happened," she said.

"I've been thinking of you since then too. Or maybe my constant emails let you know that." James looked down too, at his hands clasped in his lap. Big, warm hands; Megan imagined what it would be like to reach out and hold one. She would not do that.

"I appreciate them. I feel alone sometimes. I mean Doug and I get along well, except for that one thing, but that is something I haven't been able to talk with people about. I would sound like I was complaining about my husband, and I don't want to be that person. He's good to me, and to Phoebe. And of course, the obvious question would be, why don't I leave him? Why do I put up with it?"

James looked at her then, his eyes behind the black-framed glasses searching. He waited. "I've thought of it," Megan said. "But . . ."

"You love him," James said, the statement a question. A hypothesis.

"I love our life. I love Phoebe." She paused. "And I'm tired. The thought of moving out, starting over again as a single mother . . ." She shook her head slowly. "In most ways our life together is good. It works. And he might change. I keep thinking he will change. He is working on it."

"You don't have to explain yourself to me," James said. "Those are private decisions." He sat up, looking out over the trees. "I can almost see our house over there," he said, pointing.

She took a breath. "Thank you," she said.

"For what?"

"For not judging me."

"I would never judge someone for trying to make a marriage work. We're all involved in that enterprise." He gave her a wry smile. Megan wondered if there was something more that he wanted to say. She thought of the way Abigail smiled at Douglas, the way she held her body when she was around men: shoulders turned to one side, back slightly arched. She thought of James looking at his wife, then looking away. She didn't ask.

They said goodbye outside the museum. This time Megan reached up tentatively for a hug, and they held one another for a moment. The feel of his solid body reached through his shirt, her jacket, warming her.

That evening, Megan picked up a notebook and pencil. Something made her want to draw lines across the page. She kept thinking of the woman wearing the collar made of sticks. She, Megan, was not in a cage; her life did not imprison her. Still she could not get it out of her head. She sketched the woman's head as she remembered it, but without the stick collar, just a small necklace. She changed the eyes, the mouth, until it looked like a self-portrait.

They had remained talking on the museum rooftop until the sun began to go down. Other people came up the stairs occasionally, glancing at them. What did they see, Megan wondered? A couple in young middle age, talking intently, looking at one another, then away. As the afternoon light lengthened, they would see the couple loosen up in their conversation, become more comfortable. More smiles, laughter. Warm glances. But no touching, no arms brushing arms, none of that.

Doug came down from upstairs and settled into the leather armchair, opening a newspaper. He had changed from a suit into his old khakis. "Phoebe was having trouble getting to sleep," he said.

"I heard you two talking up there. She was watching a scary show, right?"

"Right. We shouldn't let her do that. No tv before bed, I think. She's out now, though; I just checked."

"Good," Megan said. Doug, looking at the newspaper, said, "Oh god, Bush spoke to the United Nations today. How embarrassing." Megan picked up a book; he turned the page of the newspaper. The evening passed in the warmth, the familiarity of home, while outside their windows the air thickened, thunder rumbled, and fat raindrops began splatting an irregular rhythm against the windows.

Chapter Twelve

Megan finally brought up what had happened with Abigail's father years ago. They were shopping together at the mall. Abigail wanted to buy a dress, and Megan was looking for comfortable shoes. "Old-lady shoes," she said. "Nurses' shoes. My body won't allow me to have pretty shoes any longer." When Abigail asked what was wrong with her body, Megan deflected: "Just achy sometimes. Nothing important, but I'm tired of wearing uncomfortable shoes." She didn't want to talk about her muscle weakness, the fact that she sometimes fell unexpectedly. She didn't want to say she had an appointment coming up to see what was wrong. She had barely mentioned that to her husband.

Abigail helped her choose shoes. Megan was looking at conservative flats with good arch support. "Look at these," Abigail said, picking up a lace-up black shoe, a sleek boot. "You can wear them with dresses or pants. Just try them on." They were comfortable, had good support, and looked good with the skirt she wore. Feeling reckless, Megan paid for them. Abigail had that effect on her. She would ponder later whether it was reckless, or brave, or silly. But she did like the way the shoes looked and felt on her feet.

THE SYMMETRY OF HUSBANDS

Megan sat outside a dressing room while Abigail tried on dresses. It felt good to sit down. Abigail wanted something new for a university dinner that she was to attend with James and other faculty. "Do you think I need to look professional?" she asked, shrugging a navy blazer over a red knit dress. "Modest? This dress is kind of tight, and my figure isn't what it used to be." She smoothed the dress over her middle, her hips. "Not all of us can stay as tiny as you do."

"No," Megan said decisively. "I like the red dress, without the blazer. You don't need to be modest; you look fantastic."

They took a break in a café in the mall. Over coffee, they talked of the upcoming election. "It looks as if Obama could actually win," Abigail said. "Wouldn't that be amazing?"

"I think of what some of the people we know from high school would think about that. Matt Rowe, for example. Remember how racist he was?"

"I do. I hated high school," Abigail said. "I was so glad to be done with that and to leave town."

Megan glanced at her, then around them, to the half-empty coffee shop, the bags at their feet. No one within earshot. "You had good reasons to want to get away," she said.

Abigail sipped her coffee. "Yeah, high school wasn't a raging success for me."

"That's not what I mean. I mean your family situation." Abigail's face went impassive. "We've never talked about it," Megan went on. "But I remember it, I think about it often. I just want you to know that I remember what you went through."

"My parents' bankruptcy. . ." Abigail said.

"You know what I mean," Megan interrupted. "I mean, I understand your parents' financial problem was a big thing."

"It was," Abigail said.

"But I'm talking about what I saw with your father."

"He didn't actually do anything, you know. I mean, I lost my virginity to Alex Reynolds."

"Alex? Really?"

"Yeah. Why do you look so surprised?"

"I just didn't know . . ." Megan laughed. "I could see it, though. He was handsome."

"And I knew he wouldn't spread it all around. See, he didn't. Megan, that stuff with my father was so long ago. I don't dwell on it, I put it behind me and you should too."

"Right. But still, what happened with him was important. It matters, even if . . . even if your father didn't do more than you said he did. It's still a big thing."

Abigail stared into her cup. "Okay. It's a big thing."

"You made it through. You were strong, I know. You deserve credit for that."

Abigail looked at Megan, and this time her cheeks were pink and she was blinking, furiously. "*You* deserve credit. I never properly thanked you for what you did. A little thing like a lock–I never would have thought of it or had the guts to buy it and put it up, if you hadn't given it to me. I don't want to talk about it, but since we seem to be talking about it, I should thank you. You saved me. It was that lock that did it." She swiped at a wetness on her cheek.

"Hey, no problem." Megan smiled at her. "Happy to be of assistance. I'm glad I did one thing that was helpful in this world." She lifted her coffee cup and tapped it against Abigail's. "You survived. We survived our adolescences. Cheers."

Abigail told Megan that James was applying for a six-week residency in Dublin for the spring semester, during his sabbatical. Megan didn't mention that she knew it already. "What do you think of that?" Megan asked. "You wouldn't go with him?"

Abigail shrugged. "We've got our house here, we've got Callie."

"You'd really stay home with a cat instead of go to Dublin?" James had told Megan that he didn't think Abigail wanted to go with him.

"And my classes. I have two lined up, and they might lead to something more. And besides, I don't think he wants me to go." She said this last defiantly, with a little shake of her head.

"Really? I'm sure he does." She said this slowly, thinking: *did* James want his wife to go? He'd told Megan he'd be fine there alone, it would be all right, but now that she thought about it, it seemed he might have said this with a certain relish, a secret delight at the thought of being alone in Ireland.

"And maybe it would be good for us to be apart for a while. For me to be by myself. It's been so long, I've forgotten how to do it."

"I've never lived alone," Megan confessed. "After college I lived with a roommate until I moved in with Doug."

"I think sometimes I'm happiest living alone."

◆ ◆ ◆

As Megan drove home, she thought how, in a way, she felt protective toward Abigail. She always had. Abigail had always been jealous of her. She thought that Megan was smarter and prettier when they were younger, and now was jealous of Megan's motherhood. And, though of course Abigail wouldn't admit it, she was attracted to Megan's husband, too. Megan thought Abigail's feelings were like the jealousy a daughter feels towards a mother, a daughter who loves her mother but has a girlish crush on her father and wants him to love her best. It could be dangerous, she supposed, to remain family friends with someone who felt this way, but Megan didn't believe that Abigail would do her any harm. She was like a little sister, one who needed her big sister Megan to help her make it through the world.

◆ ◆ ◆

Megan's job was working with copy editors, cover designers, and authors to create beautiful, finished products. When she finished a project she thought of a child or young adolescent, someone Phoebe's age, lifting a book Megan had worked on from a shelf, maybe at a bookstore, maybe a library. Maybe unwrapping a gift. Seeing the colorful, compelling cover, reading the title, opening the book, reading the first lines, wanting to read more. Smelling the crisp pages. It gave her pleasure to think that the work she did, the emails and the phone calls, would lead to that pleasure. Though Phoebe was getting too old to be read aloud to, she still sometimes curled up with her mother on the couch and let her read to her. The warmth and softness of Phoebe's body leaning against hers, the language of the book reaching across from mother to daughter—it reminded her of nursing, the shared enjoyment of nourishing her child.

Megan could feel the yearning in Abigail when they were together and Phoebe sat next to her mother or gave her a hug. "Hug Auntie Abby too," Megan would prompt, and the girl would obediently reach out her arms. Abigail took Phoebe on outings sometimes, just the two of them. They went out for a lunch, to a movie, or shopping. Megan would try to ask, without pressure, what the two of them had talked about, but didn't get much in response. "Stuff," Phoebe would say. "I had an éclair. It was *so* good."

Being together with Abigail and James, the four of them, had its difficulties. Knowing Doug as she did, living with him for thirteen years, she saw him exert his charm on other women even when he thought he was being discreet. Or perhaps he himself wasn't aware; perhaps he did it without thinking, without acknowledging to himself what he was doing. It became more and more clear to Megan. The angle of his head, his posture, the expression of his face gave him away; he was flirting, whether he was aware of it or not, whether he could help it or not. It was part of his approach to the world, part of the way he managed and conquered the world. It was part of his success with both men and women, but especially women. How did she not notice it when they first got together? She was young, she thought it was directed at her alone. She thought she was the one.

Abigail always had an outrageous streak. Marriage and experience had tamed her, but when Doug leaned next to her at the dinner table, making a low-voiced joke, Megan saw how

Abigail responded, sending that smile in Doug's direction, eyes crinkled in merriment. Abigail couldn't help putting out her own kind of energy, a crackling, lit-up, sexy glow. At those moments Megan would glance at James, wondering what he saw. He'd mastered the poker face, the absent-minded professor air, his eyes wandering off into corners, but she thought he saw everything. He took it in and looked the other way. When James interacted with Abigail, Megan tried to parse his feelings for her: parts of admiration, humor, affection, and something else . . . sadness? A sad awareness? Maybe she imagined it.

Sometimes when Megan spoke and he looked at her, his look surged through her, like a jolt. It was *her* he saw. He knew her. It was different than flirtation, she thought; at least, she hoped it was. The thought of their friendship, the four of them, being some sort of Peyton Place story, or Desperate Housewives (a show she never actually watched), was repulsive to her. She would not let that happen, and she also would not give up her friendship with Abigail.

Chapter Thirteen

"What do you think of Miley Cyrus?" Phoebe was walking backwards in front of her on the sidewalk in their neighborhood, filming her mother. Megan shook her head, kept walking. "What does that mean, when you shake your head?"

"I don't like the way she presents herself anymore. Look out." A man was walking toward Phoebe. She ducked to the side, kept filming, camera on her mother, walking. They passed neat houses, flowering shrubs, full trees.

"How about Taylor Swift?" Megan considered, trying to remember what she knew of Taylor Swift. Blonde, wholesome? "Good, I guess. Good music, I think. Ah!" Her leg suddenly went out from under her, and just like that, she was sprawled on the sidewalk. She rolled to her side, clutching it; it had been feeling numb, and she'd tried to ignore it.

Phoebe ran to her. "What, what are you doing? What happened?"

"I don't know. I'm all right, I'm all right." She needed help up. Her back hurt. "My leg just doesn't want to work right for some reason." She laughed, wanting to reassure Phoebe, who was alarmed. Phoebe slung her camera strap over her shoulder and put an arm around her mother's waist, and they walked toward home. "You're just the right height," Megan said, and she was, her arm resting on the girl's shoulders. She gradually was able to walk on her leg, but it felt weird. At home she rested on the couch.

"What was that about?" Phoebe asked.

"My leg just felt weak. It happens sometimes, don't worry about it. It's all right now."

Other things happened, things she tried not to stress about. If she waited, the problems went away, so why get in a tizzy? Her right eye went out of focus one day, and then went back to normal. Her leg felt weak again suddenly, and though she didn't fall that time, she took care, holding onto the backs of chairs until she could sit down.

She didn't mention these things to anyone. It was easy not to mention them to Doug, as he was gone so much of the time, and easy not to mention them to Phoebe, who was still a child. Usually Phoebe didn't notice, or thought all parents did weird things like occasionally fall down.

When Megan did acknowledge a problem, she thought it originated in her emotions. Her body was feeling bad because she was sad. She sometimes felt a vague sense of dread. Her physical issues, she thought, sprang from her inability to deal with the ups and downs of life. She was sad or depressed, not sick. Or she was having a bad body day, like a bad hair day, something everyone had to deal with as they grew older.

She finally made an appointment. Her doctor, a white-haired man with erect posture who called her "Mrs. Adams," agreed with her that her emotions were probably driving factors of how she felt. "Take a vacation, if you're able," he'd suggested. "Sunshine and relaxation will help. Vitamin D." He asked her about alcohol use, drug use. She shook her head.

It was healing to be in Phoebe's presence. Just looking at the girl's smooth skin and shiny hair, hearing the lilt of her voice, watching her dance around the living room, made Megan feel young and strong. She remembered the joy she used to feel in using her muscles the way Phoebe did; the assurance of taking them for granted, knowing they would perform as she needed them to.

Megan and Doug had finally given in to Phoebe's desire for a dog. They considered a puppy, but on a visit to the Animal Shelter, they came across a young dog of indeterminate breed sitting quietly in his cage. A large, furry, yellowish-brown dog with darker ears and muzzle, he tilted its head quizzically at Phoebe. Phoebe stuck her fingers through steel mesh, as Megan said sharply, "No!" But the dog just walked forward calmly and sniffed her fingers. He gave them a tentative lick, then sat back down again, grinning happily at the three of them, as if they were already friends. "Aw," Phoebe said, and looked at her mother, then her father.

Now Frank sat beside her chair, looking at her attentively. It was walk time. Phoebe had named him, thinking the name hilarious and appropriate. When Megan got up to brush her hair, Frank walked into the bathroom and stood looking at her. When she took the leash from its hook, he stood by the door, tail swishing back and forth. With Frank in the back seat, his nose pushed out the open crack of the window, she drove to the park where they had Phoebe's birthday parties and parked in a lot close to the beach. She hooked the leash to Frank's collar and they wandered through the park, past the gazebo and down to the beach.

It was a breezy, cool day in late fall, clouds scudding across a sky that showed itself blue when they parted. With her winter jacket and sturdy shoes, Megan thought she probably looked like an old lady, walking on the rocks. She didn't care. The beach was empty, so she unhooked Frank's leash. He stood for her, tense, as she unlatched it, then shook himself free and bounded across the sand, exuberant. He ran down to the water, attacking the surf as it came in, then up the shore full speed. The clouds chased one another, and everything around her was movement, freedom. She laughed. A person appeared, a man walking slowly along the shore, zipped up in a jacket. Frank ran up to him, jumping up.

"Frank, no!" Megan shouted. "Sorry!" As the man came closer she saw James' wide grin.

They walked, near where they had walked before. It made her feel warm to see his face, to see how he couldn't stop smiling. It made her smile, too, and they walked along like a couple of fools. He paced his steps to hers naturally. "I'm a slow walker," she said, and he just nodded.

"I hope you're feeling well," he said after a moment.

"Well enough. Better now that I see your face." She felt immediately embarrassed at saying that, but it was true. "Frank is happy, too," she added.

"Such a good boy." The wind blew, and Megan thought of leaning into the warmth of James' body but held her distance. They walked slowly along the shore. His words, his presence, warmed her.

The next day Megan had work to do and wasn't able to walk Frank, but the following day she took him to the beach the same time as she had before, and again James was there. She didn't mention the coincidence, and neither did he, but after that they often just happened to run into one another there, as if by accident. Megan took Frank out in all but the worst weather. Using her muscles made her feel stronger, not giving in to their weakness. One day as they walked, the muscles in her left leg felt suddenly weak. She slowed and stopped, holding onto the arm of his jacket. It was a cool, wet day. The water and the sky were the same grey, the rocks below their feet a darker, wet grey and black. "Just a moment," Megan said, catching her breath. She didn't trust herself to walk yet.

James waited, watching her. "What is it?" he asked.

"My leg," was all she could say. "I don't know, it just does this sometimes." Frank ran ahead, lapped at the water, then looked back at them. After a bit Megan put weight on her leg and they continued walking, but slowly, Megan still holding onto James' arm. "My body, this rough beast," she said, knowing that would bring a smile from him.

Chapter Fourteen

Megan finally asked her doctor for more tests. Blood tests ruled out some diseases, and a neurological exam was scheduled. The doctor, a woman with curly grey hair, asked about her symptoms and family history. She did motor coordination tests, an eye exam, even a smell test. The doctor held tubes of water against Megan's skin, asking whether they felt warm or cool. She asked if Megan had voted in the presidential election recently held, and what she thought of the outcome. "I'm delighted," Megan said. "Couldn't be happier. Obama will be a great president, and I'm happy Massachusetts relaxed the laws about marijuana, though that doesn't affect me personally." She thought the question was strange, until she realized that she was being tested for her mental acuity. She hoped she passed. Finally, an MRI was scheduled.

Megan told Doug she was being tested, but didn't mention the diseases they were testing for, and he didn't ask. Since she hadn't told him much about her symptoms, perhaps he thought she was malingering, worrying overmuch. She would have thought she was, too, except for the fact that her leg kept giving out on her. She started using a cane on her walks. She met with her regular doctor, Dr. Connell, to talk about the results.

He was extra solicitous, asking her how she was feeling. "Well enough," Megan said, curious.

Sitting in front of his computer, Dr. Connell said "The radiologist has confirmed Multiple Sclerosis. He had a high degree of certainty." He looked at Megan for her reaction, but she just nodded. "I'm sorry," he said.

Megan didn't know what to say to this. "Thank you."

As if he was aware that he had minimized her concerns earlier, Dr. Connell took time with her, outlining treatment options, asking what questions she had. He sat patiently, waiting for her response. Megan considered asking what the ultimate outcome of the disease would be, and how long that would take, but decided to hold off on that. She would research when she felt up to it. She shook her head. "I'm sure I will have questions later," she said. "But I think this is enough for now." He prescribed some medication and set up the next in what would be an ongoing series of appointments with medical professionals.

That night, after Phoebe was in bed, Megan told Douglas of the diagnosis. When she said it was Multiple Sclerosis, he sat silent for a time. He asked, "What does this mean? What will happen?" and she saw fear on his face.

"Well, it will get worse over time. But I'm fine now. I will be starting on some drugs." She couldn't remember their names, or what they did. "But Doug . . ."

"What?"

"I don't want anyone to know yet. Not my parents, not Phoebe. Not our friends, not anyone I work with. Not yet, not until I have to. I don't want their sympathy, their pity."

Doug stood up and walked over to where Megan sat on the couch. His movements were deliberate, thoughtful, as he sat beside her and folded her in his arms. "Will you take my sympathy?" he asked.

"Yes," she said, putting her arms around him. "You're my husband. That's your job."

"I'm sorry," he said. "I'll be here for you, all the way." As if realizing how that sounded, he added, "Wherever it takes us."

◆ ◆ ◆

Doug bought her a polished handmade walking stick, and Megan carried it with her on her walks. The next time she walked with James, she told him she was seeing a physical therapist for a knee problem. Arthritis, she said self-consciously. "Pretty cane, isn't it?" she asked, holding it up and waving it.

"It is," James said. "Beautiful." He watched her face as she spoke, then looked out to the hazy ocean. "Maybe we should walk on the sidewalk," he said, motioning up to the sidewalk on the grass beyond the beach.

"It's okay on the rocks here." The part of the beach where they walked was covered with small rocks, not sand. "It's fine, really." She shifted the conversation to the cover of a book she was working on. "Dark words scribbled across this brilliant painting . . . I can't describe how beautiful it is, but the author and I are really happy with it." James listened, half-turned to her. He was hearing what she said but also seemed to be listening if he could discern what she was really saying behind her words.

They met once or twice a month at the same place, through the winter and into the spring. Over time, their conversation on their walks deepened, took unexpected routes. She didn't tell him about her diagnosis, but she told him about the darkness that came over her in the night sometimes. She didn't complain about her husband, but she felt as if he understood. She would turn over James' comments in her mind, finding hidden facets as they walked, and she would think of them later, searching for hints of his own marriage, of the secret of his inner life, and of his feelings for her.

When he spoke of Ireland, his face lightened. "I actually spend times in pubs there, something I never do here at home. I just walk into a pub and sit at the bar, and before long I'll be involved in a conversation."

"You could do that here," Megan said. "Right?"

He shook his head. "People here aren't like people in Ireland. A conversation here with a stranger in a bar would get political before too long." He looked at the ground as they walked, hands held behind his back.

After a few more steps, Megan said, "So Abigail isn't going with you?" She was careful not to say, "doesn't want to go with you."

He looked up to the sky then, to a spot near the horizon in the distance where a light flashed. "We're still working that out. A little time apart might be good for us. You know?"

"I don't know," Megan said. "I would think time spent together in Ireland might be good for the two of you." She thought maybe she'd gone too far, but he just smiled, and let it drop.

Sometimes Megan took Frank for his walk in the early morning, when she knew James wouldn't be there. And sometimes she would let herself go in the late afternoon, and would see his figure approaching her on the beach, shrouded in fog or bright in the sunlight. And it always made her happy.

When she felt alone, when darkness or fear descended on her—as it did, increasingly, over the years—even after their walks had ceased, she would think of their footsteps, measured and even, on the rocks, of his scuffed, worn leather shoes. She would think of the wind in their faces and their foolish smiles, the rhythm of their footsteps like a slow heartbeat, and she would feel calmer, and would not feel alone.

◆ ◆ ◆

If the light dimmed over the next few years; if her vision worsened; if she felt dizzy and weak and uncertain of her body or the future, there were moments when the clouds parted and light came flooding in. She stood in the sunshine on the back deck of their house on a late summer Sunday, feeling the humidity in the air. Her dreams from the night before, thick with longing, stayed with her. She took a small bite of dark chocolate, followed by a sip of hot milky tea, and pleasure flooded her. Thick green branches reached above her, unmoving. Phoebe and Doug played a game of badminton in the yard, batting the white plastic birdie over the net to shouts and laughter. Phoebe's legs were long and white as she jumped around, laughing, and Doug's face was creased in a smile. "You dork!" Phoebe shouted, as her father waved his arms in the air madly, mimicking her, teasing her. He was never this loose with his body, this unself-conscious, except around his daughter. The heavy warmth of the sun reached deep inside her, like the love she felt for Phoebe—the love she felt for *both* these people. She didn't allow herself to think of bodies ducking through the woods, or the color chartreuse: just sunshine, warmth, the aftertaste of the chocolate. Their closeness to her just now; their laughter, their voices.

Chapter Fifteen

Megan felt no guilt, for there was nothing to feel guilty about. Because of this, Doug's fury caught her off-guard. "How long have you been doing this?" he shouted–shouted! Douglas shouting!–waving his arms in the air as he paced around their living room.

"I don't think I've ever seen you like this before," Megan said. She sat on the couch staring up at him, transfixed. "I've never heard you shout. Be quiet, you'll wake Phoebe. And what exactly do you think it is we've been *doing*?" He had read her email on her laptop which Megan had left open on her desk. She didn't know how many he'd read, but the recent ones referred to walking with her, to conversations they'd had. James never signed "Love," but the tone of the emails was affectionate and familiar.

"It's obvious, isn't it?" He looked at her challengingly, then turned away and sat down.

"I would run into James walking when I took Frank out. We'd talk." Megan crossed her arms over her stomach. This conversation, or fight, or whatever it was, was making her queasy.

Doug sat in the armchair, looking at her. "I don't feel I can trust you anymore."

This made Megan laugh. She didn't mean to be mean, but she couldn't help it. "Oh come on, how can you say that? Seriously? After all you've done, and are probably still doing, you can't trust *me?*"

He sat back in the chair, shoulders turned inward as if he were collapsed, or protecting himself. He looked young suddenly to Megan, like a child. She was afraid, for one horrible moment, that he was going to cry. When he spoke, he muttered, "What did you talk about?"

She stared at him. "What did we *talk* about? What did you talk about, with Anna? With Eileen? With . . . Clara?" She saw him flinch; she had never mentioned Clara's name to him before. He put his head down and was silent. Megan had a yearning for a cigarette, something she hadn't had in years. Doug's distress, his pain, was disproportionate to the situation, and she didn't know whether she wanted to slap him, or apologize, or comfort him, or say something mean. She finally said, "I shouldn't have said that, it's not a fair comparison to make. I never slept with James or did anything close to it. I never had any intention to, and I never would."

He looked at her, assessing. He believed her, she thought. "Did you talk about . . . me?" he asked.

This was a Douglas she had never seen before. Uncertain, defenseless, some unhealed wound raising itself. "About you?" "Yes, me. Did you talk about me, did you tell him about me?"

"You mean . . ." your infidelities, she was going to say, but Doug interrupted, saying, "About me and Clarice."

"About Clarice. Your aunt." Megan's mind was racing, trying to understand. Doug just looked at her, nodding slightly, waiting for her to catch up. So that would be the real betrayal, to tell James about Doug's affair with his aunt. "Oh. No, I didn't tell him about that. I haven't told anyone about that."

He caught his breath and turned away from her. "Good," he said. "I find it . . . embarrassing."

◆ ◆ ◆

Megan went to bed early while Doug still sat downstairs, a glass of scotch at hand and a book open before him. One of his murder mysteries, which he read before he went to sleep. She lay awake for a long time, staring into the darkness. She was trying to make sense of what happened, of Doug's strange reaction. She supposed a husband would object to his wife's taking long walks with another man, being alone with him— even a husband with Doug's past—but he'd been so childlike, so emotional. A tantrum, followed by the collapse. She didn't know him as well as she thought she did.

She heard his footsteps on the stairs. The sound of running water, brushing of teeth, toilet flushing. He undressed in the dark bedroom and lay down beside her. She lay on her side turned away from him, and he curled up behind her, his body against hers. She felt the warmth of his chest against her back through the nightgown, his arm around her. His voice, close to her ear, low and trembling. He was sorry. He knew he was irrational. He believed she hadn't slept with James, but he was jealous of their friendship. His relationship with his aunt was a deep sore inside himself that Megan couldn't understand. "I don't want to lose you," he said. "You hold my life together."

Megan felt no need to respond. She put a hand over his, and that was enough. He talked on, his voice becoming a ragged, sleepy whisper until it slowed and stopped, replaced by his even, steady breathing.

Chapter Sixteen

The summer Phoebe turned twelve, she became obsessed with making videos. Her little flip camcorder was always in front of her face, recording. It was daily life that fascinated her: her mother, stirring soup while listening to the radio, stopping to scratch her head, absently staring out the window. Phoebe biking, the road whizzing toward her. Her father, arriving home from work, standing outside the car looking toward the house before he came in. The videos, loaded onto Megan's computer, were oddly moving. It was the fact that Phoebe valued these everyday moments that was touching, wanting to capture them as if she was aware of them being temporary, soon lost.

Phoebe's body was changing, growing tall and slim, alternating between a new grace and control and a staggering, coltish awkwardness. She spent hours in front of her mirror, trying out her mother's eyeliner and blush, videotaping herself making faces. Her face was changing, reforming itself almost daily into something new.

Megan leaned against Phoebe's bedroom door, watching her try on eyeshadow. The girl looked over at her mother. "What?"

"You don't need it, that's all."

"Oh, I know. I look *beautiful* without it, right?"

"Is that something I often say? Well, if I do, it's because it's true. Yes, you do look beautiful without it."

"Excuse me." Phoebe walked with determined steps to the door where Megan stood. "I would like some privacy, if you don't mind," she said, closing it.

Megan drove her to school and picked her up most days in the afternoon. In the mornings the girl would put earphones in, nodding her head slightly and looking out the car window so her mother would know, just in case she got the notion, that she was not available for conversation. In the afternoon, Phoebe came out of the school door surrounded by her friends, and she was a different person, her face alive, laughing as she shoved a girl's shoulder (who was that, Megan wondered, Lily? Maura? It was hard to keep her friends straight, especially as Phoebe rarely invited them to her house). The girls all wore their hair pulled up or back or to the side in various ways; didn't anyone just let their hair hang down anymore? Phoebe wore leggings under ripped jeans and she looked cool, with a sort of teenage toughness. *Too soon,* Megan thought. Phoebe would still be laughing at her friends as she got into the car, and when her mother turned to her, smiling, to say "What's so funny?" Phoebe would just shake her head, as if her mother wouldn't understand, or care.

"Oh, Sarah. She's such a geek." And the headphones would come out of the bag and go into the ears.

◆ ◆ ◆

After Doug's blowout, Megan cut down her walks at the beach with James, walking Frank in the mornings. But she wanted to see James before he left for Dublin. He would be gone for six weeks. She met him at the beach one afternoon, and they arranged a visit to the same museum they'd visited before. They walked the hushed, nearly empty rooms, Megan's cane tapping the floor with her steps. Their attention was more on one another than on the art.

They stopped in front of a large painting of a man and woman lying on the grass of a park. The woman held a red flower towards the man, and the sidewalk on either side of them narrowed to a meeting point in the distance. Though both were fully dressed, the man in a suit and the woman in a red dress and hat, and they didn't touch one another, there was a sense of intimacy in the painting, of a tender closeness. They looked at it without speaking. Megan felt the air between her and James like a substance, a carrier of warm electricity.

The museum gift shop was empty but for the clerk. Standing before a glass shelf, Megan picked up a small brass kaleidoscope. She held it up to her eye and looked toward the window. The street outdoors fractured into shards of colored light. She remembered having a kaleidoscope as a child; she'd felt it meant something profound, though she wouldn't have been able to say what. It was as if by looking through the kaleidoscope, a person made a choice: you could see the purpose of light as something to illuminate highways, scruffy grass, a kitchen table with dirty dishes, or you could see light as made to fall through pieces of colored glass to turn the world into a series of never-ending, incomprehensible but meaningful colorful patterns. James picked up another one and looked through it, turning it to see the patterns change.

On an impulse, Megan took both kaleidoscopes to the desk and paid for them with her credit card. Outside the shop, the sunshine fell on the parking lot, lighting up the rows of dusty cars. She handed one small box to James. "A going away gift for you. Put it in your suitcase. It won't take up much room.

Chapter Seventeen

Abigail texted a couple of weeks after James left for Ireland, asking if Megan wanted to get together for a drink. Megan sighed. It was after dinner; she was tired, exhausted, and a drink was not appealing. *I'm lonely,* Abigail texted. She rarely let herself sound needy.

Where should we meet? Megan texted back.

Abigail was in a corner booth, drink already in front of her, when Megan arrived. Megan stood just inside the entryway, looking through the glass of the closed door. Abigail leaned her face on her palm and played with the stem of her martini glass with her other hand, a picture of melancholy. She could have been playing a depressed woman in a movie, Megan thought. She lifted her head when Megan came in the room and smiled.

Abigail asked about Phoebe. "Ugh," Megan groaned. "She's such a teenager. Makeup, boys. I can't stand it. One of her good friend's parents found a baggie of marijuana in their daughter's drawer. And Phoebe won't have anything to do with her father all of a sudden."

"Really? Why? They were so close."

"Who knows?" Megan said. She watched Abigail lean into her drink, as if it were her best friend. "So enough about Phoebe," she said. "What's going on?"

"Something happened," she said, and raised her hand to the passing waitress for another drink. For a brief, crazy moment Megan was afraid that Abigail was going to tell her that something had happened between her and Doug. They were in love, Abigail would say; she couldn't help herself. Whatever it was, it seemed hard to get the words out. Then Megan was sure that it was about James; James and she were breaking up.

Abigail bit her lip, her eyes swimming. She finally spoke. "I had a miscarriage. A second one, I mean."

"Oh, Abigail," Megan said, reaching out for her friend with a hand on her arm, guilty for the quick wash of relief she felt. The miscarriage had happened recently, after James had left for Dublin. "Were you able to talk with him about it?"

Abigail shook her head. "No. He doesn't know. He didn't know I was pregnant. I don't want him to know about this, yet. You're the only person I've told." When she looked up, Megan saw the pain on her face.

"Honey." Megan reached over impulsively to give her a hug. "Why can't you tell him? Are you all right?"

"We just haven't been talking much. I think sometimes he doesn't even like me."

"That can't be so. I know he loves you." As she spoke, Megan was searching her memory for things James had said about Abigail, any indication of his feelings toward her. He avoided talking about her, she realized.

"It's just one of those periods in a marriage, you know, the bottom of the sine wave. Maybe it will go up again and be hot." Abigail leaned back against the booth, resting her hand on her middle. "I've felt so bad. I mean, I know I shouldn't complain, when you deal with pain all the time . . ." Megan had told Abigail her limping was from arthritis. "But it was so hard." She closed her eyes tightly, to hold in tears. "I wanted that child, you know?"

"I know. I know you did."

"Everybody can get pregnant, it seems. Any teenage idiot can get pregnant. It happens all the time. All these people getting abortions. Women in the grocery store, yelling at all these babies crawling around their cart, more than any one person could ever need or even want. But I can't, apparently. I've got a room ready for it in the house, it's been ready for ten years. I thought it would finally work out this time, after all this time. I thought it would fix things between James and me. I should have known better. I'm 41, I'm too old." She sat up straighter, ran her hands over her face and took another drink of her martini. "I know I'm being a whiner. Something in my body doesn't want to support a child, apparently. It's my fault, or my body's fault, at any rate."

"It's not your fault. You'd be a wonderful mother. You're such a good auntie to Phoebe; she loves you." The inevitable question, she had to ask: "You don't want to adopt, then?"

"No. I feel like if my body can't support my own child, then maybe I was not supposed to be a mother."

Megan wasn't so sure of this. She said, "Our bodies aren't always smart about things. Maybe you shouldn't listen to it." She ordered another glass of wine, even though she didn't want it, to keep Abigail company. She lifted it in a toast. "To bodies that don't understand their owners." Like her own, she thought. "And to marriage. Long may it last."

"And to Phoebe," Abigail said. "Thank you for letting me be her pretend mom sometimes."

"Anytime," Megan said. "Anytime." As Megan sipped, she was thinking of her friendship with James. Maybe when he returned, she should try harder to avoid running into him. She pushed away the sudden emptiness she felt at the thought.

◆ ◆ ◆

With James gone, Doug working long hours, and Phoebe retreating into her teen culture, Megan found herself alone in a new way. She worked online in the mornings and took afternoon rests. She lay on the couch with a book face down on her lap. She paid attention to her body, to the difficulty swallowing sometimes, to her leg tingling and to pain in her back from her falls, to her tiredness, to the ache in her chest. Lying still, paying attention, was a way of listening to her body. She didn't know what would happen in the future, didn't know how she and Doug would handle things when she became more ill. He said he would "be there" for her, but she didn't think that taking care of a sick person would be one of his strengths. He wasn't comfortable being around another person when they were weak or in pain. He couldn't bear it.

She closed her eyes and let her thoughts drift. Let it go— life would take its course. How lucky she was to have Phoebe as a daughter! She was allowed that gift of a child. A bit of music, twisting around her head, what was it? *Yesterday, a child came out to wander, caught a dragonfly inside a jar.*

Megan felt her body was telling her that she had never been a strong person. Maybe her body *did* know her, knew more than she did, and was reminding her. Frank padded over from his spot in front of the door to lie on the floor beside her, with a sigh. She reached a hand down, stroking his head. She and the dog were both alive, moving through this mystery of consciousness. She lay with her eyes closed, her muscles relaxing. Megan had been a good student, a good daughter, then a good wife; good at her job, a good mother. But really, she had not accomplished much. Did her husband love her? Maybe, a bit. Did she love him? Don't think, she told herself. Just relax. Everything is all right. Her worries were just her tiredness talking to her, her achy body, trying to infiltrate her thoughts.

She stretched her legs, rubbing the tops of her thighs to relieve an ache. Life was not easy for anyone, right? *Fearful, when the sky was full of thunder, and tearful at the falling of a star.* She still, after everything, looked forward to Douglas coming in the door, or walking into the room; she looked for his face, the sound of his voice. There were things, every day, she saved up to tell him.

And she had Phoebe. She had given Phoebe to the world. She felt a settling in her chest. There was no doubt of the love she felt for Phoebe. That girl would make the world right.

Book Three: The Absurd Forgiveness

Chapter One

The winter of early 2017 never seems to come to an end, and Abigail can't stop reading news stories on the internet. The election in November hit her like a physical blow, making her head hurt and her joints ache. She is obsessed with outrages of the new administration, with fear and dread of what is to come. President Trump—it hurts her to say it, but she says it and reads it, over and over, like digging fingernails into a wound. It's like a TV show she would never choose to watch, but now she has to. She wakes up at night from a dream of talking with Megan, then starts worrying about the Supreme Court, and can't get back to sleep. She stays awake, hearing him brag in his hoarse voice: "I just start kissing them. . . I don't even wait. And when you're a star, you can do anything . . . Grab 'em by the pussy. Do anything."

It pains Abigail to know that her own mother, the kind, non-political woman who loves sewing and lemon cake, had voted for Trump. Both her parents had voted

Republican most of their lives, her mother following her husband's lead. She confronted her mother when the "Access Hollywood" tapes came out. "Did you hear what he said?" she asked. "How could you possibly listen to him after that?"

"I don't listen to that stuff," her mother said. The fall weather was mild, and Abigail had talked her mother into stepping outside. They were walking in the courtyard outside the apartment complex, bundled up in winter coats.

"Listen." Sitting on a bench, Abigail took off a glove, pulled out her phone and found the audio. "Sit down," she said. "Just for a minute." Her mother sat slowly. They listened to the tape, Trump saying he moved on a married woman, tried to "fuck her," and how he felt free to grab women anywhere, because he was a "star."

"That's stupid," her mother said. "But men talk like that. They do. He's not the only one. It doesn't mean he'll be a bad president."

Abigail gave up. Her mother would continue to believe in this man, just as she had continued to believe in her husband.

In the morning she sits at her desk intending to work, but opens her Twitter feed instead, and is lost in the wormhole of news stories, one post taking her to another. When Trump was elected, she took comfort in the fact that he'd done so many stupid and venal things—so many illegal things, in fact—that he wouldn't be allowed to continue as President for very long. Now, life seems to be moving on as normal, with a seeming President overseeing a seeming democracy, but everything does not feel normal. Everything feels very wrong. She has the need to do something, but what?

In January, she bought three knitted pussy hats from a woman selling them on the street: one for herself, one for Phoebe, one for Megan. On the day after the inauguration, she and Phoebe marched in the parade through downtown Boston wearing their hats. She sent Megan photos of the two of them leaning with their arms around one another, grinning. Megan returned one of herself, sitting in her rocker wearing her pink pussy hat, her thin face alight with a smile. Abigail felt silly putting on the hat, hating the need to be part of a movement that had to do this, but when she found herself surrounded by women wearing similar hats, she felt a fellowship with those around her, a sense that something good was happening. The signs around her read, "Girls Just Want to Have FUNdamental Rights;" "Nasty Women Unite;" and one young girl dressed in pink carrying a sign as big as she was, "Fight Like A Girl." For that moment Abigail felt as if she were part of a movement, part of something that would go somewhere.

Then in early March, Megan died—it feels strange to say that too; she can't believe it. It's as wrong as saying "President Trump." *Megan died.* But she did, she is gone somewhere inaccessible, and since then Abigail finds it hard to focus, hard to do anything that requires much thought. She calls up Instagram and looks at photos, hoping for the rare post from Phoebe. She reads outraged, funny, ineffectual tweets about the President and his staff by people she doesn't know; she reads about how the Russians stole the presidency; she reads about the travel ban against Muslims. She feels outraged for Hillary, for Muslims, for people of color, for the disabled, for women. For her students, for the world climate, for the poor. For herself. She stares out the window at cars swishing by on streets which seem to be always wet with sleet or cold rain. She thinks of Megan, wanting to hear her voice.

She decides to change the syllabus for her course in the Contemporary Short Story, again. She's changed it twice already since the semester began, but it's been a rough semester.

Besides, as a part-time adjunct, she sometimes feels as if no one is actually paying attention to what she does in her classes, as long as her student evaluations at the end of the semester are not atrocious. As long as she is not accused of sexually abusing her students, or offering them heroin, or never coming to her classes, chances are she will be rehired in the fall for the small amount they pay adjuncts. She wants to talk about another story by Raymond Carver that isn't on the syllabus: "A Small, Good Thing."

In this story, a young couple's son is hit by a car on his birthday and falls unconscious. As the boy moves toward death and the parents sit a tormented vigil, a baker keeps calling their home leaving taunting anonymous messages about a cake they've ordered and forgotten. The baker doesn't say why he's calling, and the couple doesn't know who it is. At the story's end, the couple realizes who it is after their son has died. They confront the baker, enraged, wanting his blood. At the end the anger fades away and the three of them eat warm cinnamon rolls in the bakery and talk, in a kind of communion.

She enters the bright green basement room, flinching as always at the fluorescent lights. Students are reluctant to begin talking, but Morgan, whose hair is hot pink this week, says, "This story is so *sad!* Ms. MacDonald, why do you assign such sad stories?"

"Because life is sad?" Abigail suggests.

"But life is sometimes happy too," Morgan says. "Why isn't that ever shown in these stories?"

"Well, remember that all fiction moves forward by conflict. But does anyone see any happiness in this story?" Abigail asks.

"The boy gets hit by a car. His parents can't talk to one another. The doctor's a dick. Another kid gets stabbed and dies. The little boy wakes up, shrieks, then dies. And then, to top it off, the parents are tormented by this baker asshole. What could possibly be good?"

Abigail knows Morgan well enough by now to know that she is not actually upset by the story, she's just making an argument, in her typical colorful language. "Ok, if not actually happiness, anything good at all?" Abigail asks. "Anything good happen?"

The class is quiet, turning pages. A few students sit staring at the pages, daydreaming; one stares at his closed book. Robert says, tentatively, "I think the couple love one another." He points to a passage where the man takes the woman's hand. "It makes him feel better to hold her hand. And then they pray."

"So?" Morgan asks, derisively. "That's good?"

"Well, yes," Robert says. "She said she hadn't prayed in a long time, then she did. And her husband did, too. Then it says they felt like they were in this together."

"That's what prayer does," Malik offers. "It brings people together." Morgan looks at him skeptically but doesn't say anything.

Sarah raises a hand slightly, then puts it down, then raises it again. Abigail calls on her. "That moment at the end . . ." Sarah says.

"Yes?"

"I mean, the baker is awful, he does terrible things, but then it's like he helps them at the end. He apologizes and gives them some of those cinnamon rolls that sound so yummy."

"I know, right?" Morgan interrupts. "I'm hungry."

Sarah goes on, following her thought. "They finally eat. They come together, at the end. They don't hate one another. He sort of saves them. They're eating together, and that's comforting. I think it's even . . . beautiful."

Thinking of this later, Abigail is reminded of how often students in her class—not always the great students, not necessarily brilliant ones—get at the heart of the stories, more or less on their own. Abigail herself had felt comforted at that moment, Sarah offering her insight as if it were a warm piece of bread.

Chapter Two

Food had become difficult for Megan. She would accidentally breathe in a bite and choke, terrifying whoever was with her. Abigail learned the Heimlich maneuver and used it more than once.

She remembered an evening last December, a rare time when Megan had an appetite and got food down without trouble. Doug had set up a Christmas tree in the corner of their living room, with old-fashioned big colored lights. They could see snow falling through the window in the early darkness. Frank lay on the floor by the wood stove, snoring lightly.

Megan had recently been hospitalized. She'd had pneumonia, brought on by aspirating food. Abigail had visited her there, and saw how ill Megan was, barely able to say anything. Breathing seemed to be an effort, and when it wasn't, Megan just wanted to sleep, oxygen tubes in her nostrils. Now she was home and feeling better, able to walk to the chair in the living room where she sat, wrapped up in a light wool shawl. Megan had made home-made guacamole and deviled eggs. Doug was working late, and the two women were celebrating an early Christmas together. Abigail had built a fire in the fireplace. Megan advised her on how to stack small pieces of wood over newspaper and light it. The food Abigail prepared for Megan usually went uneaten, but that evening Megan ate several eggs and some guacamole spread on a piece of soft bread. "So good," she said, eating very slowly but steadily. She even had a glass of wine.

They talked of Phoebe. She was in her first year of grad school. Megan was worried that Phoebe had gone to grad school right out of college, that she wasn't emotionally ready. "She doesn't handle stress well," Megan said.

"She seems very mature for her age," Abigail commented.

"Doug says that too, but he just doesn't know. She's good at hiding things," Megan insisted. "I tell him that, if I'm no longer around, he will have to do a better job of being aware of her, being ready to help her."

As Abigail stared unhappily at her friend, Megan said, "You know, if I take off with my lover somewhere."

Abigail relaxed. "The Caribbean?"

"No, too clichéd. We were thinking Norway. Northern Norway. The fjords. Northern Lights."

Abigail smiled then, thinking of her friend with an imaginary lover, motoring a boat down a narrow fjord with high mountains on either side. "You'd be cold," she said, leaning over to arrange the blanket Megan had on her lap in spite of the fire. "Dress warmly."

"Oh, I will." Megan settled back in her chair. "But really, Phoebe takes things hard, even when it seems she's doing great. I'm just saying." Megan looked at Abigail then, who nodded.

"I hear you." The acknowledgement was a promise: if the worst happened, if Megan died, Abigail would keep an eye on her daughter.

"I'm hoping Doug might go with us to midnight mass on Christmas Eve." Megan had taken to attending mass occasionally, when Doug felt like taking her.

"But . . . why?" Abigail said. She put the last piece of cheese in her mouth. Megan was no dummy; she knew the terrible things the Church had done. She knew the hypocrisy. Abigail picked up the empty plate to take to the kitchen. She called back to Megan, "I see your guy Pope Francis reaffirmed the Church's stance on women. They will never be priests." When she returned, she saw that Megan's eyes were closed. Her face looked pale and tired. "Oh, I'm sorry," Abigail said.

"No, I'm not asleep," Megan said, opening her eyes. "Women should be allowed to be priests. But I don't go to Mass because the Church is perfect. It's not, I know that. Neither is marriage, neither are most institutions. I go because it gives me comfort. Communion—the idea of communion—reminds me that there is more to life than just me, me and my aches and pains. I feel connected with something larger. I remember my parents, remember their love. We used to go to church every Sunday. When I sit there, I feel as if they are with me again. There's nothing wrong with that."

Abigail reached over to take Megan's hand. "I'm sorry. It's none of my business. You should find your comfort any way you want."

Megan looked amused, squeezing Abigail's hand in response. "There are worse ways to take comfort."

It had been five years since Megan's parents died. They had taken a sight-seeing trip in a helicopter over Boston, to celebrate their fiftieth wedding anniversary. Her mother had been afraid to get into the helicopter, but her father assured her it would be fine. A sudden gust of wind, combined with an improperly installed part, caused the crash into the harbor. Megan didn't want to sue the company, Abigail recalled, but Doug insisted that she do it. They received a substantial sum, Megan said, but didn't tell specifics.

Abigail poured herself another glass of wine, and a half glass for Megan. "Cheers," she said, lifting it. "To 2017, and to lovers."

"And to husbands," Megan said.

They drank. Frank lifted his head, looked at them both, then rested it again on his paws. Snow fell in slanted lines outside the windows, and a flame in the stove shot up with a crackle.

◆ ◆ ◆

The days begin softening, the snow disappears. One day the temperature reaches the upper 60s, and as she walks from her office to her car, Abigail sees that the grass is turning green, and a patch of daffodils is blooming next to the library wall. It happened all of a sudden, when she wasn't paying attention. The warm weather reminds her of Phoebe as a child, playing outdoors. She was a beautiful child, running in the yard, making dandelion chains. Before knowing Phoebe, Abigail hadn't realized how beautiful children could be; were they all beautiful, she wondered, when seen by someone who loves them? Probably, even the infant she saw on the train yesterday, the one with the giant hematoma on the side of its forehead. But Phoebe had been truly, objectively beautiful, and still is.

She walks through campus, around groups of students walking, sitting on benches talking. Giddy with the warm sunshine, they are wearing shorts and flip flops as if the temperature were in the 80s instead of the 60s. A girl shakes back shiny blonde hair and looks up at the sky, closing her eyes to let the sunlight fall on her face. A young man on a skateboard swoops down the sidewalk past the students, who jump away and shout at him.

In her car, Abigail takes out her phone. Phoebe prefers texting over calls. *Hope you're enjoying this beautiful day,* Abigail writes. *Can we have lunch sometime?*

Staring out the windshield, she thinks of the months when she and Phoebe's father were seeing one another in Marisha's apartment, were deliriously in love—at least, she had been deliriously in love. They kept their romance indoors, inside the apartment where she was staying. No one, she thinks, ever saw them together outside those walls. Abigail hadn't wanted Megan to be hurt—again—by her husband.

Abigail pulls out of the parking lot and onto the street. If she'd thought hard about it at the time, she would have told herself that if it wasn't her, there would be someone else for Doug, someone else he'd be playing with. So why not her? But she didn't think that way; she didn't think hard about it. She was good at putting things aside, things it didn't benefit her to think much about. She had been in love, and in the intoxication of that, didn't want to think about anything except him. It had been so long since she'd felt that intoxication, the air of possibility filling her mind. All her thoughts were of him. The future didn't exist, didn't matter. What was outside the walls didn't matter. There was just him: his eyes, his face, his mouth. His smell, the feel of his skin on hers. She was able to finally have all of him then, and she was not going to deny herself that.

Sure, Phoebe texts back. *Saturday?*

Chapter Three

They meet at an Italian place a few blocks from Phoebe's school. It is cool, a brisk wind bringing back winter. Abigail chooses a table by the window, where she can look out on a street busy with traffic and pedestrians. More than twenty minutes beyond their scheduled time she sees Phoebe walking quickly toward the restaurant. She has a thick scarf wrapped around her neck, and hunches inside her leather jacket. As Abigail watches her walk into the restaurant, unwrap her scarf from her neck and look around, the first impression she has is one of unhappiness.

Phoebe brightens when she sees Abigail. At the table, she wraps her arms around her for a hug. Her body feels small through the jacket, her arms around Abigail tight slim bands.

Phoebe has a winter pallor and a recurrence of teenage acne, red dots along her jaw. She hangs her jacket on the back of her chair. When Abigail asks how she is doing, Phoebe looks out the window, thinking about the question. She nods. "Fine, I guess. As fine as I can be, considering."

"And your dad? How is he doing?" She can't help asking.

"Oh, all right." Phoebe picks up the menu. "He's leaving this weekend for a trip to the Virgin Islands."

"The Virgin Islands? Why?"

"Just a vacation. His friend is going with him. Hope."

For a moment, Abigail thinks Phoebe is saying something about the quality of hope, that Doug hoped, or Phoebe hoped for something . . . hoped for a relationship? So soon, mere weeks after . . . Then she realizes it is a name, a woman's name. "Oh. Who is Hope?"

"Someone he works with." Phoebe puts the menu down, folds her hands, and looks at Abigail. "I think I'll have the pasta primavera." Her face is impassive, making it clear that Hope, whoever she is, is someone she has no interest in talking about.

They talk about a project Phoebe is working on. "It's a short film about funeral homes and embalming; the 'death industry'." This afternoon she will try to find someone who will give her permission to view and film an autopsy. "It's very difficult to find someone who will let me watch," she says.

"Oh, Phoebe." Abigail leans back in her chair. "Is that something you would even want to do?"

"Why not?" Phoebe still has a detached, impassive look on her face. "It's just skin. Like cloth, like material." She dips bread into olive oil, then looks up at Abigail intently. "It's not the *person.* The person is gone somewhere else." After a pause, Phoebe says, "And, yeah, I think I'd like that. I'd enjoy seeing it."

On her way home, Abigail wonders just how, exactly, she is to keep an eye on Phoebe, how she is to help her. The conversation disturbed her; it was the look on Phoebe's face, closed off, even a little belligerent, though Abigail doesn't know why she would feel that way toward her, toward her Aunt Abby. She said she'd recently broken up with the guy she'd been seeing; maybe that was it. There was a deadness to her, Abigail thinks, except for that moment when she looked so intensely at Abigail. Depression, maybe. But what can Abigail do about that?

Phoebe could not have known about her father's affair ("romance" was the word Abigail preferred) with Abigail. But did she know about the others? Megan told her she left Doug, briefly, when Phoebe was a baby, and there was someone after that. At least one more, before Abigail.

But all that was long in the past now, and he was free to do whatever he wanted. With Hope, or with whomever.

◆ ◆ ◆

If Abigail hadn't miscarried twice, her children would be eleven and thirteen years old. She imagines a gawky thirteen-year-old boy, voice suddenly hoarse, hair grown long and curly around his ears. He would be impatient with his younger sister, who adores him and torments him. His sister would be in sixth grade, reading horse books, crying over a friend who moved away, having her first crush. The girl and Abigail talk about periods, she imagines; the girl is afraid, and never wants to have sex. "You don't have to," Abigail tells her, smiling. "But someday you may feel differently about it." She and James buy the boy a drum set and let him bang away his frustrations in the basement. The shadow children grow alongside her, with their wispy bodies, their imagined voices which sound real to her. Their hurts, their achievements. Trying to compensate for having a uterus which rejected them, for having a body hostile to their lives, she is a perfect mother, always there for them. She doesn't talk with James about this, of course; doesn't mention his daughter dancing in the living room, her son playing drums in the basement.

Abigail sometimes thinks of a particular moment, seeing Doug's long, narrow body standing in a shaft of light in Marisha's apartment, his naked skin white in the sunlight. She remembers the feel of that skin against hers, cool and smooth. She held him for a moment until he pulled away, rushing to a meeting. For some reason, this inevitably brings to mind another moment.

When Abigail was helping Megan at home, she would sometimes run water for her bath. The heat of the water made Megan feel better. She'd be in there for a long time. One day Abigail, reading downstairs, heard Megan's voice from upstairs, muffled behind the bathroom door. She went to the door.

"What is it?"

"I need your help."

"You want me to come in?"

"Yes," Megan said. "Come in." She opened the door to see Megan, naked in the tub, knees up and arms resting on the sides. "I can't get out," she said, laughing in a way she had of showing that it was just her body giving her trouble, her body doing its thing. As if it had nothing much to do with her, with Megan; it was just this body, being its cantankerous self. Abigail held her arms out and Megan pulled herself up on them, slowly. Abigail steadied her with one arm, reaching for a towel to wrap around Megan with the other.

Dripping wet, Megan was skinny, her chest bony above small breasts, and slight potbelly of a droopy stomach. Her knees were round and swollen. Still she was pretty and delicate, her skin lightly freckled, cheeks pink from the bath and her curly hair damp. Still Abigail could see how Douglas would love her. "Oh, Abigail," Megan said, laughing. "What would I do without you," and Abigail pulled Megan's slight toweled body to her sturdy full one, wrapping her arms around her, inhaling her soapy smell.

These memories sometimes occur to her, one after the other, naked elusive Doug and naked vulnerable Megan. She thinks of them as she dries her hair, or as she stands in front of the mirror, putting on skin lotion. She doesn't know why they appear to her one after the other, and she doesn't know what to do about the emotions that rise in her then, conflicting, turbulent things, bumping into one another. The emotions infiltrate her dreams at night, causing her to wake with a start. She can't identify these feelings, can't name them, and doesn't, actually, want to have anything more to do with them.

Chapter Four

Wiping down the kitchen counter after dinner, the granite smooth under the wet cloth, Abigail remembers the half-empty pill bottles. James had offered to drop them at the police station for disposal, but she hadn't given them to him yet. She turns on her desk lamp and opens the bottom drawer. The brown containers with white lids rest on top of Megan's flowered journal. She picks up the plastic bottle of oxy. She could get a good price for this, she'd guess, if she were up to that. Phoebe probably knows someone . . . she drops her hand holding the bottle into her lap.

She doesn't remember Megan mentioning this drug, and it's certainly not one that Abigail ever administered. She would remember if she had. It's a dangerous drug. Even in her reckless younger days, Abigail stayed away from it. She knew that Megan suffered from back pain, from degenerative disc disease and her many falls, but she had taken pride in handling it, in being stoic. She didn't like the feeling of intoxication. Abigail picks up the bottle again. It has Megan's name on it, with the dosage. Abigail guesses that, if taken as prescribed, it wouldn't make Megan high, just relieve her pain. It was filled just five days before Megan died, she notices. It could be refilled two times. And "QTY: 60."

Abigail stares at the bottle. Twisting open the lid, she shakes the pills into her hand and counts. There are 21 pills. If Megan took two a day, the prescribed dose, there should be 50 pills in the jar.

Abigail puts the pills back into the bottle and twists the lid back on. Clutching it in her hand, she stands up. James is in his office upstairs. She starts toward the stairs but stops herself. She needs to think about this. There must be a good reason there are so few pills.

She sits back down. Maybe Doug put some of the pills away, knowing they were dangerous. But why; to whom would they be dangerous? Phoebe? Was he worried Phoebe would take them? The thought of keeping them from Megan was ridiculous; Megan was far from an addict. She thinks of the part-time caretaker, Judith. She remembers Judith's grey hair, her calm face and comforting manner, the gold cross always glinting at her neck. Judith didn't ever give drugs to Megan; that was done only by Doug or Abigail. Judith wouldn't have known they were there, and Megan felt sure she wouldn't have taken them. Was Doug an addict? Or, if not an addict, someone who liked to take drugs?

She tries to remember if he'd ever said anything that might indicate he had a taste for pills. He liked plenty of wine with dinner. When he visited her in Marisha's apartment, he always made sure they had gin on hand. They would get loose and giggly, sitting at the little kitchen table clinking the ice around their glasses. Once, after a few drinks, they brought out a set of watercolors she had in a drawer and painted, just for fun.

Doug's picture of his glass half-full was remarkably good, she thought; she'd saved it somewhere.

This leads her, inevitably, to think of the two of them on Marisha's tan couch. She can't help it. She stares out the window next to her desk, remembering. She'd close the curtains so he could uncover her breasts. He was very fond of those. He was a wonderful appreciator of a woman's body. He still is, she would imagine. Abigail had not thought, during those late afternoon visits, of what Megan might be doing at the time. Phoebe was a young girl then, maybe twelve years old.

But no, she doesn't remember him ever saying anything about drugs. He doesn't, in her opinion, have anything of a drug user about him. He is too careful of his appearance, too exact in the phrases he chooses, too careful with his exercise routine.

She recognizes most of the other medications from giving them to Megan. Steroids, an anti-spasticity drug, a gel to smooth on her skin. Others whose purpose she forgets. Megan would give herself an injection of something once a week.

Abigail leans back in her desk chair, half-closing her eyes. She hears James clear his throat upstairs. She thinks again of her friend. Something happened with Megan sometimes, close to the end. Something between them, something there in the room with them. Something more than just her, more than just Megan. A third thing, humming in the air between them.

If Megan was depressed, Abigail could not tell. She liked to talk about books she was reading, a pile of them always by her side. She said it was hard to read sometimes, hard to follow what was on the page, but she just read more slowly. "Poetry," Megan said, picking up a collection from the table. "Sometimes it's the only thing that makes sense." She read aloud: "Have you ever tried to enter the long black branches of other lives . . ." She put the book down and stared at Abigail. "I mean, really. How beautiful is Mary Oliver? And this." She held the book up again, the pages quivering in front of her face. "Do you think this world was only an entertainment for you?"

Abigail would come by in the mornings and leave before Doug came home, making sure Megan was set up with her cell phone close at hand. Megan would steer her scooter up to the kitchen table for lunch. "I just hate the looks of this thing," she grumbled, referring to her scooter. "The wheelchair was romantic and classic. Like Clara, in *Heidi*."

"Yes, but this works so much better. And you know if Clara was around now, she'd be using one of these."

Megan spooned vegetable soup to her lips carefully. "What I need is to be set free in the mountain air, in the Alps with the goats. I'd be running again in no time."

After lunch, Megan drove her scooter to the stairs, where she could walk up slowly, leaning on the handrail with Abigail close by. "My daily exercise," she called it. In her bedroom, they watched Netflix on Megan's computer, Abigail on the bed beside her. "Come on, come closer," Megan said. "I'm not contagious." They watched all of *Orange Is The New Black* together, and much of *The Crown*. "I'm getting paid for this?" Abigail said. "That's just wrong."

"You could be doing other things," Megan said. She was propped up in bed with pillows behind her back, Abigail curled up beside her with her head on a pillow. "Writing a book, applying for teaching jobs."

"I'd rather be doing this," Abigail said.

Sometimes they turned the computer off and just sat. Talking, or not talking if Megan was tired. Sometimes they sang songs from their high school choir: "The Circle of Life;" "The Lion Sleeps Tonight;" and their all-time fave, "Bohemian Rhapsody." Megan's voice was weak, and sometimes she couldn't find the breath or energy to sing at all, but she wanted Abigail to go on singing. On the days when she could, Megan would sing "Nothin' really matters to me," and Abigail would respond, "Any way the wind blows . . ." Their voices were small in the bedroom, but in their heads they were a full chorus, resounding.

"What were we thinking, when we sang that back then?" Megan asked.

"We thought we were world-weary. We knew all about life and death." Abigail took a drink of water from her glass, offered Megan hers. "And I was thinking about Kevin Williams, behind me."

"He was cute."

"Cute. Sexy. Shy. Well-hung."

"Abigail! You couldn't have known that."

'Oh yes, I could." She still liked to shock Megan, to play the sexually liberated woman. Now, remembering the faint flush that would come over her friend's cheeks, Abigail wonders, again, just what Megan knew about her and Douglas, what she suspected. What Megan had to "forgive" her for.

Maybe Megan did get a little high sometimes, Abigail didn't know. She remembers the occasional haziness of her expression, the way the words tumbled out, unobstructed by her usual reserve. She'd make Abigail laugh. When Megan laughed, she would stop to cough, then try to catch her breath. She'd talk through it as much as she could, as if her words, her thoughts, couldn't wait to be expressed. "Remember when Phoebe was small, three years old, she liked to dress up? All the time, she had to dress up, and one day she told us that we had to call her Pretty Dress Always. It was her name, you know, like Native Americans would name someone after a trait." She turned, reaching for her glass of water, and sipped it slowly, pausing to cough. "You probably don't remember when we changed our names."

"Of course I do." Abigail took the glass from Megan's shaky hand and set it on the bedside table. "I was Marcia, and you were Jan."

"From the Brady Bunch." Laugh, cough. "You were my older sister."

"Yes. Sisters." Megan sighed and was silent then, and Abigail let the silence grow. In moments like this she felt the thing between them, an understanding, a humming in the air. Something not her, not Megan, but both of them, a separate thing. She didn't need to look at Megan to feel it, and to know she was feeling it too. She stayed silent, until Megan's eyes closed and her breathing became regular.

Chapter Five

If Doug didn't take the pills, then did Phoebe? Over the next few days, Abigail contemplates this possibility. She remembers Phoebe's pallor, her deadened eyes. Her fascination with dead bodies, with autopsies. But what was Abigail supposed to do; ask her? *Did you steal your mother's pills? Are you an addict?* No. On Saturday, she texts to ask if Phoebe is home, saying she is going into the city and wants to drop off an old kitchen chair she'd promised her.

Phoebe comes to the entryway of the four-story building, looking tousled and sleepy. Her cheeks are pink, though, and she laughs at the sight of Abigail standing with a wooden chair on the front step. "You look adorable," she says. "Wait. Hold on," and she goes back inside. Coming out with her camera, she crouches and focuses.

"Oh, really." Abigail is disarmed, embarrassed. She carries the chair inside. Two chairs are pushed up to the small table in the miniscule kitchen. Phoebe takes the chair from her and places it against the wall.

"There," she says. "Now I can have two guests over for dinner, and we can all sit at the table. Would you like some coffee? Tea?"

THE SYMMETRY OF HUSBANDS

"Whatever you're having." As Phoebe puts on water for tea, Abigail watches her. She is very slim, but looks healthy in her blue jeans and tight tee-shirt. "How's life?" Abigail asks.

"Oh, all right," Phoebe says. She brings two cups into the living room/bedroom, putting Abigail's on a side table. "I've been better." She climbs on her unmade bed, leaning back against the headboard with legs crossed in front of her. Above the bed is a painting she made, a large abstract in bright primary colors. "But one would expect that, right?" She sips the tea, and asks, "What are you doing in the city this afternoon?

Abigail had planned to say she was going shopping, but what came out is, "Actually, I just wanted to see you. I was worried about you."

"Really." Phoebe observes her over the rim of her cup. "I'm all right, you know."

"I don't know." Abigail shifts on the chair, suddenly embarrassed. "I promised your mother I'd look after you. And I'm failing because I don't know how. I'm worried, and I don't know what I can do for you." She feels suddenly, embarrassingly, close to tears.

"Aw, Auntie Abby." Phoebe slips off the bed and kneels at her side. "I'm all right. What do you think, that I'm suicidal?" She smiles at Abigail. "No, no way. I'm way too chicken to do anything to hurt myself."

"No, no." Abigail sniffs, wiping her nose with a tissue. "Don't even say that, it would be too horrible. But I wasn't really thinking that. You just seemed depressed the other day. I don't know what's going on with you."

Phoebe smiles at her, and the look on her face makes Abigail feel warm and trembly inside. "Thank you, Abby. I love that you care." She leans her head on Abigail's shoulder and holds it there. Abigail reaches a hand over, and—like an auntie, or like a grandmother, or maybe even like a mother—pats the young woman on her arm. "It is hard," Phoebe said. "I miss her so much, and everything seems to just go on. People offer sympathy, and then they don't know what to do. It's like they're scared of me. And I'm just supposed to act like everything is normal. I keep wanting to call her or wondering why she doesn't call me. I remember she's gone, I know, but I don't believe it. Gone where? Where'd she go?" Phoebe stands up, puts her hands in her jean pockets, restless. "That Jonathan, you know? That's why we broke up. He couldn't handle my feelings. I bummed him out, I guess." She sits back on the bed, cheeks flushed.

"I'm sorry. But what's all this about the autopsy? Why that?"

Phoebe smiles. "Well, it would be a good film. There aren't any recent good films about it, and the science has changed since the last one was made. For me, it's a spiritual thing. Mom's death made me think about what we're made of. She was so much more than that body, you know? Not just more to *me*, but more in herself, more to herself. When I saw that old film about autopsy, it was horrible, but it was also freeing, to know that the body is stuff. Just stuff. And we are more than that."

Abigail can still feel the weight of Phoebe's head on her shoulder, her warmth, though she is now sitting across the small room, again on her bed. "I see. That makes sense. It's not morbid, I guess."

"It's a desire to *know*, to see for myself, and to understand. There's so much I don't understand. That's what the word means, you know; autopsy means 'the act of seeing with one's own eyes.' I feel like it's something I need to know, I have to see, and record."

Before she leaves, Abigail uses the bathroom. She takes a quick look in the medicine cabinet and in the drawers below the sink. The drawers are full of makeup and hair products and tampons and skin cream. In the medicine cabinet, aspirin and antacids and eye drops. Laxatives. Cough medicine. Melatonin. A couple of prescription bottles, medicines Abigail hasn't heard of. She opens them up to make sure the pills don't look like Megan's oxycontin. One has a mix of pills, green and white. She shakes a few onto her palm, trying to be quiet, but the pills are unmarked. She listens, hearing running water in the kitchen. She takes one white pill and slips it into the back pocket of her jeans. Closing the medicine door, she confronts her face in the mirror.

She touches her face; the soft skin under her eyes, her neck. *Stuff. Just stuff.*

Chapter Six

The pills don't match. Abigail holds them together in her palm, turning them over to see both sides. The oxy has a scored line across one side and is bigger than the white pill she found in Phoebe's cabinet. Abigail is relieved, and vows to stop being so anxious about Phoebe. The girl will be all right. She throws the stolen pill in the trash.

She takes a book from her shelf, critical essays she is reading as part of research for a paper about sisters in nineteenth-century domestic novels. She sits at her desk and Callie jumps up in her lap, purring. Abigail strokes her. She would rather be reading one of those novels than reading an essay about it. She puts the book aside and opens Twitter, finds images of Trump and Melania participating in an Easter Egg Roll. Melania in her prom dress standing next to her glum son, Trump in his red tie standing next to someone in a rabbit costume. She reads that he will cut business tax from 35% to 15%. Anger pumps through her, makes her feel alive.

She gazes out the window, thinking of the time she stayed in Marisha's apartment. She had borrowed Marisha's life, her single, dog-owning life. The life of a young woman with a secret lover. What could be better? What is more dangerous, more fantasy-producing and fantasy-fulfilling, than to have a secret lover. She remembers looking through drawers of things Marisha left behind, trying on clothes and borrowing scarves and jewelry, not because she loved them, but just to enter into that imaginary life, the life of someone other than herself. It was the pleasure in reading books, in watching movies, in travel: to leave her own life behind, to take up someone else's. And then to switch lovers, to take up someone else's husband. To borrow that life, and then return it carefully cleaned and folded, unharmed.

And Doug took up the role of secret lover so readily. He was good at it, he made it easy. He was funny and tender, and there was always an edge of longing that their relationship could be something more, that if their situations were different, if they'd met at another time . . . It all added up to good times, good sex. Fun sex, exciting, always knowing he had to leave soon, so not a moment wasted. Knowing that he would leave, and really, she was okay with that. She was borrowing, not stealing. And off he would go, one more hug, the scarf wrapped around his neck, a wry joke and a tender look as he went out the door . . .

She wonders if Doug had the same urge to step out of his own life, to transgress into someone else's. What lives does he take up for relaxation, for escape from his own, apart from his sexual adventures? Mysteries, she thinks. She remembers a stack of them always by the chair at his house. Murder mysteries. She could not see the attraction. Who wants to read about people being murdered, and trying to figure out who did it? She'd always wondered if people who read those books had a secret desire to murder people and see if they could get away with it.

Abigail is still slouched at her desk, Callie curled up plumply on her lap. She straightens her back. She hears the wind shaking the trees with their new leaves, rattling the window glass; she hears the occasional swish of traffic going by. She should get back to work. She should start dinner, though it's only 2:00 p.m. She should not be sitting here, thinking. She feels her mind avoiding something, skittering around it, and at the same moment realizes that avoidance is something her mind is particularly good at, having trained itself for years to avoid subjects it prefers not to think about. She is skilled at avoidance. Her thoughts circle around the subject, not looking at it. Abigail forces herself to stop, settle down, and look.

Megan's death was sudden, not expected by anyone. Doug delayed calling an ambulance. What did she die from, exactly? Abigail didn't know. Did anyone ever ask, did anyone ever say? There was no autopsy, no talk of autopsy that Abigail remembered; the first time she'd heard the word in years was when Phoebe said it. Was Megan's death intentionally caused by a husband who longed for a Caribbean beach, for another woman by his side?

She sits back, watching the computer clock click down toward 2:30. Her mind goes back and forth. She tells herself she is being over-dramatic, cooking up plots out of boredom. Cheesy, unrealistic plots, from a kind of book she doesn't like to read. But she doesn't believe herself. She should not avoid what is in front of her. Her best friend Megan is now decomposing in the Puritan Lawn Memorial Park Cemetery and has no one to investigate her death. Megan's parents are both dead; she has no angry brother, no suspicious sister. Only Abigail.

She thinks of that night. She'd been half-awake in the dark hall, hearing Doug's voice on the phone. The moon through the hallway window had been nearly full, luminous. Doug said he couldn't wake Megan; he'd asked Abigail to come over. She remembers the urgency of his voice, the strain. Why did he ask her? What did he think she'd be able to do? Abigail, feeling certain of her place of importance in their family life, hadn't questioned it at the time. She'd shouted something back to James, rushed over to their house.

And then the painful image of Doug in the lamplight leaning over his wife, shaking her shoulders, shouting her name. Megan—dear Megan, gone Megan, the pain of that loss a twist in Abigail's gut—moving like a cloth doll in his hands. Loose, flopping. What had happened to her? Why was she like that? In all the times Abigail had taken care of her, she'd never been unable to wake Megan up before, never seen her limp and unresponsive. She forces herself to let the words form in her mind: Did Douglas Adams administer unnecessary drugs to his wife, to Megan? Did he give her an intentional overdose of a powerful, pain-killing drug? Megan had said she was grateful to Abigail for taking care of her because Doug wasn't good with sick people; he couldn't stand to see suffering. Maybe he found a way to avoid seeing anymore of Megan's suffering. Maybe he thought he'd be doing her a favor.

But Doug had been distraught, pale and trembling, then and for days after. He was suffering. He couldn't have intentionally hurt Megan. Abigail tries to picture him grinding pills up in her sparkling water. Sitting beside her on the bed, handing her a coffee mug full of water and medication, urging her to drink it. *Never mind the taste, it's bitter, yes, but it's good for you. It will help you sleep.* Then when it worked, when she wouldn't wake up, he panicked—not enough to call an ambulance, the logical thing to do, but enough to call her, Abigail. A safe person. Someone who cared for him, who would see his grief, his trauma at the loss of his beloved wife, and would not question. Someone, in fact, who would field questions that might come up, who would disarm doubters. She remembers the poem he read at the ceremony; what was it? Something about forgiveness. She rummages in her desk drawer until she finds the saved program with the poem on the back. *I stand, and wait, and cry/for the absurd forgiveness, not knowing why.*

This is terrible. It is too much to think about. Abigail lifts Callie carefully from her lap, stands, and sets her on the chair. The cat, after a disgruntled *mew* and a dirty look at her mistress, jumps down and stalks into the other room. Abigail steps into the kitchen, stares at the black cylinder on the counter, and says, "Alexa, play New England Public Radio." Classical music fills the room, wordless, soothing. The clouds are breaking up, and light falls into the kitchen through the trees in the back yard. She will make something nice, a treat: chocolate chip cookies, adding black walnuts from a bag in the refrigerator. She will not think of that other business any longer.

With cookies in the oven and their smell filling the kitchen, Abigail texts Phoebe: *How are things?* It's a feeler, sent to see if she's available to chat. After a few minutes, her phone dings. *All right. Studying in the library for a test.* Abigail pictures her sitting at a wooden table while spring light from tall windows floods over her, tapping on a muted phone. *I'll let you study, just checking in,* Abigail texts. But she adds, *How's your dad? Is he home yet from his trip?* There is a longer pause this time. Abigail takes the cookies out of the oven. They are perfect, just turning crisp at the edges. *He got home Tuesday.*

Abigail sets her suspicion aside. She's not avoiding it, exactly; she's just setting it over there, like the cookies, so she can get on with her life. She imagines her suspicion in a box, a tall box, almost human-sized. It has a door, which is closed, and locked with a padlock like the one that used to be on her bedroom door.

◆ ◆ ◆

On a summer day nearly forty years earlier, Megan and Abigail lay on beach towels on a strip of rough sand at the ocean's edge. Megan sat up and stuck her legs in front of her, looking at the ocean. She reached out a thin white arm and stirred her fingers through the rocks and rough sand by her towel. Abigail lay back on her towel, watching her. They'd walked there from Megan's Maine house on the hill above, and they were the only people in sight. "I want a house like this when I grow up," Abigail said.

"You can visit me when I come here."

"No," Abigail said firmly. "I want my own. I'll build one not far from yours, and we can visit one another. We can come to the beach and hang out." She sat up and crossed her legs. "Over there, maybe." She pointed to a rocky outcropping to their left.

Megan drew her knees to her chest and wrapped her arms around them. Her body was skinny in the worn one-piece suit, and her hair whipped around her head in the wind from the ocean. "Our children can play together and be best friends. Our husbands will be best friends too. We'll have birthday parties together, and . . ."

"I don't want to get married," Abigail interrupted. "I want to come live here by myself." The thought occurred to her as she spoke, but it made sense, it sounded right. "Why get married? Men are creeps." She lifted a hand to her forehead to shield her eyes from the sun. "I just want boyfriends."

"Oh." Megan lay back down again, slowly. "Not all of them are creeps," she said a moment later.

Abigail looked out at the waves. She was thinking of Megan's father. Last night the two girls and Megan's parents had played a card game at the kitchen table called "Snap." It was a fast-moving game. At first Abigail was slow to catch on and shy to shout out, but she soon got over her shyness and was shouting "Snap!" before the others, winning hands. Megan's parents both played along with them, and her father laughed with the girls. Abigail couldn't imagine her father doing that; she didn't think he'd played a game with her since she was tiny. And if he did want to, she didn't think she would let him; he'd be creepy about it, and weird. Megan's father wasn't like that.

"Well, maybe," Abigail conceded. "If I found someone who behaved himself." She gave Megan a smile.

Megan jumped up. "Let's go in," she said.

"It's too cold!"

"Don't be a baby." She pulled Abigail up, and they ran into the cold, murky waves, shouting.

◆ ◆ ◆

THE SYMMETRY OF HUSBANDS

Abigail reads news late into the night, tapping onto Twitter and newspaper stories, leaning into the glow of the laptop while James sleeps. She is absorbed in the Stormy Daniels saga, the porn star given hush money by the man who became President. Photos show a pretty blonde woman with improbably large breasts, barely held in by the straps of a white dress.

Abigail puts a hand on her own breast, feeling its loose weight under her terrycloth robe. They have always been large, though nowhere near Stormy territory (no real breasts are, she thinks, without surgery). When she was very young she became aware of their power, and though she often wished for a body that drew attention to her other qualities—a body like Megan's, the body of a poet, a body men fell in love with instead of just wanted to fuck—she also took enjoyment in the effect they had on men. Stormy knew all about that and used it.

Abigail reads Stormy's Twitter feed, drawn in by the sassy, ironic voice that never backs down, the badass persona perfected. Stormy sells a lipstick line that "doesn't come off during sloppy blowjobs." Stormy slams back answers on Twitter to the worst kind of comments, over and over, until Abigail feels nauseated reading them. Digging deeper, Abigail finds photos that show the woman's shiny façade cracking, her eyes shadowed and lines visible on the smooth white face. She is not a porn doll; she is a real person. And she has a child, a little girl.

Abigail finally clicks off the computer and turns away after its light fades. She spends too much time caught in its glow, outraged and helpless. She turns off the lamp, and the house is silent and dark around her. She will not think of her suspicion,

256

that human-sized box in the corner. She walks up the dark stairway and sees the half moon through the window at the top of the stairs, white and lit with a silent judgment.

Chapter Seven

Abigail's mother is concerned. "You can't keep reading that stuff," she says. "It doesn't do any good to get yourself all upset."

"Mom, we *have* to read it. We can't just ignore things. It will only get worse. That's how fascism happens, when we look away."

Her mother shakes her head, looking down at her coffee and the remaining crumbs of lemon cake. "All that bad news can make a person unhealthy. There's too much anger there, and just rottenness. You have to preserve your health. You won't live forever. Enjoy life." She looks up at her daughter and Abigail sees the pouches under her eyes, the dark lines around her mouth. "What good does all the obsessing do?" her mother asks. "The world has always been full of problems, and now we see them more because of the internet. You can make yourself unhappy about them, but if there's nothing you can do to change them, then don't think about them."

Abigail remembers her mother sleeping through her father's night-time journeys up the stairs. Did she really not know anything? Abigail could not think that her mother knew and didn't do anything. That would *not* have been one of those problems she could do nothing about; she could have done something to stop it. She must not have known; she must have been sleeping soundly. Abigail wonders now if her father had other issues that her mother could do nothing about, other "problems" that she needed to sleep through.

Her mother smiles, a mischievous look on her face. "Carolyn's daughter is getting married next month, and the bachelorette party is going to a male strip show. Carolyn's going along and wants me to come too. So she's not the only mature person there. What do you think?"

Abigail stares at her mother. "You don't mean it."

"Why not? Want to come? If could be fun, what do we have to lose?"

"Our dignity," Abigail says. "Our money. My job. Who would ever hire me to teach young people if they saw me at one of those?"

"Oh phooey." Her mother flaps a hand. "No one you know will be there. And if *they* were there, then they couldn't hold it against you for being there, too."

"Well, good job taking the discussion off politics." Abigail says. "Sex always works for that." She stands, leaning down to kiss her mother. "There are other ways to have fun, you know. Find yourself a real man."

She watches her mother's face turn pink. "How do you know I don't have one?"

"I hope you do." Abigail doesn't think her mother has had sex with any man but her father, ever. They married when they were both nineteen, and in the years since her father died, her mother has not mentioned anyone. It would do her good,

Abigail thinks, though she doesn't want to think too closely about her mother being with a man. The air is mild, the sun coming out from behind clouds. She starts the car and turns a corner to drive the long way home, past Doug's house.

It has rained for two days straight, and now the grass glows a brighter green. The street is quiet, with no other cars. As she approaches Doug's house she sees the flower garden in front sitting untended, piles of last year's leaves covering any new growth. Abigail slows her car to a crawl. The shades are pulled, curtains drawn, and in the drive sits a car she doesn't recognize, a light blue SUV. In front of the garage, she sees Doug's car. As she drives past, the front door pushes open, and someone leans out and bends down. A slight woman with long dark hair, picking up the newspaper left on the stoop. She stands, pushing her hair behind one ear, and glances toward Abigail's car. Abigail looks away, to the road ahead. The woman is younger than Abigail, much younger than Doug, and seems to be wearing a bathrobe.

◆ ◆ ◆

Abigail stares into the bathroom mirror. She needs a change. She has been thinking of dyeing her hair to color the encroaching grey. Maybe a dark brown, like the young woman at Doug's house. Or maybe a vivid red like her students do, unconcerned about whether the color looks real. The more fake, the better. How would it feel to have orange hair, what signal would that send to the world? It would show that she is not concerned with trying to pretend that she is genuine; that she embraces the artifice of a construction of self. That there is no self, only color and shape and sound, words and images unattached to essence. There would be a freedom in that, a lightness, a sense of not being connected to a past that ties one down. It's the kind of thing she would have talked with Megan about, analyzing the message that hair color sends.

She won't dye her hair any wild color, or at all. She will let it grow, showing her age, showing who she is. Instead, she brushes it back off her forehead. Noting the horizontal lines deepening there, she opens the drawer of the vanity, pauses briefly to consider the name of the furniture, *vanity,* then finds a pair of shears. She carefully cuts an angled line of bangs.

◆ ◆ ◆

"Maybe we should have Doug over for dinner." James is uncertain as he says this. They are standing at the kitchen counter, eating crackers. Though it's after dinner, the sky is still light over trees in the back yard.

"Yeah?" Abigail asks. "Why?"

"Well, you know. His wife died. We haven't had him over in a long time. We're old friends."

The idea doesn't appeal to Abigail. She imagines him bringing his new girlfriend, the awkwardness of that. No, it will not happen. The box of her suspicion still sits in a corner of her mind, closed but looming. "Maybe we could go out somewhere," she says. "We'll buy him dinner. And Phoebe," she adds. "Make sure Phoebe is invited too."

"What, I should do this?" James pauses with a cracker halfway to his mouth.

"It's your idea."

"Yeah, but you're closer to him." He puts the cracker in his mouth, chews. "You worked for him, for the family. Best friends with Megan, and all." His eyes slide away, to the window. They come back to her, pausing. "Did you do something with your hair?"

◆ ◆ ◆

Phoebe is not able to come, but happily Doug's new friend doesn't come either. James and Abigail are already seated in the dimly lit restaurant when Doug walks in, light jacket flapping behind him, running a hand through his hair. "Sorry to be late," he says. He is usually late, Abigail remembers. She rises, holds out her arms for a barely touching hug. She reaches a hand around to pat his upper back, motherly. James rises also, for a handshake, then James pulls him into a hug.

"How are you doing?" James asks. "You look well." He does look remarkably well, Abigail thinks, for a recently bereaved widower. His color is good, his hair well-styled as always.

"I'm doing all right," Doug says. He sits, looking at James, then at Abigail. He shrugs: helpless, wry. Charming. "Life goes on, doesn't it?"

"Yes, it does," Abigail says. She smiles, then opens the menu, leaving James to make conversation while she studies it.

After they receive their drinks, Abigail asks about Phoebe. "How do you think she's doing?"

"Well. At least, I think she's well. She calls. She visits once in a while."

"Do you see her in the city much?" Phoebe lives a few T stops away from where Doug's office is.

"No." Doug looks sideways at her, with a half-smile. "Do you think I should? Am I being a neglectful father?"

"No, no," Abigail says, smiling, thinking *yes, yes.* "I visited her recently," she offers. "She was talking about doing a short video on autopsies."

"Really. I didn't hear that." He sits back, smoothing the napkin on his lap. "A little morbid, eh? Gruesome, even."

"I was worried," Abigail says. "But she convinced me it was part of the grieving process, and maybe even healthy, in a way."

"Maybe I *should* visit her."

"Was an autopsy ever considered for Megan?" Abigail asks, innocently. "I wondered if that's where Phoebe came up with the idea."

James looks at her. "There was no need for it, was there?" Doug has just filled his mouth with salad and takes his time before he speaks. "She was gone by the time we arrived at the hospital, and her Advanced Directive stated she didn't want an autopsy. The doctor told me it was probably a heart attack."

Abigail pauses, sipping her wine. She didn't plan to initiate this discussion, but since she has, she continues, "I know she took some opioids for her back pain." She glances around the half-full restaurant, the empty table next to theirs. "You don't thing she . . . you don't think something went wrong with that, do you?" She wipes a napkin across her mouth, watching Doug's expression. He frowns, thoughtfully shaking his head.

"There were opioids in her system," he says. "I know they found that. But it was prescribed pain medication. The pain was bad. She kept it even from you, I think, Abigail, how bad the pain was." Doug's eyebrows are drawn together, a twisted expression on his mouth. He looks as if he is fighting tears. "I don't think she would have taken an overdose. Do you?"

Abigail, taken aback, stutters. "No, no, of course not."

James reaches across the table, putting his hand on Doug's forearm. He says, "I'm sorry, Doug. Sorry you went through this."

"I'm sorry for what *she* went through," Doug says. "It was hard to see her suffer." He puts a hand on top of James' hand, briefly, then takes a long sigh.

James picks up his knife and cuts through his chicken piccata. The meat falls open, tender. "I hear you took a trip recently. Phoebe said you went somewhere warm, right?"

Doug brightened. "Yes! The Virgin Islands. St. John."

"That's good. I bet it was healing." James tells Doug about the trip he and Abigail took to St. John, years ago. He describes the cottage they stayed in, outside Coral Bay. Doug thinks he knows where the cottage is. Abigail remembers the sound of the ocean, and the way the donkeys would roam in front of their cottage at night, chewing on the grass by the side of the road under the streetlight. She remembers making love with her husband in the air-conditioned bedroom, never shaking the sense that there should be something more to this experience: more she should be feeling, as if somehow she wasn't quite giving herself up to the beauty of the place. Why was it not more perfect? What was that small knot of worry, of darkness, in all this palmy sunshine?

They talk about beaches they have all three been to, about the kennel he took Frank to, about restaurants on the island they have both been to, about snorkeling and sea turtles and fresh fish and how bright the stars are at night, and never, not once, does Doug mention anything about a young, dark-haired woman named Hope.

◆ ◆ ◆

It isn't until a month later that Abigail meets Hope. After they have turned in their final grades for the semester, James and Abigail are having dinner in an Indian restaurant. The high sides of their booth prevent them from seeing the couple until Doug and a woman are walking toward the door, past their booth. "Doug!" Abigail says. "Hello!"

Doug turns around, lifting his arms in welcome. If the moment is awkward, he doesn't show it. He introduces them to the woman. "This is my friend and colleague, Hope. Hope, these are my good friends Abigail and James."

"I've heard so much about you," Hope says, smiling. "You helped Megan and Doug through an awful time. I'm glad we can finally meet." She looks into Abigail's eyes, squeezes her hand warmly. Hope is a tall, full-bodied woman around Abigail's age. She gives an impression of vigor and energy. Abigail thinks she remembers seeing her at the house after the funeral. She has short, curly blonde hair, and looks nothing at all like the woman who took the newspaper from the steps of Doug's home.

Chapter Eight

Abigail is walking on a track circling the football field. Her steps pick up as she goes deeper into her thoughts, circling around her mind as she circles around the track. She remembers walking with Megan here, long ago, until Megan's steps slowed and Abigail turned to see her walking slowly behind, limping. She remembers Megan sitting on the grass, laughing at herself as if she were foolish or weak, not blaming Abigail for being oblivious.

She is wondering if it was love she felt for Doug. She used to think it was: that burst of energy, that feeling that took her outside of herself, into another person. There are different kinds of love, she knows, and the better love is what she feels for James: the long-term affection, the commitment. The respect. She cares for James, and he cares for her in all the little, daily ways as well as the big ways. She relies on him. She trusts him. Their lives are intertwined. She enjoys their time together. But she *was* in love with Doug, whatever that means. There was passion, the glow of fire, of a flickering excitement felt throughout her body.

The day is warm and sunny, a Sunday. A couple of boys kick a soccer ball on the field, but no one is on the track but herself. Abigail speeds up her steps. Doug would stop by in the late afternoon or the early evening. They would sit at Marisha's little table and grow tipsy while the light lengthened into the room. When he was tipsy one of his eyes opened wider than the other, while the other slightly squinted, in a way that made him look perceptive and thoughtful, witty. He had rather full lips, which when closed looked as if he were about to say something funny, or charming, or both. She adored him. There was no way she could keep away from him, no way she could not let him lead her into the bedroom, over and over again.

But then there was a way, and she was brought to it by the death of her father, and by Megan's illness. She wouldn't say she felt guilty; that wasn't it, exactly. It was need, more than anything else, that made her end it with Doug. She had need for James in her life: for his kindness, his daily care, his promise to be with her always. Doug could never do that. And Megan needed Doug when she was ill.

Abigail speeds up her walk until it is a steady jog. She hears herself panting, feels her sneakers thud against the track. She doesn't truly think that the man she knows, the man she fell in love with, could intentionally kill his wife. He is an adulterer, a lover, not a murderer. But her doubt still stands in a corner of her mind. Maybe she doesn't know him as well as she thinks she does. Megan, of course, knew him much better than Abigail does, but maybe even Megan didn't know him. Maybe they were both taken in by his charm.

She feels the vibrating of her phone in her jacket pocket, hears the muted, singing ring. She stops, unzips the pocket, takes out the black rectangle. It's James. Something in his voice makes her stop, squinting into the sky. "Doug called. It's

Phoebe. Something happened last night. He said something about an . . . overdose?"

James told Abigail not to worry, that Phoebe was all right. "What did she take?" Abigail asks.

"I don't know."

"How do you know she's all right?"

"Doug said so."

In exasperation, Abigail hangs up and calls Doug. He picks up, and sounding harassed with worry, tells her the story. "She's all right," he says. "She's going to be all right."

"Thank god. What happened?"

Phoebe had taken pain pills, not because she needed them, but to get high. She'd been with friends at an apartment, and they drank wine, and Phoebe took a pill. Maybe she took more than one pill, because the friend got alarmed when Phoebe passed out on the couch, and she couldn't wake her up. Phoebe's friends loaded her into a car and took her to a nearby hospital's emergency room. There she was given a dose of Narcan, Doug said, as a precautionary measure. Phoebe woke up in the ER scared and sick and called her father. He took her home, to his house.

"I want to visit her," Abigail says. "Would that be okay?"

After a pause, Doug says, "Wait. Give it a day, maybe two. Text her and ask; she'll let you know if she's up for it. It would be good for her to see you."

Abigail texts the next morning. *Can I visit you?* She looks at the text and adds a sentence in front of it. *I hope you're feeling all right,* then hits send. Phoebe answers *yes.* Nothing more, just one lower-case *yes,* but it's enough for Abigail. *I'll be there at one.*

THE SYMMETRY OF HUSBANDS

Phoebe answers the doorbell, and steps aside to let Abigail enter. She's wearing a grey hoodie with the hood up, and when Abigail hugs her, Phoebe doesn't take her hands out of the front pocket to hug her back. She stands motionless as Abigail wraps her arms around her. Abigail feels the life within Phoebe held tight and still, compressed inside the container of her body.

Doug's gone somewhere, intentionally to avoid her, Abigail guesses. It's the first time Abigail has been in the house since just after the funeral. She finds it odd to be there, and strangely comforting, as if she might turn around to see Megan sitting on the chair behind her, smiling.

Phoebe slumps on one side of a couch, Abigail sits at the other. There is a rumpled blanket between them, and a bed pillow. Phoebe picks them up and drops them on the floor. Used tissues scatter the coffee table. "So," Phoebe says, and shrugs one shoulder. She leans into the couch, a stockinged foot resting on the coffee table. She is exaggeratedly nonchalant, Abigail thinks, as if none of this matters, or she's trying to pretend it doesn't. "Sorry," Phoebe says, "but it is what it is."

"What does that even mean?" The words come out too quickly, a sharp tone that Abigail didn't intend, and it is exactly the wrong tone to take. Abigail softens it. "I'm sorry. I don't know what you mean. And I can't imagine what you must be feeling." That was something she'd planned to say, practicing the words on the way over.

Phoebe looks at her, her face pale inside the hood. "I feel pretty stupid," she says. "But I'm not addicted."

"No?"

Phoebe shakes her head, vigorously. "It was just the second time I ever tried those pills. I took one once before, a week earlier, and hardly felt anything. So I took more this time. I had finished editing my film and was celebrating. I was just careless. I thought they wouldn't do anything. My friend gave them to me. And I was drinking some wine too, which made it worse."

Abigail has never known Phoebe to lie, even when she was a little girl, but she knows that this is something a person might lie about. The stakes are high. "What were they?"

"Percocet. She had them for some back pain. She's a dancer." Phoebe frowns at Abigail. "You won't get her in trouble? I asked for one, and then I guess I took another without asking. I don't really remember. But she took me to the Emergency Room."

"No, I won't. I don't even know your friend's name." Abigail leans on her side into the couch, facing Phoebe. She toys with the fringe on the end of the throw blanket. "You said it was the second time you'd taken those. Had you ever taken other pills, other . . . substances?"

"No. I mean, I got high before. I smoked weed with my friends in high school. And drank sometimes. But not anything else, until this. I never had the chance, or the desire. I don't even know why I took these. Boredom, maybe. Just wanting to feel happy . . ." She lifts her hands, and drops them on her lap, a helpless motion.

Abigail reaches over and takes one of her hands, squeezing it. "No, not boredom," she says. Phoebe squeezes Abigail's hand back, and they are silent. "I understand," Abigail says, and she does, in a way: she imagines Phoebe feeling not only the loss of her mother, but the loss of her childhood. Abigail remembers her own youth, the sense she had after dropping out of college that nothing really mattered. "It's not boredom, it's pain. And loss," she says softly. "And it will get better. I promise. I super-promise."

Phoebe looks at her with a half-smile, the most animation Abigail has seen in her today. It's mid-afternoon, the light falling through the new leaves on the tree outside onto the patterned rug, the empty wood stove with ashes from the winter. Abigail imagines Megan's spirit passing through the room, loving her daughter, and she gives Phoebe's hand an extra squeeze. "That's from your mother," she says. A breeze picks up outside, shaking the windows. The sound of old windows shaking in a sunny breeze makes Abigail think of empty Amherst afternoons, of days seeming to fall into a hollowness inside her that she thought would never be filled.

Chapter Nine

James has nurtured their old washing machine, fixing it over and over again with the help of YouTube videos. Currently, Abigail needs to push a red dot he drew on the washing machine with marker in order to make it spin. When, no matter how hard she pushes on the dot it no longer spins, she tells him, that's it. "We need a new washing machine. We can afford to buy ourselves a new washing machine."

As James drives them to the store, Abigail tells him she thinks she should talk with Doug. Just the two of them. The thought makes her uneasy, with a mix of feelings she can't identify, but fear is among them. She tells James, "Megan used to say Doug wasn't aware of how Phoebe struggled. Well, now since the overdose he might be more aware, but I don't know if he really gets it. You know?"

James says, "I guess," but he doesn't sound too sure.

"Right? Megan asked me to watch over her."

"It's just that, we aren't her parents. We aren't anyone's parents. We don't really know how to be."

Abigail straightens herself in her seat, trying not to show how angry this comment makes her. She waits, breathes, tells herself to stay calm. "I'm not being a parent. He just needs someone to talk with about this. Megan would want me to do this, I think. In some ways I know Phoebe better than he does. I'm a woman, at least."

"And he's not. That's true." They pull into the parking lot of the Sears store, and James sits looking at her. "What do you think he should do? What will you talk about?"

"Just—I don't know. I don't have anything in particular to tell him. I want to know how he sees things with Phoebe, and how he sees himself helping her. I hope he's focused on that, not forgetting about it when he gets busy." *With all those women,* she thinks, but doesn't say.

"Yeah, he's a busy guy," James says as they walk into the store, and she thinks he knows what she means.

◆ ◆ ◆

She and Doug have lunch in a small, crowded sandwich shop downtown. She takes the only table available, a small one near the counter where people order. While she waits for him (late, again), she checks the news on her phone. The President has withdrawn the United States from the Paris Agreement on climate change, as he kept threatening to do. Great, she thinks. Why not destroy the environment. The tax plan his party voted in will feed the rich and strip the poor. When she thinks of the President, his fake tan and dyed hair, his terrible grammar and his sense of absolute entitlement to anything he wants, she feels a sense of looming disaster. If something bad were to happen to their country while he was President, something unexpected, what would happen? The country would be defenseless, adrift.

Her father's weaknesses wrecked their family's life, and she doesn't know what this man's weaknesses could do to their country. Who would the grownup be, who would save them?

She makes herself be still then, be calm. Slow breath in, slow breath out. There are systems in place to handle him. The Constitution will protect the country. That's what checks and balances are for. And on the good side, the Penn State college president, vice-president, and athletic director were all sentenced to prison for covering up sex abuse of young boys.

She turns her phone off as Doug pushes through the door. He looks harried. Abigail didn't want to have lunch in a place that would seem at all romantic, but now she wishes she'd chosen someplace a little quieter. Doug flinches slightly when someone bumps into his shoulder. Ruffling a hand through his hair, he looks around and sees her. He gives a strained smile. "Abigail. How are you?"

They order at the counter and wait at their table to hear their names called. Abigail spreads her paper napkin on her lap. "Thanks for having me over to talk with Phoebe the other day. I've been thinking of her since then, and just wanted to check in with you."

"You've always been very important to her." A man behind the counter calls "Douglas." They bring the food to their table and unwrap their sandwiches. Doug lifts his carefully to his mouth, takes a bite, and looks at the remaining sandwich as he chews.

As Abigail watches his absorption in his food, she feels that spark, the flicker inside herself that she always felt around him. Will she always feel this way? He looks up and catches her watching. She looks down, puts her spoon into her soup. Doug, always attentive to the winds of attraction, must know how she feels. She had no intention of asking this, but says, "Does Phoebe know about you and me? About our history?"

"No. No, I don't think so. I don't know why she would." Doug is looking at her, one eyebrow lifted in that way he does. "Why, Abigail?"

She wipes her mouth with her napkin. "I don't know. It just popped out. I hope she doesn't."

"No, I'm sure she doesn't."

You can't be sure, Abigail thinks, but says, "How is she doing?"

"She seems okay. She went to the doctor as I asked her to, for a check-up. She seems healthy. And she's seeing the therapist. The psychiatrist, I mean. The first appointment seemed to go well. She will get started on an antidepressant."

"She hadn't been taking antidepressants?" He shakes his head. "Well, that's good then. It seems as if she needs them."

"We never imagined these kinds of problems, Megan and I."

"No one does. Megan worried, though."

Doug shrugs. "All parents worry."

Abigail eats more of her soup. She says, "Megan worried in particular about Phoebe not being able to handle things emotionally." She tries to remember Megan's words. "She said Phoebe had a tendency to take on more than she can manage and doesn't want to show any weakness."

"Is that right." Doug leans back in his chair. "That sounds right, I guess. But don't we all." He smiles at Abigail.

His attitude, as if none of this were serious, makes Abigail want to say more. "When Phoebe and I were cleaning Megan's room, I found some of her pills. I told Phoebe I would take them, get rid of them safely, so I took them home." Doug is sitting still, listening. "There were oxycontin. Some were missing. More, I mean, than should be missing. I wonder if Phoebe took them."

Doug rests his chin on an open palm, elbow on the table. The door opens and closes; the man behind the counter calls out "Jessica!" All Doug's gestures are unconsciously elegant; at least, she's always thought it was unconscious. "Phoebe said she didn't have an addiction problem, that it was more of a youthful experiment," Abigail says. "I want to believe her."

"Or perhaps," Doug says, and pauses. "Perhaps you think *Douglas* took them." He smiles, as if he is a roguish boy, making a joke. A teenage boy, talking with an older, sexy aunt. "Perhaps Abigail thinks Douglas took them and mixed them into his wife's drink, to do her in." He reaches out and taps Abigail's hand with a finger. The taps are not gentle. "Do you, Abigail? Do you think that?"

Abigail pulls her hand toward herself, flustered. "Of course not. Why would I think that?"

"Your questions about autopsy, as if you thought there should be one. We both know Megan was not a drug abuser, and not the type to commit suicide. So, with a mysterious death, who is to blame? The husband, of course."

"I never thought you would have tried to harm Megan." She hears the quiver in her voice. Her cheeks are warm.

Doug smiles at her. "Oh, yes, it might have crossed your mind." He drops the smile then and looks directly at her. He lowers his voice. "I loved my wife, Abigail. It should be clear what happened to those pills, who took them, for what reason. I would give anything to have Megan back here with me. Anything. You may find it hard to believe, but I did love her." Someone opens the door to the shop, and light angles in from behind Abigail. It touches Doug's face, sparking on the water glass. Dust motes dance in the air between them. For the second the light penetrates Doug's eyes, it turns the blue irises pale and translucent, as if she can see into them, see through him. "I loved her all along," he says, and in that moment his eyes look like water, or ice.

The door closes. Abigail makes herself smile, as if everything is fine, as if she's not shaking inside. "I know you loved her," she says softly. "All along." The words echo in her head throughout the afternoon, sounding like an indictment. She's not sure who they indict: Douglas, her, or both of them.

Chapter Ten

Sometimes, in a murky half-sleep, Abigail will try to scream, but can't make a sound. One night she woke to sounds in her room, and shouted out, "Who is it!"

"It's your husband," James said, amused.

Other times she sees a face above her, coming towards her in the dark room as she lies on her back. It travels with great velocity, and when that happens she finds the strength to scream, the sound echoing in their bedroom and waking James, who reaches over to comfort her.

She still hasn't told James about her father's bedroom visits. Megan was the only one who knew, and now Megan is gone, and Abigail's father is gone, and Abigail is the only one who knows. After all these years, it would feel awkward to finally say to James, "Oh yeah, this thing happened when I was a kid. I never wanted to tell you." What good would that do? And she would never tell her mother; there was no benefit to be gained by that, after all this time. It is a small thing, Abigail tells herself, and tells the memory of Megan, who tried to convince her otherwise. Much worse happens to other people. A small thing, able to fit in the palm of her hand, be tucked away in a pocket. She can handle it.

◆ ◆ ◆

Abigail has bought a guest membership for herself at the gym Phoebe goes to, and makes plans to meet her there. As she paid for the membership, she imagined Megan, nodding at her. Thanking her for keeping an eye on her young one.

She waits on a bench in the lobby, watching people check in. Phoebe pushes through the glass door into the lobby, her face breaking out in a smile when she sees Abigail. "I have news," she says.

"What, what?" It must be good, Abigail thinks, to bring this brightness to her face.

"My film. It won a prize. The autopsy film. It's a national prize for students." Abigail shrieks and jumps up, causing people behind the desk to look up, and Phoebe bounces with excitement. "I get some money, not a big amount, but enough to help pay the rent this month. Most important, I will make connections. I just heard about it."

Abigail hugs her. "Oh, I'm so, so happy for you!"

"There is a ceremony for it in New York in a few months."

"Maybe I can go! Can I go? I would love to see that, and help you celebrate!"

"Oh, that would be wonderful! But now I want to work out. I need to burn off some of this energy. I'm so *happy*. I haven't felt happy in a long time."

Phoebe's eyes are bright, her smile radiant. "You deserve this," Abigail says.

In the women's locker room, Abigail pulls a stretchy workout bra over her breasts. She tries not to compare her body to Phoebe's, or to the other sleek young women tying sneakers and combing their hair in the locker room. Phoebe and Abigail put their hair up in ponytails in front of the mirror, giving one another smiles. In the big open equipment room, Abigail finds an empty elliptical machine, while Phoebe runs on the indoor track that circles the room. As she pedals, Abigail catches glimpses of Phoebe flashing by.

The machine next to Abigail is free, and Phoebe steps up after her run. She wipes her face with a towel, and they both circle their feet up and down. Phoebe puts headphones in and hums along with the music, moving her body back and forth to the rhythm.

When they're finished, they stretch out on padded mats on one side of the large room. Phoebe does vigorous ab exercises: bringing her knees to her elbows in the plank position; bicycling; mountain climbers. Abigail watches, impressed. "No wonder you look so good," she says. "How do you know how to do those?"

Phoebe sits up, panting. "A friend showed me. I used to work out here all the time. I stopped coming around the time Mom died."

"Is that when you started . . ." Abigail searches for the right phrase. "Trying pills?"

Phoebe turns her head sharply to look at her. "No," she says, her tone surprised. "I told you, I only took pills twice. And not until well after . . ." She pauses. "She died."

"Oh, right," Abigail says vaguely, as if she'd forgotten. She hadn't. "I'm sorry."

Phoebe presses her legs straight in front of her and leans down, reaching for her toes. "And never again," she says. "That was really not a fun time." She turns her head toward the open room, and her eyes fix on something. "Oh, crap." Her voice is soft, almost a whisper.

"What?" Abigail asks. The large room is more crowded than when they arrived, people milling around the weights and machines.

"Don't look," Phoebe says, and turns her head to the other side. She sits up slowly. "It's her. Clara."

Abigail crosses her legs and turns casually to the side, stretching her back and pretending not to look. She sees no one she recognizes at first, then at the far side of the room, riding a stationary bicycle and reading a magazine, is a familiar figure. Clara, the friend of Doug and Megan, wife of one of Doug's co-workers. Stylish greying hair, slim enough to wear a tight tee shirt over leggings and still look good. Abigail turns back to Phoebe, stretching the other way. "Clara?"

"The woman my father had an affair with."

Abigail reaches an arm over her head, stretching, then repeats the movement with the other side. She takes her time responding, waiting for the pounding in her head to die down, waiting until she can make her voice sound normal. "I didn't know about that," she says. "Are you sure?"

Phoebe spreads her legs wide in front of her and stretches her torso down between them to rest her arms on the floor in front of her. "Alexandra told me. Their daughter. We were friends."

Abigail remembers Alexandra, an over-dressed, silent child. "How did Alexandra know?"

Phoebe sits up, pushing back loose hairs fallen on her neck. "She heard her mother talking on the phone once, and then she investigated. Found texts, a record of phone calls. It's easy to do."

Abigail thinks wildly of phone calls she made to Doug, of calls he made back to her, when they were seeing one another. She doesn't think she ever texted him, except for later, when she helped with Megan, and those were innocent. "Did you ever do the same with your father? Investigate?"

Phoebe shakes her head. She stands up, stretching her arms high. "Ugh. No. I thought it would be creepy, and I didn't want to. Besides, my dad always kept his phone in his pocket. But I believed Alexandra."

They make their way toward the dressing room, both of them studiously avoiding the stationary bicycles. Abigail glances over to see Clara looking at them over the book she holds on the handlebars. Clara immediately looks over their heads, pretending not to have noticed them, just as Abigail is pretending.

In the locker room two young women are zipping up jeans, combing hair, chatting noisily. They sling backpacks over their shoulders and leave, their voices trailing behind. "Yeah, as if that would make any sense at all . . ."

In the sudden silence Abigail asks, "But how do you know Alexandra was telling the truth? Some people just like to stir up trouble." Abigail very much does not want it to be true.

"No, it was true. Alexandra is a little strange, but she's a nice person. She wouldn't make something like that up. She was upset by it, too." Phoebe tugs the elastic from her ponytail and takes a brush from her bag. "I probably shouldn't be telling you this, but it's in the past, it's all over. I'm not mad at my father anymore. And I'm trying to be honest about things. It's my new mode of being. If I'm honest about myself, then I will be honest about other people, too. He can't hide from what he did." Phoebe's eyes are wide, and Abigail sees the child she remembers in her expression of outraged innocence.

Abigail pulls off her exercise tights, takes jeans from her bag, and puts them on. "When was this? When did all this happen?"

Phoebe zips up her jacket. "Oh, it went on forever, I guess. That's the thing; it wasn't a short-time thing. I was mad at my dad for a long time about it. I don't know when it stopped. I was in middle school when we learned about it, like sixth grade, I think. But Alexandra learned that it started years earlier than that. When we were eight or nine."

Abigail can't help herself; she stares at Phoebe, stricken. Phoebe was in the sixth grade when Abigail was staying in Marisha's apartment. Doug was visiting her, Abigail, unbuttoning her shirt as they sat together on Marisha's couch, at the same time he was seeing Clara. Was having sex with Clara, she assumes. And probably with Megan also. "Oh, my god," she breathes.

"It's okay, it's not that bad," Phoebe says. She looks concerned, reaching out an arm to Abigail. "I'm all right. It's all over now."

Abigail shakes her head, attempts a smile. "Sorry. It was just a surprise to me. Poor you. Did your mother know?"

"God, I hope not. That's all I can say about that. I don't know. I didn't tell her, that's for sure. That wasn't a conversation I wanted to have." Phoebe slings her bag over her shoulder, and smiles at her. "I need to go. Don't worry, Auntie Abigail. It will all be all right." A quick kiss on the cheek and she pulls open the door.

"Congratulations again!" Abigail remembers to call after her. Then she is alone, standing in the locker room staring at the door closing behind her.

Chapter Eleven

Over the next few days Abigail goes through the motions of her life as if she is wrapped in cotton balls. The word "swaddled" occurs to her. Like an infant, she is—or wants to be—swaddled, wrapped against the world, protected. She doesn't want to engage. The image of Phoebe's face as she said *Don't worry, Auntie Abigail,* her brown eyes warm on Abigail's, haunts her.

James is teaching a summer course. He is tender with her in the morning, solicitous, sensing her mood. She rallies, cheerfully seeing him off. As he leaves for school she collapses slowly, like air going out of a balloon. She drinks her coffee extra-strong, trying to wake up from the tiredness that surrounds her. The world is full of sorrow. She puts on her sneakers and takes a morning walk through leafy residential streets, to the quiet, shaded cemetery. Here, alone at Megan's grave, her eyes fill with tears, the sobs rising up through her chest. Megan was good; she deserved none of this.

When she reads the *Boston Globe* headlines about politics, her pain comes to a focus. *Outrageous,* she says to herself: *Outrage!* And her rage flows, giving her energy; she gets up from her chair and stomps around the room, waving her arms. Travel bans against Muslims! Repealing the Affordable Care Act! The head of the FBI fired because of investigations into the President's conduct! Withdrawal from the Paris Climate deal! President sued for accepting payments from foreign governments!

That night Abigail dreams of killing someone, a man she doesn't know. In the dream, she is calm, dispassionate, not angry. It's just something that has to be done. She doesn't want to do it, but she will. She picks up the knife, brings it to the man's throat.

Abigail brings herself awake to realize that she is lying in bed with her husband, not slicing into someone's throat, thank god. She forces herself to get up, to walk to the bathroom, to make sure she is fully out of the dream. She did not kill anyone; she did not almost kill anyone. It was a dream.

Back in bed, with James breathing quietly beside her, Abigail turns her thoughts to anything other than the dream. She reminds herself of the award Phoebe won, such happy news. Then—she can't help it—her thoughts wander to the President. She thinks of him grabbing at a woman standing in front of an elevator in his hotel, grabbing at a woman on an airplane sitting next to him. Pushing a woman into a dressing room, pulling down her tights. Grabbing, grabbing. Opening the door on teenagers changing for a beauty pageant, looking at their bodies as if he owns them, as if he has purchased them. She turns to her side, and then she thinks of her father. In the dark bedroom, pushing himself against her, grabbing.

She gets quietly out of bed and walks through the dark house to the couch, where she turns on a lamp, pulling a throw blanket over her shoulders. Callie pads into the living room and jumps up on her lap. The cat kneads Abigail's thighs, purring.

Abigail strokes Callie's back, staring blankly. Her father is gone somewhere else now, maybe wherever Megan is. She closes her eyes and sees the two of them together, on a grassy bank, a sunny day. People are around them, not paying attention. She wants to warn Megan to be careful, to back away from him. Then she remembers the look on Megan's face as she gave her the padlock. Megan was shrewder than anyone knew. She can take care of herself, even now in the afterlife.

◆ ◆ ◆

In the morning, James looks at her across the table. They are eating breakfast, the doors next to them open to their deck with the rickety iron table and chairs, on a sun-filled morning in late June. "You didn't sleep well," he says. She was dozing on the couch, Callie on her legs, when he came downstairs.

"Right," Abigail says, taking a spoonful of granola. "Women are insomniac, you know that."

James smiles at her. "No, I didn't realize that."

"We have to guard the world while the men sleep."

"Well, thank you. I feel safer now, knowing you're on the job."

James kisses her goodbye and goes off to teach. It's Friday, and he has just one more week of class. Abigail watches his car pull out of the driveway. His Camry, freshly washed by rain, glints in the sun. The light seems to pierce into her head. It causes the inside of her head, behind her eyes, to feel as if it's humming. Abigail feels the version of herself that greeted James this morning—wry, nonchalant—disappear, step back behind another version of herself. This one is deeper, darker, with more space for her to stretch. With more room for anger.

Abigail doesn't ask herself why she is angry because there is simply so much to be angry about. From the top on down, from back to front. But not James; he should be spared her anger. Not Megan, who also didn't deserve it. Phoebe? No, of course she can't be angry at Phoebe. She will never be angry at Phoebe.

Doug, though. Douglas Adams. In front of her living room window, with the sun piercing into her head as she leans her forehead against the cool glass, Abigail knows that what she has been trying to tell herself is not true, is actually true. Megan was ill, but not ill enough to die suddenly like that. Maybe the doctors overlooked that fact, but it is apparent to Abigail. There was life in Megan, there were books to be read, songs to be sung. Phoebe didn't take those pills. Her father took them, and he fed them, or some of them, to Phoebe's mother. He is a weak man, and he couldn't bear her illness, her need, her pain; he needed to be free. He could convince himself he did it for Megan, to keep her from future suffering. At the funeral, Douglas knew exactly what he needed that "absurd forgiveness" for.

Abigail doesn't know what to do with this knowledge. She turns away from the window and pulls the vacuum cleaner from the closet. She will clean. She will not think. She turns the vacuum on, pushing furniture aside to reach behind it, emptying out the vacuum canister when it is full and filling it up again with dust and cat hair. She's let things pile up, get dirty. Callie jumps to the top of the couch and stares at her balefully. Abigail stacks books and magazines in piles on tables and sprays lemon-scented spray on the wood, wiping it with a cloth. She scrubs the sinks and the bathtub, her head throbbing along with her gestures. She will feel so good when all of this is done. She will sleep tonight peacefully, untroubled, in a clean house.

The guest bedroom is clean enough, needing only to be vacuumed and dusted. Their bedroom, though, has dust bunnies under the bed, grime and used tissues on the bedside tables. James' dresser is piled high with clothes. Abigail stacked his clean clothes there when she did laundry, for him to put away, but now his clothes are scattered, unfolded, more a pile than a stack. She refolds tee shirts and puts them in a top drawer, socks and underwear in the second. Exercise clothes in the third drawer.

As she puts folded pants in the fourth, bottom drawer, her hand touches something in the far corner. Something metallic, cylindrical. She pulls it out, and stares at what she holds: a silver cylinder, with engraved patterns along the side. It is something she has seen before, though not up close. She holds it up to her eye, looking toward the window, and turns it, watching the light, broken by bits of glass, fracture into colors that pierce deep inside her.

Chapter Twelve

Her head still throbbing but her house clean, Abigail gets in her car. She has to get out of the house, go somewhere, anywhere. In the grocery store parking lot, she pulls down the sun visor to look at herself in the mirror, to see how bad she looks. Her hair is a mess, and she has dark circles under her eyes. She is still wearing her baggy shorts and dirty tee shirt. She pulls her hair up in a loose bun on top of her head. She will be quick, just pick up some frozen food for dinner tonight. Maybe some flowers. And wine. Lots of wine.

In the produce aisle she sees a young woman with long dark hair, picking up an eggplant and putting it down again, carefully, as if she had never seen one before, as if it were glass. Abigail must be staring, as the woman looks at her curiously before she moves on. Abigail turns away abruptly, picks up an avocado and puts it in her basket. She feels sure it is the woman she saw at Doug's house that morning, leaning out the front door in her robe to pick up the newspaper. She wears a dark linen shirt now. She is elegant, and young.

In the wine aisle, she sees Doug himself, putting a bottle of red wine into a basket already holding two bottles. He is dressed casually, in jeans and a button-down shirt. Recklessly, feeling as if she has nothing more to lose, Abigail waves. She watches his face compose itself in a smile, even as his shoulders tense. "No work today?" she asks gaily.

"Took off early," he says. "Going to the coast for the weekend."

"Good," Abigail says. "It looks like the weather will be fine." She thinks of the young woman in the produce aisle, buying food to cook for Doug in the house in Maine they inherited from Megan's parents and from Megan herself. It is Doug's house now. Abigail thinks with a pang of her visits to that house, when she and Megan were small. The confidences they shared, sitting on the sand looking out at the waves. The children they planned to have, who would be best friends. The young woman is probably not a good cook, and Doug probably does not care.

Abigail picks up a bottle, studies the label, puts it back. Doug shifts his feet, making ready to move, and Abigail says, "Hey! I just thought of something. I've been wondering about that kaleidoscope."

He looks at her quizzically. "Yes?"

"The one you had at Megan's funeral. Do you know where Megan got it? Do you still have it?"

He shrugs, tosses his hair from his forehead. His eyes roam around the store as if he is thinking, or pretending to be thinking while he keeps a lookout for the dark-haired young woman. "I don't know where she got it. It just showed up in her drawer one day. I don't remember. She bought it somewhere." His eyes focus on her, and she is aware again of her hair, her tee shirt, the fact that she is wearing no makeup.

She thinks his face softens, a look of something like tenderness crossing it. "Do you want it, Abigail?"

"What?" She pauses, shakes her head. "No, you should keep it. I was just curious." She puts a bottle of rosé into her basket, and another one. "Have fun on the coast," she says, and turns away.

◆ ◆ ◆

A week later, a small package is delivered to her mailbox. She opens it to find the kaleidoscope. James is gone, teaching his last class of the summer. She would be able to compare it to the one in his drawer without him seeing her, but she doesn't need to. She knows it is identical.

She lifts the shining cylinder from its bed of folded tissue. It reminds her of something she can't quite recall, in the poem Douglas read at the funeral. She again finds the program in her drawer, and reads: *Or, turning from the landing, I might find/My presence watched through your kaleidoscope,/ A symmetry of husbands, each redesigned/ In lovely forms of foresight, prayer and hope.* It was the two identical kaleidoscopes she was thinking of, reflecting one another in her mind, and the phrase "A symmetry of husbands."

She holds it to her eye and turns toward the window. The sun is behind a cloud, but the colorful bits inside the device glow with light. Amazing, the brilliance of the designs, like a stained-glass window in a European cathedral. She turns the raised edge at the end of the cylinder, and the image shifts, rearranging itself into another mandala, another cathedral window of colored light.

Abigail opens her desk drawer, the one on the side that holds Megan's journal. She lifts up folders of papers to find it. The cloth cover, tan with pink and blue flowers, is faded and browned, with what looks like a coffee stain on one corner. She opens it and turns the pages carefully. Phrases, read and put aside in her mind, light up on the page when her eyes land on them. ". . . your face, laughing, then still; your eyes, brown, looking, wondering, questioning . . ." She sees James' eyes, their solid brown depth. The way he couldn't look at her when they first met, when he was her teacher, and he would glance at her, then stare above her head. The way they finally came to rest on her, with interest, with kindness. Now she pictures them looking at Megan, lighting up with affection.

The sketch Megan drew of the sun, halfway above the horizon, rising or setting, and the inked words arched around it neatly: "JA today." She'd thought the "A" referred to a last name when she first read that, but of course, James' middle name is Andrew. And the neatly written, eloquent passage: *I will always remember his face, as we walked along the shore. At least I hope I will always remember it: I am writing this, I guess, to guarantee that I will. When I was younger, I could not have appreciated this moment in the same way. We wouldn't have been able to have that conversation when I was younger—we would have been too stupid, too tongue-tied. We could not have had the openness, the honesty, with nothing held back. And knowing that my days will not last forever—I mean KNOWING that as I do, feeling it like I do— gives these moments an added sweetness.*

It was April, and the wind blew wet sleet into our faces, and our socks were soaked through our shoes, and everything was perfect.

The passage is nothing less than a declaration of love. The perfection of a moment of shared love. For of course James loved Megan, just as Megan loved him. Who would not, actually, love Megan? Abigail herself had loved Megan, would always love her. Megan lives within her still, her goodness perfected by death. She pictures James and Megan on a beach, wind tossing Megan's curls around her face. Megan takes James' arm, to steady herself. He looks down at her, and smiles. Megan so small, so slight and fragile, yet with that large spirit, that inner light. Where did they go, to be alone? Abigail could imagine James wanting to go in the woods, to spread out a blanket on a dry patch, to take her gently into his arms . . .

But no, that did not happen. James was too decent, too conscientious. He and Abigail were married, even when they were living apart. He would fight against himself. And Megan—no, Abigail didn't think Megan would do that either. She was different than Abigail, Abigail always knew that. Megan was ruled more by thought and principle than impulse; she and James had that in common. Their love would have been of a different kind than that shared by Abigail and Megan's husband.

Abigail cannot bear to think any more about that. She puts the journal back in the drawer, covers it with files, and closes the drawer.

She puts the kaleidoscope, still wrapped in paper, at the bottom of her underwear drawer. She and James will have their own matching kaleidoscopes, their own symmetries. If one day he discovers hers, then they will talk. She hopes their conversation will be long and tender, open like his conversations with Megan were.

It is growing late, the light stretching through the poplars lining their yard. She imagines her children, clattering through the door into the kitchen, shouting up the stairs to her. *Mom!* Their voices fade away and the house is quiet, the only sound the occasional car passing on the road.

Abigail flips through the hangers in her closet. James' homecoming today feels momentous, an occasion that she will remember in years to come. The moment is like a tree in late afternoon when the sun strikes it, casting a shadow into the future that stretches with time until darkness comes. She wants to look nice for James, wants to look beautiful, if she still can. He deserves to have her try for his love. She chooses a flared skirt, a white fitted blouse, and sandals. She brushes her hair and puts on makeup, looking at herself in the mirror.

In the symmetry of husbands, James is her partner. What are the last lines of the poem? *Lovely forms of foresight, prayer, and hope.* It is hope she focuses on.

She hears a car turn into the driveway.

Acknowledgements

I am deeply grateful to two people who helped this book come about: Kitty Burns Florey, for her perception, generosity, and novelist's eye; and April Guagenti, for her hard-earned knowledge of MS and her willingness to share.

Thank you to the Tyrone Guthrie Centre for peaceful days, and a desk with windows looking onto an Irish garden.

And to my siblings, who continue to love me in spite of everything.

I'm also grateful to the people at Unsolicited Press, who do all they do for the love of good books.

About the Author

Patricia O'Donnell lives in the small town of Wilton in central Maine. She has ties to Boston's North Shore, where the novel is set. She is Professor Emerita in Creative Writing at the University of Maine at Farmington. Her books include a prize-winning collection of short fiction, a memoir, and two previous novels.

About the Press

Unsolicited Press is based out of Portland, Oregon and focuses on the works of the unsung and underrepresented. As a womxn–owned, all–volunteer small publisher that doesn't worry about profits as much as championing exceptional literature, we have the privilege of partnering with authors skirting the fringes of the lit world. We've worked with emerging and award–winning authors such as Shann Ray, Amy Shimshon–Santo, Brook Bhagat, Kris Amos, and John W. Bateman.

Learn more at unsolicitedpress.com. Find us on twitter and instagram.

Printed in the USA
CPSIA information can be obtained
at www.ICGtesting.com
LVHW040258130224
771717LV00005B/156